Bad Beginnings

SHADY SPIRITS BOOK 1

Bad Beginnings

SHADY SPIRITS BOOK 1

JEN BAIR

Copyright © 2025 by Jen Bair

All rights reserved.

No part of this publication may be reproduced, distributed, or transmitted in any form or by any means, including photocopying, recording, or other electronic or mechanical methods, without the prior written permission of the publisher, except as permitted by U.S. copyright law.

The story, all names, characters, and incidents portrayed in this production are fictitious. No identification with actual persons (living or deceased), places, buildings, and products is intended or should be inferred.

Book Cover by Ljilja from Fantasy Book Design

For my husband and minions, who have loved and supported me all along the journey. Never stop being all of you.

Chapter 1

I liked my job. I liked my cousin, Lexi, who I'd been living with for all of a month. I liked living on the outskirts of Atlanta, far away from my parents and sister in Denver.

Everything was going great until Ollie showed up. As usual, ghosts ruin everything.

The Retro Cafe had been a Waffle House until a few years back when my boss, Theo, bought it.

He'd put in black-and-white checkerboard floor tiling, red booths, and walls full of Coca-Cola memorabilia, not hard to do with the Coca-Cola factory of Atlanta less than an hour away.

It was a quaint, old-fashioned diner that fit the quiet city of Peach Grove. One of the best things about it was it had zero ghost residents.

That fact had made me careless.

Ollie showed up on a Tuesday while I was waitressing. I looked him straight in his supernova-blue irises a heartbeat before I registered his telltale aura. Those eyes were so breathtakingly luminescent, I'd have thought they were photoshopped.

The moment his face lit up in delighted surprise, I knew I'd screwed up.

There is a moment of undeniable connection when two people make eye contact. When they're not looking at something in front of you or behind you, they're not looking at your forehead or your nose. It's the recognition of one sentient being to another. An understanding that draws the attention.

If you've ever tried to ignore someone staring at you, you'll know what I mean. Even if you *don't* look at them, even if you ignore them, there's that itch in your brain telling you to put your attention on them because their attention is sure as hell on you.

When his ghost status sank in, I tried to play off the connection, blinking rapidly, rubbing my eye like I had something in it.

It was too late. The damage had been done.

Nothing was harder to get rid of than a ghost who'd found out a "living" could see them.

"You can see me," he said.

I kicked myself for being fooled by his modern clothing.

Last century's ghosts were easy to spot, but this guy was in tan chinos and a teal polo with a geometric pattern woven into the fabric. The brown Chelsea boots paired with the untucked shirt gave him a laid-back, modern classic style.

"I'm Ollie," he said, checking out my name tag. "Enid. Is that your real name or did you pick something old-fashioned to go with the diner?"

I did what I always did. I ignored him.

That sounds easy. It's not.

Determined to get some sign from me that I had, in fact, seen him, he talked to me, stood in my way, and bobbed his head around, trying to get his eyes directly in front of mine until I wanted to scream.

Knowing my workplace by heart was the only thing keeping me from bumping into things I couldn't see because he was blocking my view.

If ghosts had been smoky and transparent like they were on television, my life would have been easier. Unfortunately, they looked just as solid as the living, only with an aura. Most people would find it disconcerting to see them walk through solid objects, but I was used to it.

Still, the amount of work it takes not to react, flinch, smile, shrug, fidget, speak, or shift your weight away from a ghost trying to invade your personal space takes a ridiculous amount of discipline. I had twenty-two years of practice and it was still exhausting.

Ollie was friendly, with a cheerful innocence that gave off Tom Holland, guy-next-door vibes, but without the British accent. He spent the night chattering over my shoulder, asking questions, and commenting on the patrons, my boss, and my co-workers.

Occasionally, he repeated an order back if I got it wrong, which was infuriating, because correcting it indicated I'd heard him.

Getting the order right the first time would have been easier if he'd talked less, but my luck wasn't that good. By the time my shift ended, my head felt like it had been squeezed in one of those big car-crushing machines at a junk yard.

When I left, I was lucky Ollie didn't try to follow me home.

Fortunately, I had Wednesday off. I'd requested it because my cousin Lexi had set me up with a blind date. If Ollie hadn't shown up the night before, I'd have preferred work. Lexi and I were not built of the same stuff. I was private. She had a robust social life.

My date, Gregor, was friends with someone from the parade of men Lexi interacted with. I wasn't sure who the connection was and didn't really care. I was only going on the date at Lexi's insistence.

Gregor picked me up in a fancy sports car that he'd either rented or borrowed, based on his skill at driving it. He stalled it three times getting out of the neighborhood.

He hadn't bothered to tell me where we were going.

He'd given me a critical glance at the door, then started scrolling on his phone. I assumed he was pulling up directions to our venue. It wasn't until he mounted the phone to his dash that I realized he was making a video.

"I'm out tonight with a beautiful lady. We're on our way to a restaurant, which will remain unnamed until the end of the date. If you recognize it, don't say anything. This is a private date tonight, folks. Any of my followers dying to meet me will have to wait for another meet-and-greet."

He proceeded to talk to his phone the entire drive. When we arrived, he asked his followers to wish us luck, told them he loved them, thanked them for their support, and turned off the live stream.

Without so much as a glance at me, he got out of his car and started taking pictures of the restaurant.

Judging by the fancy red awning over a matching carpet lined with black velvet roping, Bartleby's Culinary Experience would have at least four dollar signs next to it on a Yelp listing.

Gregor wore a shiny black shirt with vertical rows of silver sequins, buttoned to the top of his band collar in some strange parody of a pin-striped-tuxedo-wearing priest stripper costume. His solid black pants would have been considered a good option if they weren't also jeans.

I didn't know much about fashion, but I imagined jeans and sequins don't typically go together.

Comparatively, my ecru turtleneck and dark brown slacks were seriously understated. I imagined neither of us fit the recommended dress code for an upscale boutique restaurant.

Inside, we were taken to our table by a woman in an elegant blonde braid wearing a burgundy button-down shirt and black pants.

A waiter came by in a matching outfit with a white cloth draped over his forearm to better display his proffered bottle of wine.

"Would the madam and mister be interested in champagne tonight?"

Champagne, not wine. I hated to think what the bill at this place was going to be. Lexi had assured me a proper date would pick up the tab. I hoped she was right, since Gregor had picked the restaurant without my input.

If we'd been splitting the tab, I'd have gone with Arby's.

Even *not* splitting the tab, the pretentious atmosphere at Bartleby's would not have been my first choice. It wouldn't even have been on the list.

"Of course," Gregor said, glancing up at me briefly. "Only the best for my honey."

I almost threw up in my mouth. I'd met him twenty minutes ago, and he was calling me cringey nicknames?

"Enid," I said.

He gave no indication he'd heard me. His attention was already back on his phone.

He was busy taking selfies from every angle to get shots of the various decor in the background. The wall closest to us was covered in a silvery-blue metallic wallpaper carved to look like fish scales. The placard on our table informed us the art on the wall, currently focused on ocean themes, had been painted by local artists and rotated every month.

I wondered if Gregor brought dates here just to get new shots of the rotating artwork.

Overhead, spiral bands of metal hung from the ceiling, sporting embedded light strips that let off a soft orange glow, giving the place a candlelit feel, along with the single tall candle in a floral setting placed atop each table. The candle flames were electric.

After the third shot of what I assumed was me looking uncomfortable, I asked Gregor to point his camera elsewhere. My turtleneck looked plain enough next to his blinged-out shirt, I wasn't sure why he was photographing me at all.

My expectations for the night were dropping rapidly.

Not that they'd started high. I was far too weird for guys to get attached to. I'd been born with the ability to see ghosts, so I'd been weird even as a baby, giggling at things nobody else could see. As a toddler, I talked to them. To my mom's horror, I'd occasionally wandered off with one.

Ghosts were an unfortunate constant for me. They weren't quite everywhere, but they were plenty common and ignoring them could be tricky.

Case in point, one of them was sitting in Gregor's seat. *Inside* Gregor.

He was an older man, portly, with sallow skin. He wore a tattered business suit with extended lapels from around the 1970s, if I had to guess. I wasn't all that accurate with timelines, but he gave off post-Woodstock vibes.

"You can be my honey," the ghost said. Like a small-town mayor at a harvest festival, his voice boomed loud enough to drown out something Gregor said to the waiter.

Please let this date end quickly. I needed to go home and bury myself in a book.

Books were quiet and relaxing. They only imposed on you as much as you let them. Otherwise, they sat quietly on a shelf and didn't interfere with your life.

"I don't have my gal anymore," the ghost said. "I proposed to her in this very spot, and she turned me down. Can you believe it?"

I fiddled with my cloth napkin to keep my eyes off the ghost, wondering idly if he'd choked on his dinner that night. I doubted this bougie restaurant had been around back then, but it might have been a different restaurant.

The waiter filled our fluted glasses with two fingers of golden liquid. Gregor waited in expectant silence. The waiter gave a respectful bow of his head. I returned the gesture. Gregor ignored him.

Was Gregor too good to interact with the help? He was a dental hygienist, for heaven's sake, not a playboy millionaire.

I wasn't sure if he knew I was aware of his day job. Maybe he just wanted to let go of his mundane life for a night. If this was his fantasy, it was the opposite of mine. I liked monotony. It was a rarity for me.

So far, Gregor struck me as pompous and fake. Not the best foot forward, but then I was just as happy to let him ruin our chances before I could.

"I hope you're going to grab another glass!" the ghost hollered after the waiter.

He was going to make this night intolerable. I was already hard at work inventing reasons to bail as soon as possible. Preferably before we ordered food.

I looked up to see Gregor had lifted his glass, holding it out to me. For a moment, I thought he meant for me to take it. By the time I realized he wanted to clink glasses, the pause had been long enough for his smile to look forced.

I picked up my glass and presented it. I was a year past the legal drinking age, but didn't have much occasion to imbibe. Other twenty-two year olds went drinking with friends. Or dates.

"A toast to new beginnings." Gregor's phone whipped out to the side and he expertly took a shot of the raised glasses with only our wrists showing.

"New beginnings," I muttered, glad he hadn't tried to get me to smile for the camera this time. My request not to be in photos didn't apply to my hand, apparently.

He sipped his champagne. I set my glass back down without drinking. He didn't notice. He was busy taking side-shots of himself and his wine glass while he gazed away from the camera as if he'd hired a photographer to accompany us on our date.

When his photo shoot ended, I tried making conversation. "You're really into photography."

He gave me a practiced grin. "We're living in the future, baby. The people want to know." Like a magnet, his attention was drawn back to his phone, where he scrolled through his photos.

"Right. The people want to know what, exactly?"

Without looking up, he said, "Everything. Either they don't get out much and they live vicariously through me, or they get out a lot and they want to know where to go next. We are the information overlords."

"We?"

He raised his eyebrows like he was surprised I had to ask, but his eyes never left his phone. "Yeah, we. The social media generation."

The jilted ghost asked, "What's social media?" His face stuck out past Gregor's, creating a disturbing image.

His banana-yellow aura gave his sallow complexion a jaundiced look. He was shorter than Gregor by about an inch, so it was Gregor's blonde side-swept locks I saw atop the ghost's face.

I ignored his question. If he realized I could see him, he'd pester me non-stop. Then, if he wasn't bound to Bartleby's, he'd follow me home, and I'd have to move to another state again.

I'd been living with Lexi for less than a month. Coming to Georgia had been my second move in under a year. I was running out of places to crash.

Looking for my menu, I realized it had disappeared. "Where'd the menu go?"

"I already ordered for us," Gregor said absently, still scrolling on his phone. "I checked out their menu before I came. I know what'll look good."

For the camera. Of course. "Thanks for that." So much for bailing early.

"I hope you didn't want a salad. Girls always want salads, but you can get a pile of lettuce anywhere. They always end up looking like an advertisement for a grocery store."

"Salad?" the ghost asked. "Who goes to a steak house for salad?"

A headache was forming behind my eyes.

"I'm going to the restroom," I told Gregor. "I'll be back in a minute."

He gave no indication he heard me, but the ghost cheerfully stood, his crotch sitting in Gregor's wine glass. "Good idea. I haven't checked out the ladies' room all night."

I wasn't sure which way the bathrooms were, but with the ghost as my guide, I didn't have any trouble finding it. I entered a stall, sat fully clothed, and pulled out my phone to read a chapter of the ebook I'd checked out from the library that morning, an epic fantasy with a new character every chapter. I was on chapter six. The story was slow, but the writing was good.

The old ghost went stall to stall. The bathroom was empty. When he peeked his head in my stall, he stared at me for a minute before muttering, "Most boring broad ever. Mark my words, you'll die lonely."

I sighed. Didn't I know it.

Sounds from the dining area filtered in when the door opened. A pair of high heels click-clacked across the floor. They stopped at the sink.

The ghost disappeared to check out the newcomer. "Well, hello, gorgeous," he said from the sink area.

I'd finished my chapter before I realized the woman had gone. The ghost was gone, as well. Hopefully he'd followed Heels back to her table.

"Stupid ghosts," I muttered. I hadn't heard him criticize Gregory, who had his nose glued to his phone so firmly he probably hadn't even noticed I'd left. Was this how dating was supposed to go? No meaningful conversation, just fake pictures where people pretended to have a good time?

Maybe so. Maybe my lack of proper socialization was the problem.

I washed my hands and headed back to Gregor, only to be startled by a row of three waiters clapping rhythmically as they followed me.

Was it someone's birthday? The whole singing-waiters gig didn't fit the ambiance of Bartleby's, but here we were.

Gregor stood when he saw me. The waiters stopped two tables down, singing a merry tune, generic enough to fit any occasion. It almost sounded like a commercial jingle.

I ignored Gregor, who had his phone out, ready to take more selfies, but when I tried to sit, he grabbed my hands and pulled me to him, wrapping one arm around my waist. Shocked, I froze, leaving him to sway back and forth alongside my stiff body.

People were staring at us. Panic fluttered low in my gut. I hated when people stared at me. I'd spent too much time as the weirdo who talked to herself, who stared at empty space and laughed at nothing.

"What are you doing?" I hissed, my hands pressed to his arms. His biceps were on the slender side, but hard, probably from all the exercise he got with the camera.

"Living in the moment," he said, flashing that practiced smile. His hand lifted to the side and he took another photo of us.

I thought I managed to turn my head away from the camera in time. "I'm good living in the shadows."

Gregor backed up a step and shoved his phone in his pocket. He grabbed both my hands in his before turning at an angle and stepping in, then back out in a move that looked straight out of a country line dance.

I was wholly unfamiliar with whatever he was trying to accomplish, so I did my best mannequin impression. We looked ridiculous. For someone so focused on image, he was surprisingly oblivious.

"Can we just sit?"

The waiters stopped singing, and the patrons clapped politely, half of them still watching us. When Gregor turned his backstep into a low bow, like we were in a low-budget remake of Beauty and the Beast, I pulled my hands from his and sat, face flaming.

My single bit of luck for the night was that the ghost was nowhere to be seen. I could handle one date with a living person, right? *Right?*

The three waiters filed back the way they'd come, passing two more headed for our table, dishes in hand. One waiter set an over-sized plate down in front of me.

A perfectly round ball of what looked like whipped cream cheese sat in a three-inch puddle of orange sauce full of frothy bubbles. It looked like dog vomit, complete with green specks of what I assumed were fresh Italian spices.

The smell was odd, citrus with a smokiness that made me think of curry.

Gregor's plate held a cube of meat that he could probably fit in his mouth in one bite. It was topped with a single broccoli floret and drizzled with an avocado-colored sauce. The portions looked comically small compared to the enormous plates.

"Madam," my waiter said. "Tonight, we have for you the chicken bolete pâté in a chorizo froth."

Gregor's waiter said, "And for you, sir, we have the foie gras with citrus chervil béchamel."

I had no idea how much this farce of a meal cost, but it was going to be way more than the three dollars I felt it was worth. One bite? Maybe two. It didn't even look appetizing.

Even Gregor, who had lightning-fast reflexes whenever a picture-worthy image appeared, hesitated. "This looks different from your pictures online."

"Our house chef enjoys using his artistic talents to modify each dish in order to present a unique creative concept to every patron," my waiter said smoothly.

"Yeah, but the entire point of coming here is to get something that looks awesome." Gregor pointed at my plate. "Where are the green and orange vegetables sticking out of the chicken ball? Where's the burgundy sauce this goose liver is supposed to have? It's not just presented differently, it's a different dish entirely. The pictures on this are not going to be impressive. Are you sure you want me to post this for my followers to see?"

The waiters exchanged a look before flashing him matching smiles that told me they wanted to smack him, but couldn't.

I waitressed. I knew that smile.

"If you'd like, sir, we can advise the chef you're looking for a less original presentation. I'm sure he could arrange your food to copy what we've already posted online." His tone was free of inflection, which only highlighted the words and their implication—that Gregor wasn't sophisticated enough to recognize artistic genius when it was right in front of him.

Gregor frowned down at the food. After a long beat, he said, "No. I'll do my best to make it work."

"If you're sure, sir."

Gregor didn't answer. He just pulled out his phone and started snapping photos, trying to get the lighting right.

I pulled out my purse and handed a ten to each waiter. "First date," I said, as if that explained everything.

"Of course," my waiter murmured politely. The two headed back to the kitchen.

Gregor hadn't even noticed the exchange. He was busy scraping up a spoonful of the green sauce drizzled across his plate and dripping it on top of my white ball of chicken. I wondered if they had used a melon-baller or a silicon mold to get it so perfectly round.

When the green sauce was placed to Gregor's satisfaction, he took pictures of my plate. Thankfully, he left me out of them.

I sat back and watched the tables around us. One held a couple in their forties, stiff-backed and silent as they ate, their eyes anywhere but on each other.

The table where the singing had taken place sported an elderly couple, shoulders hunched toward each other, heads together as they spoke in cozy tones. The woman chuckled and gave the man a playful slap on the arm.

Their body language spoke of a bond strengthened over years together. I imagined their past. Youthful dating, marriage, kids, empty nesting, sharing the many stages of life. It felt right.

A familiar sensation of yawning emptiness swelled within me. I would never have that life. I couldn't keep friends. My family could barely stand me. I flinched in public places. I had difficulty following conversations or relaxing around other people. I was a mess.

Blinking, I turned away from the sweet elderly couple. Back to my date, whose camera was on my face. "Are you taking pictures of me?" I was already too mentally drained to sound upset.

"You looked so dreamy just then."

He sounded low-key excited, probably pleased with the shot.

"Can I see?" I held out my hand for his phone. He handed it to me. I scrolled back through the pictures. He'd taken six of me in under a minute after I'd asked him not to. The last four had me in profile, the elderly couple in the corner of the photo. I looked melancholy. Heartbroken.

I couldn't stand the thought of him posting my pain online, getting comments from random strangers who felt entitled to publicly state their opinion of me. It made me feel vulnerable.

"Huh," I said, deleting the pictures of me.

"You like them?" he asked.

I kept scrolling, deleting the earlier ones he'd taken of me. He'd even managed to get one with the clapping waiters walking behind me. I looked like their leader.

Once I'd deleted all the photos with me in it, including the picture of our wine glasses, which looked advertisement-worthy, I lifted the phone and took a picture of him.

In an instant, his fake smile was in place. Hopefully, he wouldn't notice photos were missing until after our date.

"I've enjoyed tonight," he said, taking his phone back. He set it on the table, using the kickstand to stand it upright. "I hope you'll do the honor of coming home with me for more entertainment."

By entertainment, did he mean a more intimate photo shoot?

To my horror, he stood, took a step away from the table, and dropped to one knee, hands wide.

He looked like he was proposing. Everyone around us thought so, too, judging by the attention we were getting.

My eyebrows climbed toward my hairline.

From across the room, the old ghost shouted, "She's gonna say no!"

It didn't take a high level of intuition to know he was right.

Chapter 2

"Be with me, Erica," Gregor said dramatically, a hopeful look plastered to his face.

"Enid," I corrected.

He shifted a couple inches to his right to center himself on the camera. "Be with me, Enid."

Was he serious? He was the most non-genuine person I'd ever met.

I pulled out my own phone, holding up a finger in a "one sec" gesture. He held the pose, probably assuming I was going to take a picture of his grand gesture.

Instead, I dialed Lexi on video chat and immediately muted her so he wouldn't know she was on the line. I flipped the camera so she could see what was going on.

To Gregor, I said, "You've ignored me most of the night while you took pictures of everything in the room, including me after I asked you to stop. Then you complained about the food because it wasn't picture-worthy enough for your tastes."

Granted, it hadn't been picture-worthy in my book either, and I was far more easy to impress, but that was beside the point.

"You ordered food for me without asking what I wanted, or if I had allergies or food aversions, because you were afraid I'd order a salad, which wouldn't photograph well for your social media page."

Gregor looked around nervously at all the eyes on him. The stiff-backed lady looked disgusted. The kind, elderly couple looked sad, the old man shaking his head in disappointment.

"I paid for the food," Gregor said under his breath.

"You put the sauce from your plate on top of my dish without bothering to ask if I was okay with it. That was your prop, not my meal. Now you're recording yourself while you get down on one knee like you're proposing marriage, but without a ring, so you can ask me to sleep with you while everyone is watching, hoping I'll feel too pressured to say no. I'd ask if you know how sleazy that sounds, but I don't think you do. You are a special kind of oblivious."

Gregor finally dropped his arms, hobbling forward on his knees to get closer so he could whisper. "Look, I know you don't get out much, but it's not that uncommon to ask a girl home at the end of a date."

"No," I said firmly. "I wish I spoke ten different languages to say no in, that's how firm my answer is."

"Is this about the camera? Because the spotlight and I are a package deal any time I'm on a date."

"This wasn't a date," I said. "It was an extended photography session. You are socially challenged and your personality is as attractive as homemade soap. You need to find a tree and apologize for wasting its oxygen." I tapped the button on my phone to flip the camera around.

Lexi looked ready to carve steel with her nails. Her phone was mounted somewhere, her eyes focused on something in the distance.

I unmuted her. "Could you come get me, Lexi?"

"Already on my way. Meet me out front. Your date better stay inside or he's going to end up as my new hood ornament."

I raised an eyebrow at Gregor. That would make a good picture.

Either his survival instinct kicked in or his preference for photography won out. He didn't follow me to the parking lot.

Lexi picked me up in her silver Toyota and apologized profusely all the way home. I assured her it wasn't her fault, but told her we could call it even if she was willing to leave me in charge of my own love life.

Reluctantly, she agreed.

With so much of her free time taken up with dating, my desire to be alone must have been baffling.

I fought hard for my privacy. Dating wasn't in the cards for someone who was different in all the wrong ways.

Lexi didn't have that problem. She was appealing in all the *right* ways, with her topaz eyes and dark, wavy hair framing a face that belonged on a cover magazine. She made guys stop and stare whether they had all the rizz or none of it.

To top it off, she had amazing fashion sense—simple and elegant with just a touch of whimsy—and she always seemed to know what to say and do.

Essentially, she was the opposite of me with the exception of the dark, wavy hair. We had that much in common, thanks to our shared paternal grandfather, who was an eclectic mix of European, Asian, African, and Middle Eastern.

My eyes were dark brown instead of light, and though my skin was around the same medium tan as Lexi's, hers was enhanced, with a brighter, creamier shade that gave her that flawless look makeup alone couldn't replicate.

As cousins, we looked just enough alike to showcase the potential I failed to reach.

Which was fine. Again, I didn't need attention from guys. I looked just good enough to get unwanted attention, mostly from guys who would run the second they spot-diagnosed me as schizophrenic.

If I ever met the right guy, I could always explain ghosts were real, but if it hadn't worked with family, I had no reason to hope it would work with romantic partners.

The next day, it was back to work. I crossed my fingers and hoped Ollie had moved on.

I parked in my usual spot around the side of the Retro Cafe, next to the dumpsters, and held my breath to avoid the smell of decaying food.

When I stepped out of my car, an eager whine drew my attention.

Between the dumpster and the cafe, a German Shepherd sat with its dark eyes locked on me. A subtle, ethereal glow emanated from it.

That was weird. Ghosts didn't normally come in dog form. Animals typically moved on after death. Across the Rainbow Bridge, as it were. They were too carefree to get stuck in the ghost realm. At least, that was my theory.

The dog whined again. Its ghostly aura was a bronze color that blended with its coat. Bronze was good. It felt regal and warm.

"Nice doggy," I said, then gave myself a mental kick. I knew better than to acknowledge a ghost. Any ghost. Even a dog.

At my greeting, it perked up, which was hard to do considering it was already about as perky as a dog could get. It was more accurate to say it grew more alert, practically vibrating with the force of its projected attention.

It gave a short, gruff bark as a return greeting. With another whine, this one impatient, it turned and disappeared behind the cafe, only to return a split-second later to give me a hopeful look so earnest I could have sworn it was trying to communicate telepathically.

It wanted something. Big surprise. Every ghost I'd ever met wanted something.

"Sorry, pup. I'm due in for work." I turned my back on it and headed around the front of the building.

The dog barked at my back.

I ignored it. A ghost dog couldn't hurt me. The most it could do was follow me inside and bark incessantly until I lost my job because I couldn't hear orders from customers. Just like human ghosts, only with barking instead of talking.

My curse was why I moved around, mooching off distant family members. Why I wasn't in college. Why I couldn't keep a job. Why I had no friends. Why I'd never have a boyfriend, or a husband, or children.

Even if I miraculously ended up in a stable relationship, I'd never pass my curse along to kids. My lonely life was mine to live. I'd spare future generations.

I'd only had this job for a few weeks, and the dog was already the second ghost I'd slipped up on.

"Keep it together, Enid," I muttered.

When I entered the Retro Cafe, I kept my head down as I made my way behind the counter. If I could spot Ollie's feet, limned in his midnight blue aura, I'd know where he was and better avoid eye contact.

Unlike people with lives, ghosts didn't have anywhere to be. They didn't get bored easily. The smallest hint of intrigue would have them glued to me like a book-worm to a library.

I couldn't screw up again. With luck, Ollie would find something new to entertain him. He would not tell his friends he made eye contact with a living person. He would think he imagined that moment of connection and get on with his afterlife.

The smell of brown sugar bacon filled my nose, guiding me to the grill. It was the Retro Cafe's specialty. That and grits, cooked the right way in heavy cream with enough butter added in to clog a pig's arteries.

"Hello, Enid."

My boss's deep, accented timbre brought a smile to my face. "Hey, Theo. Busy day so far?"

A quick scan showed the cafe was fairly empty, but that was expected for early afternoon.

Three customers sat on stools, two at the low bar, one at the high bar, all drinking coffee. The one at the high bar had just finished a plate of eggs. His napkin sat crumpled atop the remains of golden yolk.

No sign of Ollie. Good. My outlook grew brighter.

I generally tried to be a happy person, but few things could ruin a good day faster than snagging a ghost's attention.

Theo flashed me a grin, his teeth stark white against his dark skin. "Very busy. If we are lucky, we will get another good rush for dinner." His accent made dinner sound like "dinnah." I couldn't place the accent, but that wasn't unusual for me. I'd become intentionally ignorant when it came to historical and regional identifiers.

All I needed to know was that Theo was my boss and a damn good one. His affable smile and easygoing personality made him a dream to work for. His fatherly demeanor combined with his uplifting nature created an atmosphere of teamwork, which was the golden recipe for happy customers.

The quality, down-home cooking didn't hurt, either.

"I'll grab my apron and check on the customers," I said, heading for the back.

"No worries," Theo said. It was his mantra. "Enjoy the slow time. It will be busy soon enough."

Smiling, I pushed through the swinging door leading to the small back room that doubled as a food prep area. I walked right through Ollie. Only years of training kept me from reacting.

When a ghost was trying to get your attention, jump scares were not far down the list of obvious things to try.

"Oh, good. You're here!" Ollie sounded overly excited to see me. He was like a lost puppy who'd found his owner after a long search. He looked like a puppy, too, with those sparkly blue eyes and floofy brown curls.

He had boy-next-door good looks, but with a jawline that could have sliced bread. He wouldn't have given me the time of day if he'd been alive. I'd have returned the favor since I'd learned the hard way nobody wanted to be friends with a crazy person.

"You were on the schedule but I wasn't sure if you'd try to swap shifts with someone," he chattered. Ollie was very good at carrying on one-sided conversations.

I was supposed to be taking over Alicia's shift and was surprised she wasn't in the back room. She hadn't been on the floor, either.

As for changing shifts, it wouldn't have mattered. Ollie was a ghost. He had nothing but time to kill. It's not like he'd have to clear his schedule to wait for me. I could either quit my job or try to ignore him in the hopes he got bored.

To date, that tactic had been useful zero times.

"I was hoping you wouldn't call in sick or something. I know you don't like talking to me, but if you would just give me a minute to explain my situation, I'm sure you'd be willing to help. You're a good person. I can tell."

There was no way in hell I was helping him with anything. That would require me to confirm I could see and hear him, which was cardinal sin number one.

While I liked to consider myself a good person, I could only do so much. Ghosts were everywhere and they all had big mouths. Word would spread, and I'd have a line stretching all the way to Kansas of ghosts with their hands out.

Besides, any favors I did wouldn't put food on my table. I had rent and grocery bills to pay. I needed to focus on me. Just because I was the only one who could see the ghosts didn't make their problems my responsibility. That path led to Crazy Town.

I tuned Ollie out, humming a song I'd heard on the radio. It took a lot of practice to haze out parts of my reality while being present for the rest of it. I had that down pretty well.

Or so I'd thought until I slipped up with Ollie.

Now, I was planning my next move. I'd grown up in Colorado, then moved to Wyoming before heading to Georgia. I was running out of family to stay with.

That being said, I wasn't completely without a plan. I could always live on the road, sleeping out of my car. Driving cross-country from Wyoming had opened my eyes to the fact that highway rest stops tended to be low on ghosts.

Living in my car sounded uncomfortable, but I'd only need money for gas and food. I needed a nest egg to get started, though, which required me to keep my job at the cafe long enough to save up. My chances were looking slimmer by the day.

A thump on the side door, which granted access to the little hall of bathrooms, was followed by a knock. The door was usually kept locked.

"Who is it?" I called. Nobody was allowed in the back room except staff.

"Hey, Enid." Alicia's dull voice came through the door.

I unlocked it for her. Alicia had stringy black hair and permanently hunched shoulders. She was probably in her forties, but looked downtrodden enough to be in her late fifties. She was a single mom with two kids in elementary and it showed.

"Hey, Alicia. How'd your shift go?"

She gave a heavy sigh and sat in one of the three chairs pushed against the wall. "Same old, same old. The guys at the low bar have been here an hour. Coffee, black. Keep it coming."

"So just enough work to keep you from a decent break, but not enough of a tab to make the tip worth it?"

"Exactly." She gave me a wan smile.

I pulled my long, dark hair up into a ponytail and slipped my apron—firetruck red—over my head and tied it at my waist. "I got you covered. Take a load off." My shift didn't officially start for another few minutes, but I was fresh and ready to work, in part because Ollie was hovering.

He wasn't as bad as some ghosts I'd met, who liked to interject their commentary while I was mid-conversation.

There's a difference between a tension headache, sinus headache, and cluster headache. Trying to stay focused on the living while the dead talk over them brings a special kind of headache. A rhythmic, pulsing pain centered on my forehead, right at the hair line.

When Alicia had come in, Ollie went silent. He stood in front of the swinging door that led to the grill area, his head blocking the little window that let us check on customers.

Careful not to look directly at him, I walked through Ollie with my hand out, feeling for the give of the door.

It slammed into me as someone, probably Jenna, came through, shoving the door harder than was necessary.

My hand crumpled painfully, and the door kept coming. It stopped after slamming into my forehead, rebounding back into Jenna, who let out a startled "Oof."

I hissed, stepping back to shake out my injured hand. I fought the urge to kick the door a second time, just so Jenna could get the full effect. My head throbbed and my knuckles stung, but luckily nothing was broken.

"Ouch," Ollie said, moving in close. "Are you okay?"

I ignored him, focusing on my hand, which was hard considering this was his fault.

The door opened more slowly and Jenna stuck her head through. "Oh! Sorry, Enid, I didn't see you there."

That was because Jenna was scatterbrained and never looked through the window before walking through the door. Together, the two of us were a collision waiting to happen.

Without a valid excuse for my own ineptitude, I couldn't scold Jenna.

I flexed my hand and rubbed my forehead. "No worries. Glad you made it in today." It came out more grumpy than I'd intended with my hand still hurting.

Jenna had missed two shifts in the past week. I'd had to cover both halves of the cafe. Theo had been a big help, but he ran the grill most days, which limited what he could do. The fact that he worked so hard earned him my respect.

"I know," Jenna said in a whiny voice. "I'm sorry I've missed so much lately. My car's been on the fritz. I've taken it in twice to get looked at, but they're telling me it's a bust and I'll have to get a new one, but I don't have money for that kind of thing."

Her chatter sounded so much like Ollie's it was hard not to tune her out. There hadn't been a shift I've worked with her where she hadn't had an excuse of one kind or another. You couldn't always help car trouble, but it was going to mean more work for me. I knew that much.

"I had to get a ride here today," she said in disgust. "I don't know when I'll be able to find a new vehicle. With my luck, I'd be better off buying a bicycle."

"You need me to cover deliveries," I guessed, tone flat.

Theo had offered food delivery for a fee when he first opened, hoping to increase his customer base. It had worked, though most patrons preferred coming in to get their food fresh. Jenna had been hired in part as a driver, but she hadn't done a single delivery in the past couple weeks that I knew of.

Her face brightened. "Would you?" She made it sound like I'd been offering instead of stating the obvious.

"Yes. I'll deliver your orders."

"Fantastic. You can keep the tips, too," she said, as if she were being magnanimous instead of stating the obvious. "By the way, you have customers at table two. They have a baby with them." She wrinkled her nose like she smelled dirty diapers.

"Right." I skirted past her and Ollie, looked through the window that was now visible, and headed out the door.

Ollie followed me past the grill, talking to my back. "I know it's a lot to ask, but the love of my life is dead, and I could really use your help."

That was the problem with ghosts. They had no sense of boundaries. It wasn't okay to walk up to a complete stranger and ask for help with your dead girlfriend. Even if it was something simple, like asking for advice on what to write on a sympathy card for the girlfriend's parents.

With ghosts, nothing was ever simple. I wouldn't blink if he asked me to learn necromancy and try to revive her.

Not that zombies are a thing, but still.

I continued to ignore him. It was one of my favorite acts of self-preservation. One I had yet to regret.

I hadn't made it halfway to my booth when the front door swung open and a scrawny man with scruffy blond hair entered. His eyes locked on me and his pasty pink lips pulled back in a leering grin.

My spine stiffened reflexively.

Theo had warned me about this guy. His beady eyes gave him a predatory, opportunistic look that made my skin crawl. I'd nicknamed him Smiles because Shark was too obvious.

He saw the direction I was going and headed for my section, crossing my path as I made my way to my other customers. He paused in the walkway, momentarily blocking me. "Hey, darling. I'll take a sweet tea. Maybe with extra sugar." He ran his eyes down the length of me as he said it.

I fought back a shiver.

It was going to be a long night.

Chapter 3

"Ew," Ollie said, eying the guy. "I'd take his order last."

I gave Smiles an uneasy nod. He sat in a booth, allowing me to skirt by. Theo typically took over any table Smiles occupied. He didn't like the way the creepy guy spoke to his waitresses. For a semi-regular, Smiles didn't come in that often. This was only the third time I'd seen him in a month.

A glance at Theo showed he was already pouring tea. It was the only thing Smiles ever drank.

I focused on my customers in the corner booth. Their baby was old enough to stand on the bench seating, bouncing his legs in that loosey-goosey way little kids do. He'd already drooled all over the menu. The woman, presumably his mom, gave me a tired smile. The dad was busy making sure the toddler didn't fall over or smack his face on the table while he bounced.

"Hi, folks. What can I get you started with?"

"Coffee," they said in unison, sounding as tired and frazzled as they looked. "And we're ready to order," the mom said. She looked ready to be done with the meal, done with the day, done with life. Raising kids sounded exhausting.

This knowledge did nothing to fend off my sense of sour grapes. Maybe I'd have decided not to have kids, given the choice. Having the decision made for me was embittering and stoked my longing for what I couldn't have.

The baby's knees buckled, and the dad's hands circled under his armpits was the only thing to keep him from a split lip. Lucky kid.

"Sure thing. I'll get your coffee before I put in your order. What'll it be?"

They started rattling off their order, but the mom's voice triggered the baby, who started loudly chanting, "Ba-ba-ba-ba-ma-ma-ma."

"I'm sorry, could you say that again? White toast or wheat?" By the third time I asked them to repeat themselves, Ollie started parroting their order whenever my pen paused.

"Over easy, not over medium," he said looking at my notebook. "Waffle dark."

I read the order back to them to make sure I had it right. I did. Careful not to look at Ollie, I slipped off to get their coffees, then put in the order.

Mid-pour, the phone rang. Jenna rushed out of the break room to grab it. When she hung up, she handed me a slip for a delivery order. "I'll take over your table while you run this out."

Of course, I'd already done most of the work for my table. She'd end up taking the tip for it, though. I gave her a cheerful smile, hoping it didn't look as forced as it felt, and started prepping to-go boxes.

Ollie chattered at me as I worked, which had me moving faster than usual. I was out the door in record time.

He followed me to the parking lot where the dog was still waiting for me. "Huh. I've never seen a ghost dog before," he muttered.

I wasn't sure how long Ollie had been a ghost, but the fact that he'd never seen one either made me inexplicably uneasy. In my experience, strange occurrences in the ghost world were never a good thing.

I climbed in my car, an older model Kia Soul, pre-wrapped by a previous owner in "midnight plum" vinyl, a deep purple that passed for black on a dark night.

The Soul had sounded like the perfect car for me. I'd bought it on sight and immediately dubbed it the Phantom. It was my first car, and it held up well, though the vinyl was beginning to peel in places. It would probably look like trash in another year or two in this southern heat and humidity.

Rotten smells from the dumpster had seeped into the Phantom, so I held my breath while starting the engine.

Ollie stepped through my passenger door and sat next to me.

Before you ask, even ghosts aren't sure how they manage to go through things at will. I'd asked an old lady back when I was young and trusted ghosts. Before I realized they were using me. The ghost lady had said it was automatic, like how I adjusted my balance on a moving escalator instead of on stationary ground.

With nowhere else to put the two bags of food, I set them on the seat. I felt mentally icky about shoving my hand into a ghost body. It didn't feel like anything, but it looked disturbing, like I was trying to massage his guts or rip out his heart.

"Really?" Ollie asked, looking down through his body to where the outline of the bags could be seen through his stomach.

My eye twitched with the effort of keeping my commentary to myself.

I pulled out my phone and plugged in the street address. 21 Primrose Circle.

"Primrose Court," Ollie said helpfully. "Not Circle."

Dammit. I stared at my phone and weighed the cons of driving to the wrong house over indicating I'd heard Ollie. "Hmm. Was that twenty-one or twenty-seven?" I muttered, looking at the receipt stapled to the food bags. It was hard to make out through Ollie's dark teal shirt, but since I only needed to pretend to look at it, that didn't matter. I changed the address and brought the Phantom purring to life.

While my eyes were glued to the pavement, my attention was on Ollie's blue glow in my periphery.

Ghosts had rules that governed them. Like most things in life, they always seemed to have exceptions. They couldn't be seen by the living, except for me and my now-deceased grandmother. They couldn't touch the living world, but I'd once met one that could move objects.

The majority of ghosts were bound to where they died. Clearly, Ollie wasn't required to stay inside the Retro Café. I hoped he couldn't leave the parking lot. Or the property boundary. Even being bound to one city block would be useful. Where his leash ended would determine if I needed to get a new job or move to another state.

He hadn't followed me home, which meant it was unlikely he could go anywhere he wanted. I suspected the few ghosts who could travel around were still limited in some degree, otherwise they'd all be off on a tropical island somewhere. Who hung out at a diner in Peach Grove, Georgia when you could be literally anywhere in the world?

One thing about Ollie bothered me. If he was bound to the cafe, why hadn't I seen him before?

Often, bound ghosts would disappear for a while. They didn't go anywhere, they just stopped being around. I'd always imagined them lying underground like vampires. Ghosts didn't sleep, but everyone needed a break from stimuli on occasion, right?

After a month of work, I'd only just now seen him? That whole first week of work I'd expected new ghosts to pop up, but by now I'd spent countless hours working. It was strange that I hadn't seen him around.

I pulled out onto Highway 70, which ran the length of Peach Grove, all the while watching Ollie's aura out of the corner of my eye. Had I been wrong? Had he been traveling around all this time, not bound to anywhere? I hoped not.

He shifted to face me. "Now that we've got some alone time, I'm hoping you can talk to me without anyone judging you."

I turned on the radio.

"My wife is dead," he said, raising his voice to be heard over the pop song blaring on the radio.

He was married? He was around my age. Not that people didn't get married in their early twenties, I just hadn't pictured him with a wife.

I didn't usually do music. I much preferred silence, which was harder to get.

"She's not technically my wife anymore since she only recently died. I've been dead a bit longer than that, so she's had other boyfriends, which is good in a way, since I never wanted her to be lonely."

He was preaching to the choir. Nobody *wanted* to be lonely, but somebody had to draw the short straw.

"Some of her boyfriends haven't been the best choices, though," he said.

Could she top a blind date with Gregor? I didn't care enough to find out. I cranked up the volume, irritated he hadn't hit the end of his tether yet.

If his wife died, shouldn't he be happy? They could be together again. Maybe she didn't love him anymore. Maybe she moved on. If he thought I was going to play matchmaker for him, he was in for a rude awakening.

The dead handled their affairs fine without me, despite their complaints to the contrary. I didn't owe them anything.

Peach Grove wasn't that big. Soon I was tick-tacking down back roads. I pulled up to a stop sign across from a corner gas station, where a man was pumping gas into a pickup truck, his arms propped on the side of the bed, watching something on his phone. A ghost watched over his shoulder, laughing at whatever was playing, while his female ghost friend scowled at him few feet away.

The male ghost threw back his head, laughing uproariously the same time as the living guy chuckled.

The female ghost stomped off into the darkness, her brick red aura disappearing with her.

Auras looked like they glowed, but they didn't shine like light in the darkness. Whatever created the effect wasn't actual light.

The male ghost glanced briefly at his companion's retreating back. He didn't follow. By the time I'd rolled past the gas station, his attention had reverted back to the show on screen.

Everybody had problems. My biggest one was ghosts. If they weren't courteous enough to stay invisible to me, I'd have been happy if I'd been invisible to them. That would at least make things fair. Not that I thought the powers that be were much interested in fairness.

Primrose Court turned out to be a long, meandering road ending in a cul-de-sac. I found the house I was looking for near the end.

I turned down the radio so the neighbors didn't complain about the volume, which had gotten to near deafening levels. I snatched the bags of food from the seat and left the Phantom running, my thoughts in turmoil as I walked up the path to the front door.

Ollie was still with me. He could travel farther than I'd expected. Not only did I need to find a new job, I definitely needed to find a new place to live. Far, far from here.

Lexi probably wouldn't mind having her couch back, but the list of other relatives with houses I could crash at was slim. The chances of me building a nest egg before bailing was even slimmer.

21 Primrose Court was a single-story beige house with a plain white door devoid of the decorative glass embellishments most of their neighbors sported. I knocked on the door before noticing the doorbell had a built-in camera. I pressed that, too, for good measure.

Musical notes echoed through the house. A ghost stepped through the door, yipping when she almost ran into me. She stumbled sideways in a flash of wavy auburn hair. Her jerky actions told me she was new to being a ghost.

I closed my eyes and hoped the sinking feeling in my stomach would dissipate.

"Oliver? Oh my gosh, is that you?" the ghost girl gasped. "I can't believe you're here!" With that, she burst into noisy sobs.

I held the bags of food up to my face, squinting at the address, which very clearly said Primrose Circle. Not Primrose Court. Which is where Ollie's wife had recently died, if I had to guess.

"Sneaky bastard," I muttered. I should have known better than to rely on a ghost.

Pulling out my phone, I navigated to Primrose Circle. It was a block away. Why street planners stuck similarly named streets next to each other was beyond me. Maybe they got a kick out of knowing how many people would end up at the wrong house.

"Peyton, I'm *so* sorry you died," Ollie said from behind me, the pain in his voice real over her muffled sobs. "I wanted you to have a family and a long, beautiful life."

I stood facing the door, determined to stay out of their business while they talked on the walkway behind me. Ollie had tricked me to get a ride to his wife's house, and now I was standing here looking stupid.

Fine. He wanted to be here. Now he was. For all I cared, he could stay here. Maybe I'd finally get some peace at work.

"I can't believe you're here," Peyton repeated, her voice going up an octave. "You died. I thought I'd never see you again, but now you're here." She started crying harder.

Ollie made shushing noises, and her crying grew muffled again. I pictured him stroking her hair. "I never meant to leave you." His pain was so raw. Utterly heartbroken.

My eyes started misting up. I gave my head a quick shake. No. I wasn't going to get caught up in whatever they had going on. I just needed a plan for how to extricate myself.

If I turned and left, it was possible Ollie would stay. Then again, he might follow me. I was like catnip to ghosts. Meeting me was like winning the lottery for most of them. When you live in a world you can't touch, it's hard to turn down a free pair of hands.

I decided my best shot at escaping notice was to fiddle with my phone until the two love birds wandered off, deep in conversation. Then I could leave without drawing notice. Sure, Ollie knew where I worked. Since he was untethered, he could return. Hopefully, he'd be content to spend time with Peyton, at least until I'd built up a nest egg.

Ollie said, "I heard about what happened. I'm so sorry. Murder? That had to be terrifying. I wouldn't wish that on anyone."

Murder? She'd been murdered? Had Ollie told me that while I drowned him out with pop music?

A pang of guilt shot through me, but I pushed it down.

Ghosts didn't live by the rules of polite society. They weren't opposed to invading my bedroom while I changed, walking in on me in the shower, luring me into unmarked panel vans as a seven-year-old, or trying to get me to cross a busy street to pass on a message as a four-year-old. If I died horribly, they didn't care. What was death when you were already a ghost?

"Do you want to talk about it?" Ollie asked, his voice thick with sympathy.

Despite myself, I turned slowly, holding my phone up so I wasn't as obvious. I didn't look directly at them. If they paid me any attention at all, I hoped they'd think I was sussing out addresses.

Ollie stood with his arms wrapped around Peyton while she sobbed into his shirt, his blue aura blending with her rosy pink one. She inhaled a hiccupping breath and pulled her tear-streaked face away from him, flashing him a wobbly smile that took up an inordinately large portion of her face.

"It was so scary." A shiver ran through her. "It was worth it to see you again, though." She inhaled another jagged breath. "I missed you so much." The words came out half-strangled.

Facing each other, I could see their profiles. Ollie looked absolutely torn up over what had happened to her. A rush of hatred and bitterness coursed through me.

How come they got to be all gooey in love while I was left on the outskirts of humanity? They looked perfect together. Two beautiful, dark-haired people with perfect complexions and big, soulful eyes. Their kids would have looked like celebrity supermodels.

As a rule, I didn't trust beautiful guys. Their looks made them a target for all the girls, which exponentially increased the chances of them cheating. The same went for gorgeous girls. If I'd grown up with everyone telling me how beautiful I was, and how I could get any guy I wanted, it would have been hard to develop dating ethics. Why buy the cow when you can get the whole herd for free?

Not that beautiful people were never faithful, but I was convinced it was more rare the more beautiful a person was. Ollie seemed like the one-in-a-million guy. He'd kept track of his living wife for how long? Now that she was dead, he was determined to swoop in and save the day. How noble.

Meanwhile, I wouldn't get an Ollie. I wouldn't get anyone. I'd be alone my whole life unless I could find a guy who didn't mind a whacko girlfriend. That wasn't going to happen, I knew. I hated dating. It was like window shopping at a candy store when you're diabetic.

"I know," Ollie said. "I missed you, too, even though I've been here, watching over you."

She pulled back in surprise. "You have?"

"Of course. I know how hard you've had it."

"Then...you know..." She didn't finish her statement.

He gathered her in close. "I do. That wasn't your fault."

What wasn't her fault? Dammit, it was frustrating watching the equivalent of a daytime soap playing out in front of me without having any of the details.

Ollie's hand moved in small circles on her back. "Tell me about this latest guy."

Latest guy? As in, boyfriend? It hadn't occurred to me he'd be watching his ex while she dated other guys. Had he watched them in the bedroom? If so, he wasn't nearly as nice as he pretended to be.

Peyton nodded. "I met a guy a couple weeks ago." She lifted her head, talking to his chest like she couldn't bear to look him in the eye.

"He seemed nice on the first date, then he started texting on his phone a bunch on our second date. Our third date was the last one."

So maybe Gregor wasn't the only phone-happy guy out there. If dating standards had had really dropped that low, it was a wonder anyone got married.

"I broke it off. He'd left a couple things over here. He wanted to come over and get his stuff. He didn't even seem upset about the break up. Not that we were close, but he didn't even pretend to care." She rambled on much like Ollie did.

"Anyway, I stuck his stuff in a box and put it on the front step. He came over to get it, then didn't want to leave."

Ollie nodded, his face a mask of sorrow like he knew where the story was going. Probably because he did.

It was clear he thought Peyton was going to say the boyfriend killed her, but she sounded more disgusted with the guy than anything.

If some guy had murdered me, I'd have much stronger feelings than disgust.

"He kept ringing the doorbell, trying to talk to me. Said he wanted to smooth things over. I ignored him. He tried to come in. I'd locked the door. Bolted it, too. He tried peeking through windows and spotted me. I put my phone to my ear and acted like I was talking to the cops. He got the message and left."

I'd figured as much. She hadn't sounded like she was leading up to a breaking and entering, followed by murder. Her tone was way too casual.

"So who killed you?" I asked, caught up in the story.

She didn't seem surprised to have me join the conversation. I wasn't sure she knew enough to be able to tell I was still alive.

She gave me a shrug. "I don't know. Someone came into my room in the middle of the night and stabbed me more times than I can count. Not that I tried. You have bigger things to worry about than counting in situations like that. Plus I was half-asleep when it started."

Her pale blue outfit, soft cotton house pants and a matching shirt, showed no signs of blood, which wasn't surprising. Ghosts didn't hold onto the wounds that killed them.

Their clothes were sometimes torn and threadbare, but only because that had been the normal state of them long before death. Ghosts didn't appear with spears and arrows jutting from their bodies or half-caved-in skulls. They just looked like normal people.

Ollie narrowed his eyes at me. "Are you done pretending you can't see me?"

Peyton gasped in surprise. "That's right! You're alive! You don't have a glowy line. How can you see me? None of the cops could."

"Call it a curse," I said dryly.

"Are you finally willing to help us out?" Ollie asked. "I know it's an imposition, but Peyton will be stuck here if she doesn't get closure. We need to figure out who killed her."

Peyton blinked up at him. "Stuck here? But you're here. I'm happy if I'm stuck with you."

The tune to Huey Lewis's "Stuck with You" ran through my head. The lyrics fit the two of them perfectly. Sweet and sappy. I buried the urge to slap them both, fully aware that my grapes had grown extra sour.

"You don't want to be stuck here, Peyton," Ollie said seriously. "There's a better place for you."

Before she could object, I cut in. "I have my own life problems to deal with. This is a murder. Let the police handle it."

Peyton let out a sardonic laugh. "The police aren't solving this anytime soon. They have no leads. Even I don't know who did it, and I was right there when it happened."

That was interesting. Had she not popped up as a ghost after she died? Did that take a while? I wasn't sure since I'd never actually seen someone die. There was a brief time in my early teens where I'd been morbidly curious about that, but the only way to find out was to camp out beside someone in hospice, which my mother wouldn't have tolerated, or ask a ghost.

It had been well over a decade since I'd cared enough to ask a ghost about anything. The answer wasn't worth the cost.

Ollie turned to me with an imploring puppy dog look. "Please. You have to help her." He was so earnest I wondered if he'd taken acting classes to maximize the effect.

It would take more than a look to soften this heart of steel.

I held my arms out, a bag in each hand. "What do you want me to do, Ollie? I'm not psychic. I can't time travel. I can't read minds. I don't know who killed her. Are you asking me to break into the police department and steal her file? She just said they don't have any leads."

He looked around as if an answer might be right in front of him. His roving gaze froze on something across the street.

I leaned to the side to see past him to where a man was checking his mailbox across the street. He had frozen with his hand inside the box, his eyes locked on me. He was probably too far away to hear what I'd said, but not too far to see that I was talking to myself. I gave him a head nod. Hopefully he'd think I was having a phone conversation through headphones.

"Maybe he knows something," Ollie said.

I gave him a look that said, "Seriously?"

He grew more animated. "He looks like he pays attention. Maybe he's part of the neighborhood watch."

I didn't like how enthusiastic he sounded. I kept my voice low. "If he knew something about her murder, don't you think he'd have told the police?"

"Not if he thought it would make her look bad. Strange guy banging on her door and all." His hopeful look flickered into irritation. "The least you could do is ask."

"The least I could do?" I asked, my eyebrows scrunching with such force that it made my forehead ache. "Who do you think you are? I don't owe you anything. You lied to get me here. Now the food is getting cold, and I might lose my job. The least *you* could do is leave me the hell alone. You got your wife. Keep her company. At least she wants you around."

I stomped toward my car, skirting around Ollie and Peyton, who were blocking the walkway. The guy across the street watched me as I bypassed the perfectly clear path to my car so I could walk through the grass.

He probably thought I was drunk. What did I care? I'd never see him again. Peyton had Ollie, with his stupid blue eyes and his stupid sweet face. Surely he could snoop around better than I could.

As always, I was just the convenient option, but I was past my days of being used by ghosts.

Chapter 4

Ollie hurried to get in my way, his hands held up to placate me. "I'm sorry. You're right. You're totally, one hundred percent right."

He paused, as if waiting for me to stop and listen to him while he backpedaled to come up with a better way to get me to do what he wanted. Manipulative bastard. Why did no never mean no? Why did they always feel the need to talk me around to their way of thinking like I didn't know my own mind?

I kept walking, right through him.

He followed, of course. "I lied to you, which was wrong, even if I had a good reason for it. You didn't deserve that. I promise I'll leave you alone forever if you'll just please, please ask that guy if he knows anything about Peyton's death." He circled in front of me again, his body half-buried in my car. He put on his puppy dog look, his blue eyes catching the sunlight in a way that made them almost glow.

"I'm desperate," he said quietly, glancing at where Peyton stood closer to the house. "She can't stay here."

He sounded near tears. I hated myself for caring. He was dead for Pete's sake. Why did dead-people problems always sound so much bigger than mine? Boo-hoo. I'm lonely. But dammit, I had a right to my own life, didn't I?

Scowling, I set my bags down next to my car. It would have made more sense to put them inside, but the door handle was sitting right at crotch level. Stupid ghost. He hadn't even noticed. "Alone forever?" I asked, belatedly realizing that was the best I could hope for. The only attention I ever seemed to get was the kind I didn't want.

"I promise."

It was a lie. I knew it was, but at least going through with it would give me something to fling in his face. With luck, that little wedge would stave off bigger problems now that I could no longer pretend he didn't exist.

I blew out a breath and crossed the street. The neighbor was pretending to flip through his mail, though his frequent glances in my direction told me where his attention really was.

He was stocky, with shaggy brown hair and a matching beard fast approaching Santa Claus length. I couldn't tell how old he was. Somewhere around forty, if I had to guess. It was hard to see details past the bushy beard.

His eyes narrowed when I approached, so I put on my best smile. "Hi there. I hope I'm not disturbing you."

He slowly lowered the mail from in front of his face and nodded a chin at Peyton's house. "You delivering food there?" he asked, trying and failing to mask his suspicion beneath a casual facade.

"Yeah." I tried for a lighthearted laugh that sounded as awkward as I felt. "It looks like I've got the wrong street, though."

He nodded. "Primrose Circle?"

How often did they get people on the wrong street here?

"That's where I should be. You nailed it in one." I launched into the least contrived sounding conversation I could come up with. "I'm nervous about leaving now that I've rung the bell here. I noticed they have a camera, and I'd hate for them to think I was some creep. If you see them come out, could you tell them I had the wrong address?"

He tipped his head to the side in confusion. "You noticed the camera but didn't think to talk into it? They usually record messages."

I blinked. "That would have been a smart thing to do if I'd thought of it." Crap. If the police came back to check the footage, they'd probably hear me talking to myself. Had I said anything suspicious that couldn't be explained by a phone conversation?

My jaw ached from clenching it. Ghosts were the worst.

"Don't matter anyhow," the neighbor said. "Nobody lives there anymore."

I wasn't sure how to get him talking about Peyton now that I'd walked over to him.

Luckily, Ollie and Peyton had wandered over to eavesdrop. "Ask him why there's a camera if the house is empty."

I parroted the question.

"A girl lived there up until yesterday when she was murdered," he said casually, though his eyes studied my face with an intensity that was disconcerting.

"Oh, wow," I breathed. "I hope they catch whoever killed her. I'd hate to think of a murderer loose in Peach Grove."

When his eyes narrowed, I panicked. I wasn't supposed to know the killer had gotten away. "Or did they already catch them? It wasn't a murder-suicide, I hope."

The neighbor gave a single shake of his head, though he watched me like a bug squirming on the pavement. "Nope. They didn't catch him. They won't, either."

"I told you he was creepy," Peyton said, nudging Ollie. "He's as likely as anyone to have killed me."

Well, paint me stupid. Why hadn't anyone mentioned that before sending me over here? I was going to kill Ollie extra dead.

"Oh." My palms grew sweaty. I cleared my throat and fumbled for something to say. "Why not?"

The neighbor stroked his beard. A steady sprinkling of crumbs fell out of it. "Police are in on it. They're in tight with some bad people, and they got problems a whole lot bigger than a stab-happy stalker. Trust me on that one."

Alarm bells were clanging in my head so loud I almost couldn't hear myself speak. "Right. Well, let's hope everyone else stays safe." I eased my way back toward my car. "You too. Stay safe, that is."

He watched me go, only his eyes moving as they tracked me.

When I reached my car, I grabbed the food and put it in the back seat before leaving as fast as I could manage without my tires squealing. Of course, I was pointed toward the cul-de-sac, so I had to drive into it, loop around, and head back out, all the while being watched by the weird neighbor.

I gave an awkward finger-wave as I drove passed.

When I stopped watching him in my side mirror, I realized Ollie was in my passenger seat. I almost screamed.

A glance in the rearview showed Peyton standing in her yard with her hands wrapped around her like a child lost in darkness. "You're just leaving her there?"

"She's bound to the house," he said tightly, clearly struggling to keep his temper in check. "You could have given us time to say goodbye."

Was he looking for pity? "You could have stayed with her."

My estimation of him went down every time he opened his mouth. He'd honestly expected me to hang out while he caught up with Peyton after tricking me into bringing him here. No surprise. It was one example in thousands of how narcissistic ghosts were.

"Why do you hate ghosts so much?" He had the gall to sound incensed.

"There are not enough hours in the day to list the reasons," I assured him.

"You do realize you'll be one of us some day."

"And when I'm one of you, I'll be free to talk to you without getting locked up or accosted or losing every friend I've ever had. Do you have any idea how weird it is for a living to talk to invisible people? To know facts that you shouldn't know? The living have a visceral reaction to people like me. I just want to be left alone."

"Normally, I'd respect that. We're low on options. You're the only one who can help us."

"Look, I'm sorry you're dead. I'm sorry your wife is dead."

"Peyton."

"Peyton. Whatever. You need to exercise whatever options ghosts have for solving problems. I'm not getting involved. You can chatter at me until I lose my job and have to move—again—but I'm staying out of it. I'd rather be the girl spacing out in a world full of ADHD adults than the girl who talks to dead people. One of those gets me fired. The other one lands me in an institution."

Ollie went quiet. I immediately hated it. My intrusive thoughts went hyperactive. *Poor me, I don't have friends because I'm a weirdo. Meanwhile his wife has been brutally murdered, and I'm too much of a chicken to put my own neck on the line to help him.*

Grrr. That little voice in my head had talked me into more stupidness than I could stand to think about. It constantly bullied my voice of self-preservation.

Fuming at myself, I pulled up to the correct house and set the bags on the porch. This house had the decorative glass in the door, which revealed people milling around inside. I rang the doorbell and booked it back to my car. They opened the door as I reached the Phantom and waved before scooping up the bags. I waved back.

They seemed like nice people. It was too bad they were stuck with cold food.

People in Atlanta were a lot like people in Denver, heading about their business in their own little world. I felt at home here.

My brief stint in Wyoming had brought on culture shock with its small-town dynamics. I'd worked at a diner outside Cheyenne. People would come in, sit at my table, and greet me with, "I heard there was a new girl in town. You're living at the old Marston house, right?"

The Marston family had owned the house I was staying at about fifty years ago. The last Marston moved out of the area over twenty years ago, but that's how everyone knew the house, so that's what they called it. In the few months I spent living there, I never got used to people I'd never met knowing all about me.

Peach Grove was far enough from Atlanta to have its own feel, something between big-city and small-town. People here drove with one hand on top of the steering wheel so they could flick their fingers up in a casual wave whenever they drove by someone walking on the street. Pedestrians love to wave. A lot.

Complete strangers would chat each other up at the store, but the community wasn't close enough to know houses by their original owners' names from half a century ago. That was hard to do with a population of thirty thousand.

While I'd appreciated Wyoming's slower pace, it was hard to keep a secret with everyone in your business. The ghosts there were twice as nosy as the living. It hadn't taken long before I needed to move on.

Peach Grove was the perfect blend for me. I didn't want to leave.

I parked beside the dumpsters, careful not to run over the German Shepherd who remained standing guard. It was on the small side. And kind of skinny. It might make a good ghost guard dog, though.

Guilt washed through me. Here I was complaining about how ghosts used me all the time, and the first thing I think when I see a ghost dog is how it might benefit me. For shame.

Ollie had stayed silent the entire twelve minute drive, which was a feat for him. I knew it wasn't going to last.

"Look," I said, my hands gripping the steering wheel. I refused to look at him. If he flashed me those puppy dog eyes, I would not be responsible for my actions. I had enough trouble keeping my thoughts straight without him manipulating me. "I need you to not talk to me while I'm working. Or when I'm around people. If you need to say something to me—and I really hope you don't—but if you do, tell me when I'm in my car. Don't follow me into the bathroom or anything."

When he didn't answer, I risked a glance. He was looking out the windshield with a thousand-yard stare and a haunted expression.

"Can you do that?"

"Yes." He said in a monotone voice.

"And I need to keep my ghost ability private. Word tends to spread quickly. I don't need to get swarmed again. I'm just trying to live my life in peace."

Ugh. Live my life in peace. That was at the top of the list of insensitive things you could say to a ghost, but dammit it was true.

His gaze flicked to mine. "I'll do my best not to bother you any more than necessary."

The phrasing introduced enough loopholes to make a lawyer twitchy, but I let it slide. In the end, I couldn't *make* him leave me alone and I knew that.

When I pushed open my door, the dog started barking at me.

Ollie planted his feet on the ground and stood in place with my car through him like his head was stuck out a sunroof. He frowned at the dog. "It's weird that he's so focused on you."

The German Shepherd ducked behind the building only to reappear a moment later, the same as he'd done earlier.

"It's like he wants you to follow him."

Fat chance. "I have work to do. Why don't *you* follow him?"

Ollie shrugged and walked through the front end of the Phantom to crouch in front of the dog. "Hey, there. What's up, boy?" He tipped his head, then corrected himself. "What's up, girl?"

I was late getting back to the cafe. My extra stop had taken more time than I had to spare.

Heading off, I'd only made it a few steps when the dog's bark turn to a growl. I turned back in time to see it snap at Ollie's face. He scrambled back, tumbling to the ground inside my car. I bit my lip, trying not to laugh.

The dog seemed to like Ollie as much as I did. Maybe it liked guarding the cafe. I wouldn't complain if it did.

With my mood lightened, I headed inside.

Ollie stayed outside, either to make friends with the dog or to respect my wishes and steer clear of me.

Despite my long absence, Smiles was still eating his dinner. Theo sat with him. Other than them, the restaurant was empty.

I'd seen Smiles twice before. I'd only tended to him once. He was tall, in his thirties, and looked creepy as hell but otherwise pretty average. That first time, I'd asked him what he wanted to drink, and he flashed his teeth at me in one of those over-the-top smiles like he was a game show host, then waggled his eyebrows in a poor attempt at charm. "I'll take a sweet tea from a sweet lady."

Theo had taken the tea from me before I'd filled the glass. "I will take care of him. You still keep the tip, though."

It was just as well since the guy only tipped a dollar. He probably thought his charm was worth more than money, heaven help him.

With nothing better to do, I headed for the back room, then watched them through the little window.

Jenna sat at one of the chairs, playing on her phone. She didn't bother to acknowledge me.

I focused on Theo, who hadn't bothered to make himself food, even though it was around the time he usually took his dinner break. He'd sit with the guy, but he wouldn't eat with him. That was telling.

Smiles talked with his mouth full, gesturing the whole time. Theo listened a lot and talked a little, his expression abnormally serious.

When the meal was over, Smiles made a show of paying his bill, pulling out his wallet, waving his credit card between two fingers before handing it to Theo with a flourish like he was a stage magician.

Theo rang him up, ran the card, and handed it back, all business.

Smiles tipped an invisible hat and sauntered out the door.

Once he'd gone, I went to stand by Theo. "What's with that guy?"

"He is not a man you want to know. You let me deal with him."

From behind me, Ollie spoke up. "I could find out more about him if you want."

I almost jumped out of my skin. How long had he been behind me?

As for his offer, I didn't want to know anything about Smiles. Besides, Ollie would just use what he found to guilt trip me into digging into Peyton's murder. Did he think I had friends on the police force?

I shook my head, not bothering to look at him.

"You sure? It's no problem."

A trio stumbled into the cafe, two men and a woman. They headed for Jenna's section.

I turned on my heel and shot Ollie a dark look as I passed him, heading for the back room.

"Right. No talking at work. I'll wait."

And wait he did, standing in the middle of the highest point of foot traffic with his arms crossed, lost in thought. He stayed there all through the dinner rush. I walked through him fifty times before my shift ended, leaving me irritated. Was there some reason he couldn't wait in the break room or stand somewhere less obtrusive?

Jenna wrapped up washing a batch of dishes as the last of the customers left.

We closed at eight. On slow nights, we managed to get most of the cleaning done while the stragglers finished eating. We still had mopping to do when Jenna said, "Oh, look. My ride's here. Theo, do you mind if I head out? There's not much left to do anyway."

Of course, he said yes. He was too nice for his own good. Normally, that wouldn't have bothered me, but I was itching to leave as soon as I could. The suspense of waiting to see if Ollie would let me go home alone was killing me.

When we finished mopping, Theo escorted me to the door. We walked around to the side of the building, Ollie trailing behind us.

I chewed my lip, knowing Theo would wait for me to drive off first. I needed to lay out more ground rules with Ollie before I went anywhere.

"I appreciate your hard work, Enid." Theo's accent grew thicker late at night, like it took effort to add the proper inflections. He seemed extra tired tonight.

He managed his usual cheerful smile. "I am grateful to you for taking on deliveries last minute. It is a shame Jenna's car is not functioning properly."

It wasn't the first time Jenna flaked out, and we both knew it wouldn't be the last.

"I'm happy to help where I can," I said, doing my best to keep my snide commentary to myself.

A single overhead light illuminated the back end of the parking lot. Theo's teeth were almost all I could see of him in the dim lighting.

"It is difficult to find good help. You are very good for my business. I hope I never make you feel underappreciated."

"Never. You're a great boss," I said. I meant it.

Theo always had a good attitude. He never got stressed when things got busy. He didn't snap at his employees or make demands, opting to ask for what he wanted instead. I hadn't known him long, but he seemed like a genuinely good person. He fit the Peach Grove mold.

He patted my shoulder and headed for his tan Chevy sedan. "I will see you tomorrow," he called.

"Yeah. See you then."

As soon as I situated myself in my car, I pulled out my phone, pretended to dial, and held it to my ear for Theo's sake. Ollie sat beside me. "Theo's going to wait for me to leave first, so talk quick."

Ollie bit his lip and grimaced. "I need a ride back to Peyton's."

"No. Anything else?"

He looked hurt by the speed of my response. "I can't leave her like that. She's upset."

"You could have stayed with her," I reminded him. "In fact, you could have walked to her house at any time today. It's not like you get tired or dehydrated. You don't sleep. Your feet don't hurt. You don't even need to rest. You could walk there now."

"I can't." He ran his hands through his hair, frustrated. "I'm bound to you."

I blinked. "You're what?"

"Bound. I'm bound to you. I have to go where you go."

"Ghosts aren't bound to people. They're bound to places."

"They can absolutely be bound to people," he assured me.

"Not that I've ever heard of. Besides, I'd never seen you before this week. You died a while back, right?"

"Yes. I wasn't bound to you when I died. This is...new." He squirmed uncomfortably.

I sat there for a long minute, trying to make sense of this. My mind swam with images of him at my house, hovering over me while I ate, beside me when I slept, in my bathroom, waiting impatiently on the other side of the shower curtain while he relentlessly pestered me about helping his dead wife.

"No, no, no," I chanted.

This was a nightmare. *Please let me wake up.*

Chapter 5

"You are *not* coming home with me."

Ollie's tone got belligerent. "Hey, I'm not happy about this either."

"I guarantee you're not as not-happy about this as I am."

"Calm down, okay? I don't need to be in your house. I'll stay outside. I'm not a stalker." He let out a huff of irritation. "I just have to stay within range of you. You can be all cozy in your house while I hang out in the yard, twiddling my thumbs."

He didn't say "and not investigating Peyton's murder," but it was clearly implied.

I glowered at him. "What changed?" I demanded.

I wasn't completely convinced he wasn't lying about the whole thing. He was desperate to be with Peyton. Being with me was not going to help him with that. "How come you're suddenly bound to me? Did you do this on purpose?"

"Sort of?" he said dubiously. "We don't always have control of these things."

He didn't meet my eyes, which I found suspicious.

"If you bound yourself, then you can unbind yourself."

"Like I said, I don't know how it happened. I don't know how to undo it."

I chewed my lip, thinking hard. "Ghosts are normally bound to something familiar, right? Like the house they lived or the place they worked. If I take you to Peyton's, can you bind yourself there?'

"Maybe. It's worth a shot." He didn't sound all that confident.

I'd worked a full shift. I wanted to go home and unwind with a hot shower and a book. There was no way I was taking him with me. As far as I knew, he didn't know where I lived. I'd prefer to keep it that way.

"Okay, fine, but you need to figure out a way to bind yourself to Peyton's house. You are not coming home with me."

"You already said that."

At my look, he held his hands up to ward off my anger. "I'll give it my best shot. Cross my heart."

"And hope to die?" I rolled my eyes, then put my phone away, muttering, "Doesn't mean much when you're already dead."

I started the Phantom and pulled out onto Highway 70 with Theo behind me. He lived near the cafe and pulled onto a side street two blocks later. I continued on to Primrose Court, parking down in the cul-de-sac so I didn't look obvious in front of Peyton's house. It was late enough the neighbor guy might be asleep, but I didn't want to risk it.

"I'll wait here," I said. "Tell me when you're unhooked."

"Unbound," Ollie corrected absently. "And you're most of a block away. I need you closer to the house."

My teen years weren't so far gone that I held back my dramatic sigh of exasperation before climbing out of the car, careful to turn off the overhead light before opening my door. I closed it softly. The neighbors were probably on high alert after having someone murdered up the street.

Luckily, the walk to Peyton's house only included one street light, which was across the street, so I was able to stay in the shadows. I cut through the corner of her yard. When I was seated in the darkness along the side of her house, I said, "Be quick. I'm not sitting here all night."

"Right," he said. "I'll have better luck inside."

"Stay focused." I pulled up a book on my phone and put it in dark mode to keep the screen from giving me away. Ollie disappeared through the wall.

I was less than a chapter into my pirate witch story when a noise caught my attention from the back of the house. I held my phone against my chest, blocking what little light it gave off.

The noise was probably a squirrel.

Denver had birds. Wyoming had birds and cows. One month in Georgia and I'd seen a thousand birds and squirrels, plus deer, coyotes, armadillos, turtles, frogs, locusts, and giant yellow spiders as big as my hand with webs wider than both my arms outstretched. I'd even seen a bear meandering along the shore of the Chattahoochee River a mile out of town.

The abundant array of wildlife in Peach Grove meant almost anything could have made the noise.

I was contemplating the chances of a hungry bear prowling Peyton's back yard when I heard a foot scuff. Someone rounded the corner from the back of the house, their details cloaked in darkness. The shoulders seemed broad enough to be male. He was carrying something in one hand. A bag, maybe?

My throat constricted. This could be Peyton's killer. It certainly wasn't a cop. Not that a cop would be much better. I had no logical explanation for hanging out in a recently dead girl's yard at night.

The figure was on a direct collision path with me. It wasn't hard to tell when he spotted me.

He jerked to a stop. Heartbeats passed where we both stared at each other.

Slowly, he moved his empty hand, placing it in his pocket before withdrawing something. I heard a 'snick' that sounded far too much like a knife blade for my comfort.

"Uhh," I said, hoping to stall him with my wit.

He lunged at me before I could think up a way to talk myself out of danger.

I scrambled sideways, half-falling as I kicked out with my foot. I landed a glancing blow off something. A muffled curse was nearly drowned out by the blood pounding in my ears.

I turned and ran, my foot pushing off a tree root, launching me like a sprinter from the blocks. I didn't realize I was screaming until I hit the street. Running for my car might have been the smart move, but it seemed too far, the path too dark. Instead, I made a bee line for the nearest street light just past Peyton's driveway.

Before I made it there, the neighbor's house lit up with huge floodlights. It was like the sun popped up out of nowhere, momentarily blinding me. I kept running.

The front door banged open. The weirdo neighbor came out swinging a baseball bat. He spotted me, dismissed me as clearly *not* the threat he was looking for, and continued to scan the furthest reaches of Peyton's yard where his lights didn't quite reach. "I'm calling the cops, but only after there's a body!"

I stumbled into his yard, then turned to scan the area behind me. Something moved a dozen yards from me. My attacker was there, watching from the darkness. Could he throw his knife from there? Did he have a gun?

Not wanting to find out, I sprinted for the neighbor. I wasn't sure how useful his bat was going to be, but he'd at least be a second target for the creep. That alone would increase my chances of survival. Plus, it's harder to hit a moving target than a stationary one.

The neighbor wore a purple nightgown with a matching nightcap, complete with a pompom dangling over his shoulder. With a little barbed wire on his bat, he'd be the perfect mash-up of A Christmas Carol meets Walking Dead.

He looked ridiculous. Hopefully that would make my attacker think twice before messing with him.

"Get inside," he said, holding his door open.

Three steps led up to his front porch, which was a five foot square of concrete barely big enough for one person to fit on, much less the two of us. His doormat said "Visitors are Unwelcome. Go Away."

Like Peyton, his door didn't have fancy glass. The door itself was fancy, though, made of solid wood if the grain was any indication.

What is with my obsession with glass in the doors? I never seemed to notice unless I was in this neighborhood. Considering I had bigger things to worry about, I pushed the thought aside.

From the doorway, I scanned the yard. Not only was there no sign of my attacker, there was no sign of Ollie. He had to have heard me scream. He couldn't have done anything to help.

That never seemed to be relevant when I told him the same about his ghost problems.

Maybe he was in the middle of a binding spell to get him out of my hair. I hoped that was it. If it wasn't for him, I wouldn't have been here in the first place.

The bat-wielding neighbor backed inside. "You okay?"

My heart was still racing. I couldn't tell if that was from the sprint or the adrenaline. Despite that, I couldn't stop staring at his fuzzy purple bunny slippers. Was that a sign of shock?

"Um. Yeah," I managed.

"What happened?"

"I was—" How did I explain being over at Peyton's again? This made twice in one day and had to look suspicious as hell.

"You were peeking in windows? Wanted a look at the crime scene?" He waved a hand dismissively, still facing the yard. "People get curious. It happens. What scared you?"

I wasn't the least bit curious about the crime scene, but it wasn't like saying a ghost demanded I take him here so he could bond to his recently-deceased wife was going to win me any points. "A guy came around from the back of the house. He pulled a knife on me."

The neighbor nodded as if he'd expected as much. How much action did this guy see in a week's worth of neighborhood watch?

Enough to have floodlights and a baseball bat ready, apparently.

"Probably the perp. Did I tell you the victim in that house was stabbed multiple times?"

I'd known she'd been stabbed, so someone had. Was it Ollie? Or Peyton? Either way, it wasn't the neighbor.

He saved me from answering by herding me further inside. "Go on into the kitchen. I'll make you some tea. Chamomile will help with the shaking."

Shaking?

It wasn't until I crossed my arms that I realized my hands were shaking. With bat-man breathing down my neck, I had second thoughts about disappearing into his house, but there was nowhere else to go. My attacker was out there somewhere. Surely he was more dangerous than bat-guy.

I'd heard a joke about a man driving down the road who stopped to pick up a hitchhiker. The hitchhiker said it was brave of him to pick up a stranger. He could be a serial killer for all the guy knew. The driver laughed and said, "The odds of us both being serial killers is pretty slim."

The joke had been funny the first time I'd heard it. Thinking of it now, it was hilarious. I bit my tongue to keep from laughing. Something dark hid behind that urge to laugh. I wasn't sure it would let me stop once I started.

I tried to focus on my surroundings. I stood in a small living room with two couches facing one another. Generic art prints hung on the wall, blank white with steaks of red, blue, and gray. A gray area rug and a coffee table finished the sparsely furnished room.

On the far end of the room, an oversized archway led to a breakfast nook with a four-person table. Everything looked neat and tidy and not at all like what I expected after the number of crumbs that had fallen from bat-guy's beard earlier.

Given the fact that he was essentially wearing a purple dress, I didn't think making assumptions about him was wise. If he could carry a bat, wear a costumed nightgown, and eat like a slob, he could certainly clean up nicely and be a serial killer while he was at it.

I'd just convinced myself that last part wasn't true when I heard a series of clicks and thunks behind me. Suddenly hyper-alert, I watched as he engaged the better part of a dozen different locks on the door. Nobody was getting into his house without a battering ram.

Of course, that meant nobody was getting out, either.

My body, which had been working hard to rid itself of excess adrenaline, greeted a new flood. My mouth went dry, and I wondered how much trouble I could get into in one day.

It made sense to have the cops pre-dialed into my phone in case bat-man tried anything. A quick pat down of my pocket brought on the realization I'd dropped it beside the house. I'd been reading a book, which meant there was a good chance it was unlocked. If knife-guy managed to find it, I'd have a new record for how deep a hole I could dig myself.

This was bad. Really, really bad. Would my attacker know where I worked? Where I lived? Probably. At least my secret about seeing ghosts was safe. That information never saw the light of day. Yay?

The crazy neighbor interrupted my spiraling thoughts.

"You want chamomile with or without lavender?" he asked, passing by, headed for the kitchen.

I studied the locks. It would take me far too long to undo all the bolts to escape. His house was Fort Knox.

Trying not to panic, I followed him to the kitchen. My fingers were cold. I clenched and unclenched my fists, trying to get the blood circulation going. For as hard as my heart was pounding, I should have been warm enough to melt snow caps.

I was probably overreacting. He'd passed right by me, bat in hand. If he wanted me dead, I'd be dead. He was trying to keep me safe. He wasn't locking me in. He was locking the bad guy out. That was a good thing.

If only my nerves would get on board with my logic.

When all else failed, I did what I did best: compartmentalized. I focused on what I wanted to and blocked out the rest. I wouldn't worry about the attacker or my phone or where the hell Ollie had holed up. Instead, I would just breathe and follow the conversation at hand.

The kitchen was larger than I expected. Bat-man had set his weapon down somewhere out of sight. He stood in front of an open cabinet full of stacked boxes of tea in every flavor imaginable. He turned to look at me with an expectant air.

He'd asked something about tea, I remembered. "I'm not picky."

Without looking, he grabbed a box, closed the cabinet, and opened the one next to it, which was full of coffee mugs. "We didn't get to introductions earlier. Name's Randall."

Uh oh. I debated whether to tell him my name. Enid wasn't exactly common. My grandmother had insisted on it because Enid meant 'spirit.' She'd had the same curse. It skipped my mom. Or possibly, by the sheer power of her delusion, she'd nullified it. If anyone could imagine ghosts weren't real vividly enough to make it manifest, it was my mother.

The sound of hot water percolating came from behind the counter. A minute later, Randall brought me a steaming cup of tea.

If I was going to trust him enough to drink his tea, there wasn't any point in hiding my name. The tea would be the bigger danger. "I'm Enid."

He nodded at the table behind me. Once I was seated, he slid the mug over. It was warm, but not hot enough to burn.

I wrapped my fingers around it, the soothing warmth momentarily making my hands shake more before they settled into something resembling a relaxed state.

Randall sat across from me, his chair turned to the side, offering a good view of his profile. His shaggy beard made him look frumpy. In the light of the breakfast nook, I could see little bits of pale chip glistening through his brown beard hairs.

"You wanting to call the police?" he asked. "Not that it'll do you much good."

The offer made me feel better. Maybe that was the point. Either way, I thought about it. "I didn't see the guy well enough to identify him, but it seems wrong to let some crazy guy with a knife run off. What if he stabs someone?"

Randall huffed out a laugh. "There's a lot bigger things out there to worry about than a guy with a knife. Trust me on that."

Motion at the front door caught my attention. I twitched before I realized it was Ollie coming through the front door.

Randall caught the motion, his eyes going from me to the door. He must have chalked it up to nerves because he didn't say anything.

Ollie looked around the living room before heading my way.

"Reporting the guy isn't going to help anything," Randall assured me. "My rule of thumb is you only call the cops if you are currently in immediate and overwhelming danger."

I didn't want to know what Randall thought of as overwhelming danger.

"He's a little kooky," Ollie said.

I nodded, thinking the same thing. "You don't seem to have much faith in the police around here."

"Nope. Big crime has been moving in on this town for two years now. At first, I figured they weren't aware of the problem, so I pointed it out."

"And?"

"They ignored me. Eventually, the problem got so big a blind person could see it from the moon. They should have pushed it up to the federal level by now. They're sitting on their hands. The only reasonable conclusion is they're in on it."

I moved him up a couple notches in my mental estimation of his insanity levels. "What kind of big crime?"

"The cartel has outposts everywhere, for starters. They've infiltrated the whole city. You never know who's working with them. People who used to stay home are out driving around at all hours of the night. The rate of drug overdoses in nearly every county adjacent to ours has spiked. For another, cops aren't investigating mysterious deaths like they should." He gestured in the direction of Peyton's house. "That girl across the street got crosswise of someone in the Saints, mark my word."

"The Saints?" I asked.

"The cartel."

"What?" Ollie said, clearly offended. "She doesn't hang out with the cartel. That's ridiculous. This guy's off his rocker."

Ollie hadn't bothered to show up when I was screaming my head off. The fact that he could walk through walls meant he should have reached me before Randall, the bat-wielding, purple-clad conspiracy theorist. Just to poke at him, I said, "That's feasible. With Atlanta's size, there's bound to be plenty of organizations running drugs. A small town on the outskirts probably wouldn't have the manpower to take them down easily."

"You're joking," Ollie said.

Randall scratched his beard, flakes cascading down his pajamas. "Poor girl probably didn't have a clue. Most people ignore the signs. I doubt she knew what she was getting into."

"Ugh." Ollie threw his hands up and stormed off through the living room wall to whatever lay beyond.

"I tried to warn her once. I could tell she wasn't very open-minded about it," Randall continued.

"Too bad," I murmured, sipping on my tea. It was good. Warm. Soothing.

Setting Ollie off didn't make me feel the least bit guilty. He'd almost gotten me killed. He could go hang out with his wife if he wanted better company.

I needed to ask him how the binding went. The fact that he'd come into Randall's house wasn't promising. I'd been hoping he was stuck over at Peyton's house.

"Unfortunate but expected," Randall said. "People ignore signs plain as day all the time. There's stuff walking this planet most people wouldn't know what to do with."

I chuckled darkly, and my mouth moved without consulting my brain first. "Like ghosts?"

"Maybe. I don't have any proof of ghosts. Who knows what's on the other side of the veil?"

Me. I knew.

"We could probably figure it out if we didn't ridicule claims of ghost sightings. Nobody even believes in the Tall Man, despite concrete proof of its existence. People are so busy trying to block out things they can't explain that they avoid taking a hard look at it, even though that's *how* you get explanations."

"Right." I said. "What's the Tall Man?"

He raised his eyebrows, incredulous. "Bigfoot. Sasquatch. Yeti. Though that particular species tends to live up north. Tall Man is what the Creek Indians called them before the civilized people came to do what *civilized* people do."

I could hear the disapproval in his voice, but I was distracted by the fact that he was talking about Bigfoot while I was bolted in his house nine ways to Sunday.

"I'm convinced the government has satellites on the lookout for these creatures, and they've got plenty of proof they exist, but they're keeping it quiet so they can catch them and run experiments without the animal rights activists making a stink about it. Those poor creatures just want to be left alone. It's all they've ever wanted."

"Eniiiiiid!" Ollie called from somewhere deeper in the house. He burst from the living room wall, his eyes wide. "You need to get out of here. Now. The guy's got rooms back there full of murder boards, police radios, walls of monitors with surveillance cameras from dozens of places—including this room—plus weapons. Lots and lots of weapons. Guns, knives, swords, throwing stars. And a target that he's spent way too much practicing on."

The renewed adrenaline made me queasy, the taste of tea lingering in the back of my throat. "Oh, darn." I stood, trying to hide my alarm. "I forgot to meet my friend. I told her I was coming to check out the house real quick, but then we were going to meet up. I'm late." I headed for the door, leaving my cup behind and hoping he hadn't put anything in it.

Randall didn't move. He watched me, his face expressionless.

"She's going to be worried about me," I babbled. My heart was pounding in my chest as I headed for the door. "I'm sure the guy outside is gone by now, and the drive isn't far. I should be safe."

I'd managed to turn the top bolt before a hand pressed on the door next to my head.

"I'm going to need you to back away from my door."

Chapter 6

Randall snaked an arm in front of me, easing me back.

I gave Ollie a desperate look, fully aware I was in deep trouble if I was looking to a ghost for help.

"Crap. I'll see if there's another way out." He sprinted through the kitchen wall.

Why was I not surprised his idea of helping was to leave? I'd call him a waste of space if he took up any.

My breathing grew ragged. Could I jump out the window? I hadn't noticed bars on them, but Randall took security seriously. He probably had bulletproof glass or something.

Randall stepped between me and the door, his back to me. He was too tall and muscular for me to grapple with. Jumping him from behind wasn't an option. Running might be useful if Ollie could tell me where to go.

A familiar *snick* told me he'd re-locked the bolt I'd undone. It was pure paranoia for him to think one bolt would make a difference when he had so many others in place. I really, really wish I hadn't been stupid enough to leave my phone in Peyton's yard. I could have called the police after all. Assuming Randall didn't have a cell jammer in his murder lair full of weapons and techno-gadgets. Had he asked if I wanted to call the police to see if I'd pull out my phone?

At least if I'd left it outside, there was a chance Lexi would report me missing, and they'd track down my phone. Of course, finding it at Peyton's house would throw them off track. Had any of the neighbors heard me screaming? Had any of them seen me go into Randall's house?

Thoughts streamed through my head, cascading into one another like a fourteen car pileup on the freeway. I couldn't seem to stop them.

I wished I hadn't come to Peyton's house. I wish I hadn't dropped my phone. I wished I hadn't screamed like a girl and run away when the attacker had come at me.

Growing up, I'd had a neighbor who owned a martial arts studio. Master Cho tried to get me to join. My sister had, but his studio was downtown. As a child, the location had too much history and far too many ghosts for me to block out.

Master Cho knew I was weird. He'd take a few minutes every couple days to call me over on my way home from school, or on the way to play with friends, and we'd work on a move in his front yard. The impromptu lessons never lasted long and focused on no-nonsense self-defense moves.

He'd been my only sparring partner, so I got used to practicing on someone much bigger than me. My sister learned the official moves. I learned the quick and dirty stuff. Choke holds. Pressure points. Arm twists. Shots to the side of the knee. Arm bars to the throat. Master Cho knew I wasn't keen on fighting, but he insisted if I ever needed to, it was important to put down my assailant quickly and get away.

Fat lot of good my training had done me. I'd booked it out of there so fast I'd forgotten I even had a phone until I was safe. I could have been stabbed in the back. For all I knew, the tree root my foot had caught on, the one that had launched me away from my attacker, was the only reason I was still alive.

I hoped that guy tripped on it.

When I really needed my training, I'd panicked. I wasn't going to panic this time. I stepped back and planted my feet in a wide stance, ready to take Randall to the floor by any means necessary.

To my surprise, he stepped back, the door opening with him. I hadn't even heard him turn the locks.

He peeked out, then opened it further, checking both directions. Then he opened it all the way and motioned for me to exit. "Where are you parked?"

My head was spinning. I had whiplash from trying to convince myself I was safe, only to be in danger again, then turn out safe.

Numbly, I pointed to the cul-de-sac a few houses away.

"I'll walk you. Let me get my bat."

All those weapons and he wanted to keep his bat handy?

I stepped outside, my head on a swivel while I waited. I could have run, but the logic part of my brain was frayed from trying to figure out where the danger was, everywhere and nowhere all at once.

Schrödinger's danger. I'd only know it was there when I was dead.

Ollie returned. "Careful, he's got a bat. Oh, look," he said, surprised. "The door is open."

I let out an incredulous laugh. He'd been worse than useless.

Randall appeared at my side and gestured for me to lead the way.

"Thanks for walking me," I said, my voice high and nervous. "I'm sure I'd be fine, but it never hurts to have an extra set of eyes."

"Hey. That's what I always say." He grinned at me, genuinely pleased.

The panic-inducing claustrophobia from being locked in his house abated. Standing in the open air with only the one potential attacker after me I felt like I could string two thoughts together. Randall wouldn't have let me out if he'd had bad intentions. He'd had me at his mercy.

Maybe he wasn't such a bad guy. A little paranoid. A little murder-boardy. Sure, he believed in Bigfoot, but who was I to judge. I talked to ghosts.

It was a depressing thought. Just that morning, I was the girl who *saw* ghosts. Now I talked to them. Probably not a good sign.

I went down the stairs, wobbling on the second step. Randall's hand gripped my arm above the elbow.

"Careful. You sure you're good to drive?"

A nod was all I could muster until I reached flat ground. "Uh huh."

He released my arm, but continued to scan the area. His floodlights had to make it hard for neighbors to sleep. Of course, the screaming should have done the same, but nobody had seemed bothered by it. They hadn't called the police about a disturbance, anyway. Maybe they were used to Randall's peculiar ways.

Or maybe his conspiracy theories weren't as off base as they seemed. Were the cops ignoring calls?

We hit the end of where Randall's light reached. He followed me into the darkness, all the way to my car, and peeked in the back windows.

"Pop the trunk," he said. Once he was satisfied the Phantom was clear, even underneath, he gestured for me to get in. "You should come back and see me tomorrow," he said. "I've got cameras up."

"No joke," Ollie said, circling to the passenger side of my car. "So many cameras."

"If your attacker came sniffing around after we went inside, I might have an image of him. Even if you don't call the cops, it's good to know what he looks like in case you run into him again."

"That's a possibility." I winced. "I dropped my phone next to the house."

Ollie said, "That's not good. I'll go see if it's there. Don't drive off without me."

What would happen if I tried? It was tempting to see if the tether would drag him down the road after me. Or was he bound to Peyton's house now? *Please let that be the case.*

"That's not good," Randall said, almost in sync with Ollie. "We should check for it. I'll walk over. You shine your headlights on the area you dropped it. We'll see if we can find it."

Guilt washed through me. He'd saved me from my attacker, and now he was willing to walk alone through the danger zone with nothing but a bat to look for my phone, yet I kept thinking the worst of him.

I started the Phantom and followed Randall's retreating back.

Ollie waved at me as I positioned my car sideways, blocking the entire road.

"It's over there," he said, pointing.

I scrambled out of my car and followed. Randall was less than a dozen feet from where it lay in a bed of dirt at the front corner of the house where a row of bushes ended.

The screen was cracked, either from being dropped or stepped on, but it still functioned. If my attacker had found it, he'd have taken it, right? He wouldn't have snooped, then left it behind.

I pressed the button to light up the screen. My book was closed out. Not minimized. Closed. That didn't bode well.

The stress from the day pressed on me. I could feel a headache coming on, and I just wanted to curl up in bed and sleep. "Thanks," I told Randall. "I got it." I waggled the phone at him. "It still works, even."

"Glad to know the cartel doesn't have it. That would be bad."

"Yeah," I muttered. My stomach squirmed uncomfortably.

We headed back to the car. I said goodbye and left Randall behind, a lone figure bathed in radiant light.

Ollie rode shotgun. I didn't bother to ask how the bonding went. Clearly he was staying with me.

I wasn't in the mood to talk. Luckily, I was very good at ignoring ghosts. He made a couple attempts at conversation, then got the hint, and we rode home in silence.

When I pulled into Lexi's driveway, I put the Phantom in park and sat there for a long minute. "I need boundaries."

The ensuing silence worried me. Did he plan on manipulating me into dragging him back there every day until there was progress on her case? Progress I couldn't help with?

A quick glance showed he was staring broodingly out the windshield, lost in thought.

"You're still bound to me," I said. It wasn't a question. "But I know your tether can stretch across a street, otherwise I'd have seen you when I went to Randall's."

Had he known I was in Randall's house because of the floodlights or could he follow the bond back to me? It didn't matter enough to sidetrack the conversation from the point I needed to make.

"That means you can stay outside my house when I'm inside." I put steel in my voice. "If you walk in on me while I'm changing or in the shower, so help me I'll find a way to exorcise you from this planet."

His distant look focused on me, his expression appalled. "What? I wouldn't do that."

"Because it would be wrong?" I looked him dead in the eye. "Because it would be a violation? Like interrupting my life and demanding I solve your problem? The one I'm not qualified to interfere with? The one that got your wife killed? The one that almost got *me* killed tonight?"

He had the good sense to look properly scolded.

"I'm terribly sorry if I've offended your sensibilities by assuming you don't know where the line is."

Fidgeting with his hands, he said, "I know that was wrong, and I'm sorry. I really am."

I could sense a "but" coming.

"I can't promise I wouldn't sneak into your shower if it had any chance at all of helping Peyton move on." He winced apologetically. "The state of her soul is more important to me than your embarrassment. I know that's a terrible thing to say, but you don't seem to know how important it is for a soul to move on."

It was his turn to look me in the eye. "Being stuck here is torture. Imagine someone you love locked in a coffin and buried underground with an oxygen mask and an I.V. They can't die, yet they aren't really living. They're just stuck. Possibly forever."

"If I could get rid of all the ghosts by helping them move on, I would. It's not in my skill set. Besides, plenty of ghosts do fine as hold-overs. They travel around, they have friends. I know some are bound to one place and, yeah, that sounds really boring," I admitted, "But I can't help that."

"What if you can?" His desperate, pleading look told me he didn't really believe that. He was grasping at straws.

I had no way to definitively prove I couldn't help Peyton. Hope was a hard thing to kill. It was time for a different stance.

"I hear what you're saying. I can see how she's the most important thing to you. I get that. You gave me the hard, unfiltered truth, so let me do the same in return."

He turned his shoulders toward me. I had his attention. His dubious expression told me he knew he was going to regret what I said next.

"There are a million problems in this world. A million starving children. A million abandoned pets. A million people in need of a liver or a lung. I can't save them all. Where ghosts are concerned, I can't save any of them. Some want me to tell their loved ones they're watching over them. That never helps. Believe me, I've tried."

Granted, I was six at the time. The lady I'd delivered the message to thought I was too young to be believed, but somehow old enough to mastermind a plan to dig up secret, unknowable things her husband used to say to her, then use that to manipulate her feelings as a mean prank.

Blessed night. Save me from the unbelievers.

"They want me to kill their killers, raise their kids, take up the cause that they didn't even care about when they were alive until it affected them. The crime rate isn't a problem until someone breaks in your house and kills your loved one, right?"

His gaze was haunted, telling me I was right. He hadn't given the crime rate in Peach Grove a second thought to until Peyton died.

It was a cozy place. The crime rates were low. I'd looked them up before moving out here. Specifically the death rates.

I took a deep breath and blew it out. "I've had a lifetime of ghosts who don't care about what it costs me, so long as they get what they want." The night's events were like a blinking neon sign highlighting that point. Circling back, I said, "Ollie," then waited until he met my eyes. "I. Need. Boundaries."

He broke the gaze first.

"Don't come in my house." I said it gently. He'd gotten the message. Somewhere beyond his desperate need to help Peyton, the shreds of his former decency came to the surface, and he nodded.

I left him there in the passenger side, lost in his new, painful reality. I felt like the villain.

My somber mood wore off after entering Lexi's house. It was hard to maintain pity for ghosts when they were the reason for my living conditions. I couldn't keep a job long enough to get a place of my own, so I intruded on my cousin's digs. I slept on her couch and helped take care of her dog, an adorable little Yorkipoo.

Lexi never made me feel like an imposition, but who wanted extended house guests invading their space for an indefinite period of time?

She was unmarried, kid-free, worked from home, dated a ton, and had a robust social life. She was drop dead gorgeous and had an amazing personality. She was only a couple years older than me and was already paying down on her own home instead of renting. Her life was perfect.

At least, it was before I'd shown up.

She was a freelance journalist with a personal office off the living room where I slept. Her work desk was bigger than anything I could imagine needing the space for, but I was a waitress, so what did I know about office desks?

I tried to be aware of her habits and avoided disrupting them while helping in any way I could. I did most of the grocery shopping, but only a little of the cooking. I cleaned some, though Lexi was fastidiously neat, and walked her dog, Bailey, every chance I got.

Because I was so attuned to the house, I was aware the second I walked in the door that she had a man over. I knew because Bailey had peed on the dining room floor. She was a sweet dog, but she really didn't like it when Lexi brought a man home, which was a regular occurrence.

Bailey typically got a ridiculous amount of attention from Lexi. Less so when a man was over. This was her way of objecting.

I cleaned up the mess quietly. Murmuring sounds came from Lexi's bedroom.

I'd put money on tonight's man being one I'd never seen. He would make the fifth in a month. Lexi brought home someone new every week.

I put Bailey on a leash and exited the house, contemplating how to ask my cousin if she was a call girl. Not that I was judging. I talked to ghosts after all.

Ollie wasn't in the Phantom. Either he was exploring the bounds of his tether, or he was ignoring me, which was just as well. We'd both said what we needed to.

Bailey sniffed around out back. Lexi's yard was average sized, the back blending into a strip of forest that ran between the rows of houses between our neighborhood and the next one over. Bailey and I both loved the forest. I went hiking in Sweetwater Creek State Park whenever I got the chance since it was only a few minutes' drive. The smell of pine mixed with leafy trees gave the air a fresh, invigorating sense of wildness that called to me. It spoke of solitude and adventure, just me and nature with no ghosts allowed.

Deer had worn a number of game trails through the long stretch of trees. It was easy to see which ones the neighborhood kids used. Those trails were more worn and less triggering to my snake aversion, another plentiful native of the area.

I stood, breathing in the fresh air until I was pulled from my reverie by the sound of a honk coming from the direction of Lexi's house. Despite the frequency of her dates, they never stayed the night.

A car pulled off as I stepped out of the forest with Bailey. We made our way to the front door and entered. Lexi was already in the shower.

Exhausted, I kicked off my shoes and lay on the blue couch that doubled as my bed.

I was asleep before Lexi exited the bathroom.

Chapter 7

My truce with Ollie lasted less than a day.

On my way to work, he reiterated his case. "I can't leave Peyton stuck in this world. I left her once. I'm not doing it again."

His tone was so full of...self-hatred?...it caught me off guard. He had that haunted look again.

Ghosts typically got stuck because of unfinished business, though that wasn't always the case. Whatever had happened in the past to keep Ollie from moving on, he hadn't dealt with it. If he never did, it mean he'd be permanently stuck with me. Ugh.

Thinking hard to come up with a workable solution, I said, "I could go back to Randall's tonight. While I'm going over video footage with him, you need to be working hard on binding yourself to her house."

"That's not going to help. I already tried that. I don't know what I'm doing. Besides, being bound there will just convince her to stay. She needs closure. She needs to know who killed her. Me being there helps comfort her, but it doesn't help her cross over."

"Are you so sure crossing over is better than staying here?"

Not everyone who died got stuck. If that were the case, the world would be overrun with ghosts. There were too many as it was if you asked me.

Most ghosts crossed over when they died. My grandmother had been one of them. I liked to think she knew better than to linger. As far as I knew, though, crossing over was to ghosts what dying was to mortals: a big unknown.

"No," he said, frustrated. "But I know it's not healthy for her to stay here."

I knew better than to argue with a ghost when his mind was set.

Like it or not, I was going to have to help him. "Maybe Randall will have information I can take to the police. Maybe my attacker is her killer."

We rode in thoughtful silence. When I pulled into the parking lot of the Retro Cafe, he said, "I have a friend that might be able to help me."

I didn't want to know where the friend was. Probably prison. Or a crack den. Nothing was ever convenient.

"Great. Finding him will have to wait for my day off. For now, I need to work. We'll head over to Peyton's after my shift. Any idea how long she has before she's stuck here for good? Is there a time line for that sort of thing?"

"Not really. I knew an elderly ghost who stayed with her husband until he passed a year later, then they crossed over together. I know a lot of ghosts who have been stuck for decades. I'm not sure they'll ever pass over. I think it depends on what's keeping them here. The sooner they get resolution, the sooner they can cross."

"Which is why you want to find Peyton's killer," I said glumly. "Why does she care? She's dead. Does it really matter who killed her?"

"If someone took your life, you're saying you'd let it go?"

Probably, but then, I knew the alternative. It seemed like a pointless thing to worry about.

The German Shepherd was still there. It barked in greeting, ducking behind the building in its usual pantomime. It looked so hopeful.

"Sorry, dog. I don't have time to dig around for lost balls." I had enough trouble with ghosts as it was.

I was teamed up with Jenna again for the afternoon shift. She liked to chatter about trivial topics as she worked, commenting on whether a customer's shoes went with their outfit or which stores had a BOGO sale.

I hummed and nodded at appropriate intervals, grateful for the distraction.

Ollie stayed in the back room, which meant I stayed out on the floor.

The early afternoon passed slowly.

My most interesting customer was a guy at the low bar, who ordered coffee, then proceeded to call me over four time to ask for different kinds of sweetener, then whipped cream instead of creamer—a new one for me—then to see what desserts we had.

He looked fit in a snug shirt and cargo pants. His black hair would be considered long for the military, but barely.

There were no real military bases to speak of in the area. Certainly not like where I'd grown up in Denver.

I wondered if he was home on leave visiting family. He was in his late-thirties and had that disciplined feel to him, all business, no humor, zero appreciation for frivolity, and his gaze was always roving like he felt the pressure to be doing something. Die-hard military people sucked at vacationing.

Before he left, he stopped me one last time to comment on potatoes. "You've got hashbrowns, french fries, sweet potato fries, oven potatoes, sweet potato medallions, mashed potatoes, and potato salad. That's a lot of potatoes."

"It's a comfort food," I said, trying to keep my smile in place. A waitress on the clock was not a social companion. I'd spent less time on a family of six. "We try to have something for everyone." Which is why we had multiple sweeteners and six desserts, not that he'd wanted any of them.

It just went to show you couldn't please everyone.

He gave me a look that said it was ridiculous, comfort food or not, then he tossed some bills on the counter and left. Good riddance.

Twenty minutes later, I took my dinner break in the car, hoping to sit without having to deal with Ollie. To my surprise, he was sitting in the Phantom's back seat. I didn't realize he had a friend with him until I was too close to turn away.

The new ghost was my father's age, thick-set, and sporting an olive green fedora. He studied me with interest.

I'd told Ollie not to tell other ghosts about me. Had this one stopped by to chat, or did he know about me?

Standing awkwardly wasn't winning me any incognito awards, so I got in.

"You're sure you heard him right, Frank?" Ollie asked.

Fedora Frank had a Jersey accent. Or maybe Boston. Whatever it was, it reminded me of the Godfather, which I had never actually seen, but it sounded like it fit. Gangster. Mafia. Something like that.

"Absolutely. Your stalker met up with another guy I ain't seen before. He says, 'The broad didn't recognize me. It was too dark, like I told ya.' So the other guy says, 'If you're sure nobody's pointing fingers. We might need to make her disappear quietly just to be on the safe side. We don't need any extra heat after the mess you made.'"

My plan had been to put in earbuds and drown out their conversation with music, but the topic of conversation was strange enough to give me pause.

"Frank followed that customer you had," Ollie said.

Since Frank was the only other person in the car, it made sense that Ollie was talking to me. I glanced in the rearview to see him looking back at me.

Without a shred of contrition, he continued. "I didn't get much of a look at your attacker last night, but after that guy kept calling you over to talk about his coffee, I had my suspicions. I managed to pass word to Frank, and he showed up in time to follow him. It was definitely the same man from last night."

I blinked. Had Ollie overheard my customer pestering me from all the way in the back room?

"You know who I'm talking about, right?" Ollie asked. "The man who ordered coffee, then asked you for a bunch of stuff? He watched you like a hawk every second he was in there. He was trying to see if you recognized him."

Slowly, I pieced together what he was saying. That customer had been my attacker. He must have found out where I worked from my phone. I'd been afraid of that.

I felt like I was sinking in quicksand, grasping for a hand hold to keep from going under. All I could find were ghosts shoving me further in. Ollie was hazardous to my health.

My anger and frustration zeroed in on one fact. "You told another ghost about me." My rules weren't unreasonable. A little personal space and the bare minimum of privacy was all. "After everything we talked about, you thought this was okay?"

"Holy smokes, you were right," Fedora Frank said. "She really can see you." His voice dropped an octave. "The Spirit Body is not going to be happy about this at all."

I wasn't sure what the Spirit Body was. It sounded like bad news for me.

Fuming, I stepped out of the Phantom and stalked back into work.

Two tables had been occupied in the brief time I'd been gone. Jenna was supposed to be covering for me, but she was nowhere to be seen. Probably fixing her hair in the bathroom or buffing her nails in the break room. I brought both tables their silverware and took their drink orders.

"Hey, toots," Frank said, walking through the wall of the restaurant to pop out next to the soda machine where I was filling drinks.

I glared at him, and he held his hands up in surrender.

"Sorry. New age, new rules. *Enid.*"

It was laughable he thought I was pissed about being called toots. He was as clueless as every ghost I'd ever talked to.

"Your assailant's name is Gio. He has ties to Craig. You really don't want to mess with that guy." He glanced around the Retro Cafe. "Honestly, I'm not surprised you're tied up in this. Your boss has his nuts in the same vise."

Neither table full of customers was close enough to hear me whisper, "I don't need to hear anything about my boss's nuts. Theo's a good guy and a good boss."

"Don't flip your wig," he said, his accent growing so thick I could hardly understand him.

"We're a long way from Jersey. Go easy on the accent."

Frank grunted like I'd kicked him. "Woah. You're in so far over your head you can't even see the sun. I'm from Rhode Island, I'll have you know, and your man Theo?" He paused to be sure he had my attention. "His real name's Tunde. That's too different for some people. He's from Nigeria. You know, in case you thought he was Cuban or something stupid."

The word 'stupid' had enough emphasis to include all of me by association.

"Learn some geography. You ain't enough of a looker to get by on beauty alone, sweetheart."

As fun as it was to trade insults with him, I just wanted to be left alone. "Look, Frank. I'm working. I need you and every other ghost on this cursed planet to stay away from me. Got it?"

He gave me a salute and wandered off, his voice echoing through the wall. "Anyone ever tell you you're about as welcoming as a popsicle in the pants?"

The two tables didn't vacate before the dinner rush hit. Ollie came in to follow me around.

"Sorry about Frank. He's a little rough around the edges. I wouldn't have said anything, but I was worried about that guy in here. He seemed suspicious. He must have seen your phone last night or run your plates or something because he found out where you worked really fast. I was trying to keep you safe. It turned out to be the right call, though. At least we know you're in danger."

"Because of you!" I'd been in the middle of prepping a salad and the words came out loud enough to draw the stares of several tables plus Theo. "Sorry." I ducked my head and went back to making my salads.

I needed Ollie to go away before he got me fired.

"You're right. It is because of me," he said, the words continuing to tumble from him like water from a fire hose. "I take full responsibility for my actions, which is why I'm trying to keep you as safe as I can."

I closed my eyes and found my center, my shoulders curling in to block out everything I could but the task at hand. The sound of his voice became a blur in the background.

When Theo tapped me on the shoulder, I turned to him, feeling dazed.

"Are you feeling okay, Enid?"

I nodded numbly. "I'm just really tired tonight. Nothing a good night's sleep won't fix."

It took me a moment to realize the droning of Ollie's incessant chatter had disappeared. He was gone.

"We close in a few minutes." Theo looked concerned. "Why don't you head out early. It's been slow. Jenna can help with the cleaning."

I almost argued with him.

When I hesitated, he insisted. "I can't have my best girl getting sick. Go get some rest."

I didn't look forward to going to my car, but postponing wasn't going to solve anything. I thanked Theo, grabbed my stuff, and headed out.

Frank and Ollie were chatting near my car. Ollie leaned against my bumper, and Frank stood by the dog, who apparently didn't feel the need to snap at his face like he did with Ollie.

Ignoring them both, I unlocked my car.

"What about your cousin?" Ollie asked, letting the question hang in the air like a frosty breath in January.

Kicking myself, I took the bait. "What about her?"

Frank said, "You don't care about your own safety. Fine. Think about her safety."

Ollie said, "That guy found you easily. They can find her, too."

"But I didn't recognize the guy," I said stupidly. "They have no reason to come after her."

"Think, toots," Frank said. "If they decide to tie up loose ends, they got no idea if you blabbed about getting chased around with a knife at that other broad's house."

"Peyton," Ollie corrected.

Frank waved a dismissive hand. "They already said they may need to tie up loose ends by taking you out. You go missing, and the cops are gonna talk to your cousin. Maybe *she* starts talking about the guy with the knife. Suddenly more eyes are taking a closer look at Peyton's murder. That's the last thing they want. If the cops decide there's a serial killer running around, nobody's gonna ignore that. It's exactly the kind of attention Craig and his cronies want to avoid."

Well, crap. Had I put Lexi in danger? I hadn't wanted anything to do with Peyton. I just wanted Ollie gone.

That quicksand feeling returned. I'd gotten myself into several pickles over the years, but this one was fast becoming a nightmare. Most of my bad situations didn't include death threats. I'd graduated to the big leagues.

"Enid," Ollie said.

Frank cut him off. "Leave her be. You wanted her to think? She's thinking."

The only way I could see out of this problem was through it. If my attacker was coming for me, I needed to take him down first. Or at least put him on the police's radar, that way they'd know who to go after if I went missing.

I needed photographic evidence of my attacker. If I gave that to the police, my attacker wouldn't have anything to gain by killing me. It would be in their best interest to leave me alone.

"I'm going to see Randall."

"Who's Randall?" Frank asked.

I climbed into my car without answering.

Ollie took shotgun and Frank sat in back before I could drive off.

"Randall lives across the street from Peyton. He's got security cameras along with a lot of really shady stuff in his basement."

"Sounds like an interesting character," Frank said. "I'll have to check him out. Make sure he's on the up and up."

Up and up? Who talked like that? I blocked out their chatter and focused on driving.

I caught Randall as he was leaving his house.

He greeted me at the door with a grunt. "Thought you might show up." He wore jeans and a polo shirt. His sleek hairdo had a side part, and his face was freshly shaved.

My jaw dropped. "You look...different." The beard had made him look much older. Now he looked like a college student, and kinda hot. "Are you going somewhere?"

"Headed to a funeral." The look had changed, but his responses remained brusque.

"Oh." Bad timing on my part. "Sorry for your loss."

He shrugged. "Don't be. I didn't know the guy." He waved me in. "I got images of your attacker on the table."

A brown folder sat on the little dining table. He flipped it open, revealing a dark, slightly blurred image of the buff guy who complained of too many potato options.

I let out a breath in a whoosh. "Thank you. That's him." Now I had proof.

"Of course it's him. I got this image three houses down about a minute after my floodlights came on."

"You have cameras three houses down?"

"They call it a neighborhood watch for a reason."

"Right." I fingered the photo. "He came to the cafe where I work today. He sat in my section."

He let out a low whistle. "Did you kick a leprechaun at some point? You've got the worst luck."

I closed the folder and picked it up. "I'm turning this in to the police. I want them to know where to look if I go missing."

Randall ran his tongue over his teeth while he thought that over. "Okay, but first, I want you to come to this funeral with me."

I probably should have thought it over longer.

Two minutes later, we were in Randall's car. The garage door alerted Frank and Ollie to my imminent departure. They took their seats in back.

"Nice ride," Frank said. "Ollie wasn't kidding about the basement, though. This guy is super sketchy."

Super sketchy or not, I trusted Randall a hell of a lot more than I trusted Ollie. I reminded myself of that when we were riding through the dark cemetery with our headlights off.

Randall's car was black and old fashioned enough to make me think of the poodle skirt era. It would have fit in well at the parking lot of the Retro Cafe. The only thing missing would be a waitress on roller skates.

"You don't see Impalas much these days. Lost legends in the car world, I tell ya," Frank said. "What I wouldn't give to have had one of these babies when I was alive. Broads woulda been falling all over me."

I fought back the urge to make gagging noises. I couldn't imagine a 'broad' running her fingers through his flowing mane. Mainly because I didn't see much hair sticking out from under the brim of his fedora. I was pretty sure he was bald.

Old people were gross.

"I was never a car guy," Ollie said. "This one looks like it would have been impressive back in the day."

"Not that far back in the day," Frank said. "I'm old, but I'm not that old. It's no horse-drawn carriage. This car was built during your father's time."

"I know, Frank. I'm not calling you old," he placated. "I'm not calling the car old. I'm just saying it was before my time."

"Young kids these days ain't got no respect," Frank muttered.

Up ahead, a line of cars came into view, back-lit by a glow coming from over a low rise. Randall parked behind the last in the line. He hadn't said much. Just that it was a political funeral, and he wanted to see who showed up.

I'd asked why he cared. He'd declined to answer.

We got out and closed the doors, which were wide enough to put a crazy amount of stress on the hinges. Surprisingly, they opened and closed without creaking. I closed my door harder than intended, the sound loud in the night.

"Shh!" Randall hissed. "We're not invited to this funeral, we're crashing it. Try being at least a little discreet."

I winced. "Sorry."

He shook his head in disgust and made his way around the hill away from the cars.

If the lights marked the funeral, we should have been going up the hill. Maybe he wanted to put some distance between us and the noise I'd made.

Eventually, we circled around to where we could see the funeral in the distance beyond a low, decorative memorial wall covered in carved names.

We snuck up to the wall and focused on the funeral, lit by flood lights on portable poles. I wondered why they were holding the funeral at night, but knew better than to ask.

"Almost a dozen," Randall muttered. "They brought the whole crew."

Ollie stopped beside me, not bothering to duck behind the wall.

Frank continued on ahead. "Is that the mayor?" He made his way closer to the group to get a better look.

I wasn't sure how he recognized anyone. They were all crowded around the hole in the ground, most of them with their backs to us. "Why are we here, Randall?" I asked in a whisper.

"You see the guy with the shaggy hair? That's Dan Hanks."

I looked at him blankly. "I moved here a month ago. Am I supposed to know who that is?'

He pursed his lips. "Chief of police. The blond and the redhead are partners. Special Agent Wagner and Lennox. Wagner's the beanpole."

By that, he meant the blond guy, who was well over six feet and slender. The redhead guy was an inch or two under six feet, but more muscular.

"They're lead on this case."

"What case?" I was getting frustrated.

Randall ignored the question. "That short lady with the bun is Mayor Alvarez. The tank next to her is Assistant Mayor Brown."

The mayor had shiny black hair. Hispanic if I had to guess at this distance. "The tank" was a black version of Mr. Clean with broadly muscled shoulders and a bald pate.

I made a rolling motion with my hand. If Randall was going to insist on naming everyone here, I preferred he get on with it so he could fill me in on more pressing matters like why he'd dragged me out here.

Over by the group, Frank jumped down into the open burial hole. I didn't see a casket, which meant it had already been lowered.

Randall squinted at the group. "I think the rest of them are regular cops."

"Great. So what are they doing here?"

"They're *re*-burying a dead guy." He paused to look at me. "Specifically, a very high level criminal they supposedly killed last year. He was buried in that grave up until tonight when they dug him up to re-bury him."

Chapter 8

Randall had a lot of strong opinions about authority figures, but he didn't believe in ghosts. This sounded very much like he believed in zombies, though. I gave Ollie a questioning look.

He followed my train of thought. "Never heard of zombies being real. Pretty sure the Spirit Body would have mentioned something about that."

Again with the Spirit Body. It sounded like an official organization of some kind. I had questions, only now wasn't the time to ask them.

Frank's head popped out of the grave, his voice drifting over to us. "Sweet mother Mary! You're not gonna believe who they got in here!" He stepped up onto what was probably the coffin and climbed out. "That's Kevin Quill!"

I had no idea who that was.

Ollie made a sound of interest, but didn't expound, of course.

"If he was dead and buried, what happened?" I asked Randall.

"I've got two theories."

Of course he did.

"The first is they're covering up their ineptitude after claiming to have killed him when they in fact hadn't. Since nobody's heard from him since his supposed death, that doesn't seem feasible unless they made a deal with him to lay low or get out of the business."

He conveniently didn't mention what business the guy was in, besides the criminal kind.

"The second is they made a deal with him before everything went down, then they helped him fake his death."

"Who is this guy?" I had a name. That didn't tell me much.

My answer came from two mouths at once.

Randall and Ollie spoke over one another, and I had to parse through the information. Big time arms dealer. Drug dealer. Murderer. Most wanted fugitive. Master of disguises. Chased for nearly a decade before they caught him.

Or didn't, as it turned out.

"Don't you watch the news?" Frank asked after wandering up during the tail end of the explanation. "He headed up the PR gang."

I blinked stupidly at him.

"Pounds and Rounds? Pounds of drugs, rounds of bullets?"

I shook my head. I'd never heard of them.

Frank waved me off. "Whatever. Quill was flying off to countries unknown when his plane took a nose dive off the Georgia coast. He hit the water and died on impact. Supposedly, they recovered the body since they knew the plane was going down. Officials say they had someone on the inside tinker with his plane. It was supposed to make an emergency landing. The pilot botched it and killed everyone on board."

"I think I remember hearing about him on the news," I lied for Randall's sake. "PR gang leader who died in a plane crash?"

"That's him," Randall said. "PR was a tough group. Pounds and Rounds. Drugs and bullets. It made him a wealthy bastard."

"As opposed to a normal bastard?"

Randall huffed out a laugh.

Frank said, "I bet the criminal world would crap bricks if they knew he'd been alive this past year."

"Why are all the cops here?" I asked. "That looks suspicious. Why not have the night crew bury him?"

"Good question," Frank said.

"I think they were all working together," Randall said. "I think he made a deal to cut them in for a chunk of the profit if they quit breathing down his neck. They figure they can't leave him be after chasing him for so long, so they fake his death and nobody reports on him after that. In return, his business grows under a new name, and he funds his retirement plans with off-shore accounts."

"So you came here tonight to see who was in on it?" I asked. He thought the mayor and chief of police of cozy little *Peach Grove* were in on it?

Before he could answer, my phone trilled out loud enough to wake the dead.

Randall and I stared at each other, eyes wide. "Run," he hissed, then took off.

One look at the crowd of cops told me half of them had already left the circle of lights, melting into the darkness. I mashed the button to shut my phone up and took off on a different route.

Splitting up meant less chance of being caught.

Adrenaline made my feet fly. I ran straight down the back of the hill, wondering what the hell I had gotten myself into. I was an upstanding citizen. I worked my job and kept my head down. I didn't steal or drive like a maniac. The last thing I wanted was to meet the Chief of Police and the Mayor in a dark cemetery at night while they covertly reburied a dead criminal mastermind.

Footsteps padded behind me, closing in. I risked a glance to see the blond giant, his legs twice as long as mine, gaining on me fast. I cut hard around a tall stone cross statue, grabbing hold of it to lever myself in a new direction.

Out of nowhere, the redhead drew alongside me. Judging by his trajectory, he'd meant to stop me with a flying side tackle, but my altered course put us parallel to each other.

He reached for me. I kicked out with my leg, hitting the side of his knee like Master Cho taught me.

I stumbled, almost losing my footing.

He went down like a wet sack of sand, hitting the ground with an "Oof."

It had been instinct, I swear. Never in a million years would I have kicked a cop. Prison bars danced before my eyes, and fear lanced through me, giving me a boost of speed as I ran for my life.

Headlights flashed on up ahead. Randall leaned across from the driver's seat and pushed the passenger door open. He was mostly in shadow.

The cops probably wouldn't be able to identify him on sight, but his car was a dead giveaway. They'd track him down and find me by association.

I'd have to worry about that later. For now, I ran, convinced the blond's hand would snatch me any second. For a moment, it felt like that nightmare where you run down a corridor, and the door at the end recedes infinitely so you never get close to it.

Frank appeared next to the car, his arm windmilling to urge me on. "Let's go! Time to agitate gravel!"

I reached the car and hopped, tucking my legs at the last second to land in a cannonball pose.

My shoulder slammed against Randall's. He stomped on the gas, swerving around the cars parked in front of us.

The passenger door closed of its own accord. I'd lost sight of Ollie. He would be fine. Probably. He was attached to me. I wasn't sure what that would mean if he got out of range.

Ahead, two dark figures ran into the road. Their bulky hips told me they were uniformed cops.

Randall kept driving, ready to run them over. Thankfully, they didn't pull their guns.

I screamed a second before impact, but cops knew how to get out of the way in a hurry. They dodged the oncoming Impala at the last possible second.

Randall took the cemetery roads at quadruple the recommended speed limit, swerving like he'd mastered defensive driving and added a few extra moves for good measure. He cut the wheel, skidding around a sharp turn, and we shot out the far side of the cemetery.

Headlights trailed behind us. They were no match for the Impala. We took back roads the whole way home. Randall parked in his garage.

"That was fun," Frank said from the back seat. "I like this guy."

Next to him, Ollie said, "I'm glad I'm not alive for this. You're going to be in so much trouble."

Grateful he'd made it into the car, I leaned my head back against the headrest and exhaled.

Randall elbowed me. "Don't look so glum. We escaped."

"They'll track you down by your car." Even saying it, I suspected Randall was way too paranoid to get caught by such a simple thing. The fact that he was relaxed and grinning told me he had precautions in place.

When he pulled into his garage and closed the door, he said, "Come inside. I'll show you why they won't."

"Do I want to know?"

Randall chuckled and climbed out of the car.

My phone trilled again. I pulled it out only to find my hands were shaking. I was in no condition to drive myself home.

The display showed it was Lexi calling. I answered. "Hey Lexi. I meant to call you. I got caught up in some after-work activity, so I'm going to be a little late." I'd forgotten we normally went over the grocery list together on Friday nights while we caught up with how our week had gone. Granted, we'd only made it an official thing two weeks ago, but I felt bad for blowing it off.

"No worries," Lexi said, her voice light and soft, which always made me think she could make a killing recording guided meditations. "If you're going to be a while, I'm headed to bed after Bailey's walk. There's some prosciutto-wrapped chicken in the fridge."

It baffled me that Lexi managed to get her men to make fancy, home-cooked dishes every week in addition to taking her out on the town. There was no way any woman could juggle as many men as she did.

Whenever I brought up her dates, she carefully steered the conversation to other topics. I hadn't gotten around to flat-out asking yet.

"Bonus points for that guy," I said. "What's prosciutto?" Lexi knew how little cooking I did.

I could hear the amusement in her voice. "It's thin-sliced dried ham. You had it when Lenny made beef wellington."

My silence tipped her off.

"Beef wellington is what you called a steak loaf wrapped in a baguette."

"Ohh. I remember that." I wasn't sure I'd ever actually met Lenny, but he had mad skills in the kitchen. The bread loaf had had fancy criss-crossed designs all over it and had looked amazing. "I didn't like the mushroomy coating between the steak and bread, if I'm remembering right. So the ham stuff is actually steak?"

"No. The mushroom stuff was held to the meat by the prosciutto before the bread went on. Meat in the middle, then mushroom paste, ham, bread."

"Huh," I grunted. "I didn't even notice the ham."

"You'll notice it on the chicken. No mushrooms this time. I promise."

Randall appeared outside my window and motioned at me.

I held up a finger. "Thanks for saving me some. I should be home in the next hour or so."

"Sounds good."

I hung up and followed Randall. Frank and Ollie were gone, already inside I assumed.

Randall led me through the kitchen, where a short hall ended at a bathroom. A door to each side led to a small office on the right with a floor-to-ceiling bookshelf and an even smaller bedroom to the left that barely fit a full-sized bed and dresser.

He entered the office, which was tidy enough to look virtually unused. He tipped a book at one end of the shelf, and I heard a *snick* before the bookshelf rotated out from the wall on a hinge. I couldn't say I was surprised, especially when Ollie had warned me of his expansive setup, which definitely didn't fit in such a tiny room.

A spiral staircase led to a lower level, lit by an LED strip stuck to the wall. While I was short enough to walk down without hitting my head. Randall had to hunch. Light from below illuminated the bottom of the stairs, which dumped us at the corner of a single huge room.

Frank stood looking at the murder boards lining one wall, where maps were posted with red strings held up by push pins connected various points.

"Wow," I said nervously. "You really like to keep your finger on the pulse of humanity."

Frank passed by a rack stacked with weapons. He doubled back to get a closer look. Ollie was nowhere to be seen. Something told me he was over at Peyton's house.

My gaze was drawn to the most impressive thing in the room: his computer setup. Nine screens were arranged in a grid with three separate CPUs behind a multi-tiered shelving contraption that looked like one of those huge fancy church pianos—organ?—only instead of piano keyboards there were computer keyboards. The screens flickered through various surveillance videos.

"More people would pay attention if they knew what was going on around them," he said, dead serious. "Some people think ignorance is bliss. Really, ignorance is just ignorance. What you don't know will absolutely kill you. I had that printed on a coffee mug."

He gave me a few minutes to do a slow loop around the room. The corner with the throwing weapons and the targets were on the opposite corner from the computer setup, which made sense. No point taking out your computer monitors with a bad throw.

The murder boards were everywhere, some of them pinned floor to ceiling along stretches of wall. Circling back to the computer corner,

I noted a book case, one shelf filled with notebooks. I imagined they contained meticulous hand-written notes.

Randall sat at the monitors, pulling up documents. "I got my car from my mother fifteen years ago."

An image showed a middle-aged woman with brown hair and a goofy grin standing in front of a car like Randall's, but in a burnt orange color. She was posed next to a white-haired woman.

"My mom's the younger one in this photo. The car belonged to her friend Nannette. That's the older lady. Nannette decided to go on a cruise and left the car at my mom's house before she left. She ended up having a heart attack and died at sea."

He didn't pause long enough for a display of sympathy, plowing on with his story. "My mom never registered the car. She knew Nanette didn't have any family, so she kept it to remind her of her friend. I got it when my mom died about a decade after that. Mom never drove it."

"You had it repainted. They can still track it down by the license plate, right? Or is it still unregistered?" I hadn't noticed either way.

"It's registered. I have legal plates on it, they're connected to an account for someone who lives in Alaska with the same make, model, and color."

He pulled up a record of registration alongside a grainy picture of a guy with a black Impala.

"Pretty neat, huh?" Randall waggled his eyebrows at me. "They could go knocking on his door. He's probably got friends or work or whatever that'll vouch for his whereabouts. They'll figure out the plates are fake, not that it'll help them track me down. That's assuming they got my plate to begin with. My back plate has a light that's angled to produce optimum glare, so it's really hard to get the numbers on camera. It looks like light is constantly glaring off it. It activates whenever enough light hits the plate for it to be readable."

"And in the dark?" I asked.

"It stays dark."

That sounded completely implausible, but it was Randall, so who knew? "Where did you learn how do to all this stuff?"

"Like I said. If people knew what was going on right under their noses, they'd pay a hell of a lot more attention." His fingers chattered on the keyboard, and a string of images came up. One was a giant plaster footprint. Others were grainy images of a bigfoot-looking creature.

Randall pointed to one picture that was clearer than the rest. "I took that picture myself four years ago."

The picture was of densely packed forest. Rays of sunlight shone through the branches, looking peaceful and serene. "Pretty."

He enlarged the image, focusing on a series of four trees in the distance. One had a strange shape. It was straight and tall like the rest but with lumps in the trunk here and there. He enlarged it more until it was grainy, then enhanced it to make it clearer. "See these lines here and here?"

Highlight lines marked the image, then disappeared. Studying the picture, I could see what looked like legs and arms. Zoomed in, the upper portion of the arms were cut off. "Scroll out," I said.

He complied. Above the arms, branches obscured the very top of the trunk, then it seemed to narrow suddenly, like the transition from shoulders to head on a person. He scrolled out further. Above the head, the brown trunk-like figure ended.

If it was a tree, it was chopped off below the canopy. The more I studied the figure, the stranger it looked. It was the oddest-shaped tree trunk I'd ever seen. Lumpy, but without any branches.

"Weird," I said.

"Check this out." Randall pulled up an identical image. "This is the same shot one minute later."

Three of the trees were there, complete with all the branches in the correct place. My eyes sought out the odd-shaped tree. "It's gone."

"Uh huh. I've been searching for more of the Tall Man ever since. I saw that thing walk off with my own eyes. Fourteen feet tall. If I hadn't been paying attention, I'd have walked right by it."

It occurred to me that maybe Randall wasn't as crazy as I'd thought. Or maybe I was just as crazy.

"Why are you trusting me with all this?" He'd let me into his inner sanctum of crazy, something I doubted he did often.

He studied me for a minute, his eyes calculating. "You have a good reaction to me. You're open minded about things. I can tell."

I thought about how I immediately assumed he was a psycho and ran off that first night I came to deliver food. Had that only been yesterday? It felt like longer. Later, though, when I'd been in danger, I'd run right to him. I'd come in his house and listened to his talk about Tall Men. Or was it Tall Man, even in plural form?

He probably thought I was open minded because I'd come back. "Yeah. I guess."

My mother would have said another word for open-minded is naive. Naive or not, it was hard being the only crazy person around. I understood that more than most.

If he was looking for a partner-in-vigilantism, though, I wasn't cut out for that. "I should probably head home." I hooked a thumb over my shoulder at the stairway.

"Oh. Right. But hey, come back any time. I'm always here. Day or night. I don't sleep much, and I don't get many visitors."

Go figure.

We went up the spiral staircase and through the house. I grabbed the folder with the images of my attacker on our way to the door.

Randall unlocked his many deadbolts. When he opened the door, Ollie was walking up the steps. He paused when I stepped out.

"Hey," Randall said. "Did I tell you there's been a development on the case from next door?"

I could feel Ollie's attention sharpen.

"No. Did they catch the guy?"

"Not quite. There was a guy she'd been seeing. Not long. He only came to her house twice."

With all his surveillance equipment, he would know.

"They had a falling out, so she put a box of his stuff on the porch."

"Oh." I'd already known that. If the cops were just figuring that out, it wasn't going to help them much. "Did the boyfriend kill her?"

"Not sure, but earlier today, the ex-boyfriend turned up dead."

My stomach dropped. "Dead?"

Randall nodded. "Suicide, so they say."

That was coincidental timing. "If he'd only come over twice, I assume he didn't die of heartbreak."

"I'd go with guilt, but I don't think that's the case either. Especially since the bullet went through his right temple. The ex was left-handed."

That didn't take long to filter through my brain. "He was murdered."

Randall tipped his head in agreement. "I'm telling you, steam is building up around here. Something's gonna blow. My burning question is whether the cartel killed him or the cops did."

I frowned. "Cops? Why would they kill an evicted ex-boyfriend?"

"Same reason someone would kill Peyton. I think she and her ex saw something they shouldn't have." Randall shrugged. "It's either the cartel or the cops. Doesn't matter if they're working together."

I bounced the folder against my free hand. This was why he'd wanted me to come to the cemetery. I'd have to think long and hard about involving the cops in anything connected to Peyton.

And if the cops knew I'd seen their secret funeral, I could end up dead just as fast.

Chapter 9

"What the hell have you gotten me into, Ollie?"

I was speeding down Highway 70, trying to put as much distance between me and Randall's house as possible. He'd seemed like a total fruitcake when I first met him, but now the mayor was holding private, midnight funerals, and bodies were dropping like flies. I was in way over my head.

"Don't look at me. I didn't do anything," Ollie insisted.

"Yeah," Frank said. "Don't look at him. Keep your eyes on the road. And go the speed limit. You're wanting to steer clear of the police, not get arrested."

He was right. I slowed down, double-checking my rearview to make sure there were no flashing lights behind me. Why did I feel like a fugitive when I hadn't done anything wrong?

I'd never had an overwhelming sense of self-preservation considering there wasn't all that much to live for if I couldn't have something remotely resembling a normal life, but blessed night, the distance between my current life and a normal life was somewhere on the negative end of the number line.

Things had been simpler when I could avoid bothersome ghosts. Getting a new job would have been better than my current predicament.

Hell, moving states would have been safer. Now, I had a ghost bound to me. He'd follow me anywhere. Everywhere. Forever.

"Look out!" Ollie shouted.

I slammed on my brakes in time to avoid flattening a pedestrian. My bumper smacked him hard enough to make him stumble sideways. He went down in a tangle of his own limbs and rolled several feet.

"Holy shit!" I'd almost killed a guy. My pulse slammed through me like a silent, internal siren. The guy wasn't moving. Had I knocked him out?

Frank muttered, "Told you to watch where—"

"Get out of my car!" I screamed, bordering on hysteria. "I can't live like this!" I flung my door open and clambered out.

An impatient driver swerved around us, honking as it passed. They slowed when they saw the guy in the road, but didn't bother to stop.

Had they thought I'd slammed on my brakes for fun? Or did they think I was crazy?

Honestly, I wasn't completely sure I wasn't crazy. Sanity was seriously underrated.

I was halfway around the front bumper when I realized I hadn't put my car in park. I hurried back to the driver's seat and managed to hit the brakes before rolling into the man. All I needed was to hit him a second time.

I climbed back out of the car to see the guy getting to his feet. He was wobbly, one hand clutched to his thigh.

I stumbled to him, this time checking for oncoming cars. The next one in line had rolled to a stop, keeping me from getting rear ended.

"I am so sorry," I told the man. "Are you okay?"

Lean and fit, he wore blue jeans and a charcoal shirt. He was dark-skinned with olive undertones and shoulder-length, silky black hair. He was cute but probably not all that smart.

Crossing a four-lane highway in the dark without reflective gear or a crosswalk probably made the accident his fault. I wasn't about to point that out.

"Yeah. Fine. Just a bruise." He pulled up his left sleeve to peer at his arm. "Maybe a few scrapes," he amended.

Long, shallow scrapes ran down the length of his outer forearm where he'd braced himself to keep his face from getting similar treatment. With his attention on his arm, he shifted, putting weight on the leg he'd been holding. He ended up hopping on his good leg, sucking in a pained breath.

I considered calling him an ambulance, but the cops from the cemetery were probably on high alert. I didn't want to risk them showing up to snoop around and recognizing me.

The backup plan was to drive him to the hospital myself, though I'd need to be quick about it. With my luck, someone had already called it in.

"Climb in the car. I'll take you to the hospital." I tried to herd him toward my passenger door, hoping it was ghost-free.

Considering Ollie was bound to me, he wouldn't go far, but he'd be in the back seat if he knew what was good for him.

"Are you sure?" the man asked.

"I'm positive. Get in." I helped him hobble onto the seat, glad he wasn't larger than average.

"You're not going to take me to a back alley and dump me, are you?" he joked, wincing through his chuckle.

My laugh came out strained and high-pitched. "Only if your family refuses to pay the ransom."

Don't ask me why I said that. The stress had my mouth running without consulting my brain.

The man froze with his grimace in place. "What?"

"Sorry. Poor attempt at a joke."

"Poor attempt?" Frank said from the back. "The timing on that was golden."

"He's a little distracted to care about the timing," Ollie said, also from the back.

"Ahh," the injured guy said. "The old ransom joke. Funny." He did not sound amused.

"Sorry." I kept saying that. "I swear I'm taking you to the hospital. It's just up ahead."

I hadn't hit the guy hard enough to do lifelong damage. It could have been so much worse. As it was, I'd get a ticket for reckless driving at a minimum. Car insurance in Georgia was sky-high.

Luckily I hadn't killed anyone. Still, my thoughts kept jumping back to the midnight funeral and how I wanted nothing more than to avoid the police.

Selfish, I know.

I pulled up to the emergency room and hopped out to help the injured guy hobble inside to the check-in desk.

"I think I'll be fine," he said. "It's feeling better already. All I need is to rest some, and I'll be good as new."

His limp had improved, though he still winced with every step.

The lady behind the counter wasn't impressed with his tough-guy act. "Name?"

Hospitals were a hot spot for ghosts. There were only a couple in the waiting room. There'd be more deeper in the bowels of the building.

I glued my eyes to my victim's torso, watching for any hint he was going to keel over. "I can't believe I hit you with my car."

"Why do you sound like you're apologizing?" Frank asked. "He's the schmuck running across the street at night in dark clothing."

"Name?" the lady repeated.

"Guy Peterson," the guy—Guy—stated. "Really, I think I'll be fine." He turned to me and said, "Why don't you move your car. I'm here, I'm safe. You should park somewhere. Or maybe just go home. It's not that big a deal."

He was trying to stand up straight. The knee of his bad leg remained bent. He was keeping his weight off it.

"I'll park, then come right back. Are you sure you're okay?"

He gave me a forced smile and nodded, then turned to the receptionist. "She's terrible at jokes. I tripped and smacked my leg on a bench. Pretty sure it's going to leave a bruise, but it'll be fine."

"Fill out this form," the lady said.

I went to my car.

"That was quick," Ollie said as I fumbled the gears, going in reverse before flipping it back into drive.

The churning pit in my stomach was distracting as hell. I was thirsty and wanted to throw up at the same time. Guilt always made me feel an odd mix of symptoms.

Despite my shaking hands, I managed to park without crashing into anything. When I returned to the waiting room, I didn't see Guy anywhere. The receptionist saw me and pointed a pen in the direction of a sign for the restrooms.

Guy could have a long wait to get x-rays. It was smart to use the bathroom before they called him back.

Frank hadn't come with me to park the car. He wasn't in the waiting room, either. I hoped he didn't follow Guy into the bathroom.

Steering my thoughts from tracking down that path, I spotted Ollie in front of the entryway, lost in his own thoughts. It would be nice if he'd look for Frank. Unfortunately, there was no way to ask him inconspicuously.

After several minutes of fidgety waiting, I started pacing. At one end of the waiting room, I stumbled across a doorway to a little cubby with two vending machines, one for drinks and one for snacks. I scanned the selections.

"Hey," Ollie said, poking his head into the cubby.

The last thing I wanted was for a hospital ghost to know I could talk to him. "We are in a hospital," I said under my breath. "People die here all the time. I'm ignoring anything you say. Possibly forever."

"Look, I know you're upset. Things are feeling a little dangerous, and you're still among the living—"

His patronizing comment had my blood boiling before he finished. I pulled out my phone and put it to my ear, ready to give him a piece of my mind.

My phone rang. I almost dropped it in surprise. Glaring daggers at Ollie, I answered without looking.

"Hello?"

"Hi, baby. How are you?" The sugary sweet tone my mother used when she was checking up on me brought on an automatic eye roll.

My mother and I didn't get along. She liked to pretend every hateful conversation we'd ever had—and there were a lot—never happened. We had an unspoken rule. We followed a script, sticking to safe topics so she wouldn't get upset. Under no circumstances were we to discuss grandma, spirits, my childhood, the reason I moved to Georgia, or anything at all out of the norm for everyday people.

"I'm fine, Mom. A little busy right now. I gave someone a ride to the hospital. They're going to be fine, but it's not a great time to talk." Succinct. Not overly aggressive. The tone was right. There was no reason for her to get tetchy.

"Oh, no. I'm so sorry to hear about your friend. It's the middle of the night. You must be in the emergency room. What happened?"

Here we go.

There was never a way to talk around my mother. She always seemed to know the right questions to ask, and she knew my tells, so lying was out. "He was bumped into by a car that stopped too slow. Nothing's broken. He's up and walking. He's getting checked out to make sure. It's just a formality. He's fine, really."

"He? Is this a boyfriend? You've only been out there a couple weeks, and you already have a boyfriend?"

I fought the urge to scream. It was an effort to keep my tone light. "Not a boyfriend. Just a guy."

"From work? I thought your shift ended an hour or so ago?"

"It did. He's not from work. He's just a guy."

"How did you meet this guy? You have to be careful in this day and age, Enid. Not all guys are knights in shining armor. You'd know that if you were more social."

And there it was. If I had a boyfriend, it was too soon, and he was probably a bad person. If I didn't have a boyfriend, it added to the "anti-social" bit she'd been flinging in my face for most of my life.

I let my head drop back on my neck to stare at the ceiling. Why was my mother so painful?

"I'm social, mom. I have plenty of people I talk to at work, plus Lexi has friends that drop by on the regular."

By regular, I meant almost daily. By friends, I meant random men. I would keep that fact from my mother if it killed me. She'd fly down here just to call Lexi a harlot to her face and blame her for leading me astray with her bad example. Then she'd blame me for not seeing what was happening right beneath my nose because I was too anti-social and sheltered to know better. There was no winning.

"Work friends aren't social friends, and Lexi's friends are hers, not yours. You need friends of your own."

Just not boyfriends. I sighed and abandoned the vending machines to find a seat. Ollie followed.

My mother was like a dog with a bone. Getting her off the phone was a nightmare every time. "I saw the guy get hit, Mom. That's the only reason I'm here with him. He's not my boyfriend. He's not from work. He's not even a friend. I don't even know him."

She paused. "You saw the accident?" Her voice went up an octave. "Was it a hit-and-run? Why didn't the person who hit him take him in? Maybe it's best you volunteered to take him in. I wouldn't trust someone after they almost ran me over. They'd get in big trouble over that. You'd be surprised at what some people will do to get out of owning up to—"

"Mom!" My voice was louder than I intended, but I couldn't stand listening to her when I was already freaking out plenty on my own. "I'm the one that hit him."

The swivel of heads in my direction registered in my periphery. I looked around to see most of the waiting room staring at me, including the front desk lady, who had two men in suits standing by her. She pointed her pen at me and they turned my way.

"Look, mom, I'm taking care of it, okay? I really can't talk now. I'll call you later." We both knew I would never call her. I'd rather remove my eyeballs and fashion them into earrings.

I jabbed angrily at the button to hang up and shoved the phone in my pocket.

The two men in suits were watching me expectantly.

Recognition dawned slowly. The tall blond looked apologetic. The redhead wore a calculating smile, like a dog had peed on his shoes, and he was debating how hard to kick it in the head.

A wave of panic rolled through me, and the hairs on my arm stood on end. I was in so much trouble.

"Uh oh," Ollie said. "Aren't they the guys from the cemetery?"

I couldn't hear what he said next past the pounding of blood in my head. After a moment, I realized I wasn't breathing. No wonder I was lightheaded. I forced myself to breathe slowly, though a whimper slid out of me on that first exhale.

The redhead jerked his head at the doors leading deeper into the hospital.

There were more ghosts in a hospital than a police station. My desire to avoid going through those doors was visceral.

I sat there long enough they must have thought I'd gone brain dead.

The tall blond, whose name I couldn't remember, said something to his partner, then headed over to me. "We'd like to ask you a few questions."

Shakily, I stood.

He put a hand between my shoulder blades and guided me toward the doors, gently, but firmly.

I walked in a daze, trying to analyze my options. I couldn't run. The hospital had cameras. They'd have my face. They'd have my car. Traffic cameras would show I'd hit Guy. My car's custom skin was not inconspicuous. Running would only make me look more guilty.

The big question was whether or not they recognized me from the cemetery. Running over Guy would get me a ticket. That would go on my driving record and hike my insurance, which already took a sizable portion of my income.

Assaulting a police officer was a little worse than that. Probably a lot worse. My knees went weak and wobbly at the thought of how much worse. Jail time? A permanent record? Was kicking a cop a felony? Was I going to be a felon?

I was breathing hard, almost hyperventilating at the sure knowledge they were going to lock me in a hole so deep my own mother wouldn't be able to find me.

If Randall were here, he'd tell me to run before they killed me and dumped my body in the coffin alongside the criminal mastermind. Nobody would look for me there.

"Hey. You're new here," an old, hunched ghost said to Ollie. He had a buddy, a rotund, middle-aged guy who'd probably died choking on fried chicken.

The smell of disinfectant made my nose tingle. I rubbed it, noting the hall had over a dozen ghosts roaming the halls.

"Welcome, stranger," the big ghost said in a southern drawl.

Ollie didn't say anything in return, keeping steady pace at my side. I was grateful for that.

I scanned the crowded hallway, picking the dead out from the living. Where was Frank? Where was my victim? Guy Peterson was supposed to be in the bathroom, but even constipation didn't take this long.

A slow, undulating sense of terror built in me. Had Guy gone missing? Had the cops already taken him in for a statement in an attempt to get me in their clutches? It had been dark at the cemetery, but the redhead cop had been close enough to get a good look at me.

"Breathe, Enid," Ollie said. He sounded anxious, which didn't help calm me.

I hunched in on myself, blocking out everything except what I absolutely needed to focus on in the moment. One foot in front of the other, the doors and hallways passed in a haze.

Finally, they ushered me into what looked like a nurses' break room. It was vacant, with three tables spaced a few feet apart, each with a few chairs around them. A counter ran the length of the back wall with a microwave, coffee maker, and sink. A fridge sat along the wall to the right.

As soon as we were all inside, the redhead closed the door behind him. A moment later, the ominous sound of the door being locked echoed through the room.

Chapter 10

I scurried further into the room, circling one of the tables to put distance between me and the cops.

"Are they allowed to lock the door?" Ollie asked.

"Have a seat. Make yourself comfortable," the redhead said.

His calculating look reminded me of half the girls in high school when they were trying to figure out how much they could get away with. I'd been the target of their torture more than once, but only after I'd watched them torture others.

With no friends to speak of, I spent my high school years reading and observing. By the time the girls had decided to pick on me, I knew better than to act like prey.

Dealing with the police wasn't exactly the same. They had actual authority over me. That would require me to modify my tactics. I could still be confident. I just couldn't be as mouthy.

I straightened my shoulders and took a seat with my back to the wall.

They stood over me, silently watching me for an inordinately long time.

The silence was probably supposed to make me feel nervous. Unfortunately for them, I was perfectly comfortable with silence. It wasn't something I got to enjoy very often.

As the seconds ticked by, turning into minutes, I fell back on an old habit I'd developed to preserve my sanity. Since I'd spent most of my life reading books, whenever I needed to block out reality for a while, I'd take the main character from one book and have them run through the events of another book.

What would Aragorn do at Hogwarts? How would Logen Ninefingers fare if he'd gone to high school with the Twilight crowd?

I typically used this mental exercise to occupy my thoughts whenever a ghost followed me home and refused to leave me alone. The nurses' break room had three ghosts, not that they were bothering me. One lay across the counter top, one sat at the table farthest from me, and a third looked out a little window, watching nature do its thing.

That head count didn't include Ollie, of course. He hovered behind me in the two feet of space between my back and the wall.

He was talking. I wasn't listening. I'd shut him out. I'd shut everything out. Attention was a commodity. Most of the people who demanded it didn't have the right to it. That included the cops.

I started running through characters. For my character, I chose Jacky Faber, an orphan girl who was wild, extroverted, and unpredictable. I stuck her in the underground lair of the dark elves, where nobody was ever bubbly and brimming with excitement.

I was getting to the part in my imagined story where the dark elves unanimously agreed to have the girl assassinated for her uproarious behavior when the cops decided they'd softened me up enough. Or maybe they didn't like my amused smile.

A finger tapped the desk in front of me. "Hello?"

I glanced up. "Oh. Are we talking? I thought this was silent time."

The blond said, "Vehicular assault is a serious offense."

That had escalated faster than I expected. Still, it told me they were focused on the accident and not on the cemetery, which gave me hope.

"Vehicular assault? That does sound serious. Maybe I should get a lawyer." I hadn't meant it to sound flippant, but when you'd been considering dark elf assassinations, two guys in suits weren't all that intimidating.

The redhead's jaw clenched so hard beneath his smile I could see the muscles bulge.

If they were focused on the accident, I might be able to get some information from them. "What did you say your names were?"

"Special Agent Wagner," The blond said. "My partner is Special Agent Lennox."

"And you're with the Peach Grove Police Department?"

"Essentially."

The way he said it sounded cryptic. Like maybe they were working *with* PGPD without being an official part of the organization. Did the PGPD have special agents?

I couldn't put my finger on it. Something wasn't sitting right. "Do you have badges?"

The blond—Wagner—pulled aside his jacket flap to show the badge on his belt. He turned his hip toward me so I could read it.

Lennox did the same, but instead of holding his jacket open, he flicked it angrily so the gold badge showed briefly, then crossed his arms.

"Aren't you supposed to wear a uniform if you're law enforcement?"

"We're agents, not officers. We don't do traffic stops," Lennox said, as if the question was ridiculous.

"Then why are you here about a traffic issue? It's not like there's been a murder. Or even a serious injury. And how did you get here so fast? Guy didn't file a—"

Frank came through the wall at a jog, his head swiveling. He stopped short when he saw me. "There you are! Wait, are those cops? Don't say anything." He came to stand by my table. "Woah. Those are the guys from the cemetery."

I was glad he was catching himself up to speed. It wasn't like I could explain anything.

"They're here about the 'vehicular assault,'" Ollie said. I could hear his air quotes even if I couldn't see them.

"They're fishing," Frank said. "Guy just walked out of here. Didn't even check in. I'm thinking he has his own reasons for avoiding the cops. Besides, he told the lady at the desk he fell." He glared at me. "Your big mouth is the only reason anyone thinks you hit him with your car."

I blinked. That was interesting. No report had been filed. I doubted the front desk lady would care enough to call the cops when it was clear the victim was walking and talking and claiming he fell.

Dread settled in my stomach. If they weren't here for the accident, they were using the comment I'd made to my mother as a reason to start a conversation. Probably to put me on the defensive before they asked why I was in the cemetery.

"Who?" Lennox asked. "The guy you ran over?"

They didn't know the guy's name was Guy. I ran back over my conversation with them. Luckily, I'd deflected most of it. Frank had arrived in the nick of time. The special agents had almost walked me into a trap of my own making.

I stood slowly, making steady eye contact for the first time since arriving. "Who did I run over, again?" I looked from one of them to the other.

They shared an enigmatic look.

Sometimes my mouth ran without consulting my brain. This time, I let it.

"I came in here with a man who tripped and bruised his leg. He didn't even ask me for a ride. I offered it because he was limping, and it felt like the right thing to do. I've asked you if I needed a lawyer since you're in here giving me the third degree over something you think I did, only it's clear you have no idea what you're talking about, but you haven't offered to let me call said lawyer. Do you have any idea who I am? Do you know how *old* I am? Do you even know if you're talking to a minor outside the presence of her parents?"

I'd gotten offhand comments, usually from skeezy men, about how I looked younger than I was, so I knew my twenty-two could pass for seventeen in a pinch. Plus, I'd been yelling at my mom on the phone, which is totally something a teenager would do.

I wasn't sure what the legal requirements of talking to a minor were, but the idea of these two badgering an *actual* child without their parents or a lawyer present was appalling. A child would be terrified of them. Hell, I was terrified of them, and I was old enough to drink, if barely.

Special Agent Lennox forced an amused expression. "You don't seem to have much faith in law enforcement."

"I have faith in law enforcement in general. I'm not sure I'd trust *you* to hit water if you fell out of a boat." That might be going too far. I fought back the urge to cringe. Now that I had the spotlight, I wasn't sure what to do with it.

Both of their faces had gone blank. I didn't need their expressions to tell me what they thought of my tirade.

"Keep it going, kid," Frank cheered. "Don't let them gain the upper hand. Storm out of here, quick."

Frank had good advice. It was time to bail.

I shimmied my way out from behind the table while I blathered on. "Before you go judging others for not following the rules you so strongly uphold, maybe you should take a look in the mirror and ask yourself what it is you stand for. If it's the law, follow it."

I made a bee-line for the door.

"Hold it," Lennox barked. "We've got one more question for you."

I pulled down on the handle, which auto-unlocked the door. I froze before opening it.

Lennox waited until I turned to look at him. "Where were you between nine and ten tonight."

Crap. I'd been with Randall at the cemetery. They *had* recognized me, only they couldn't prove it was me, which meant they had no recordings.

Or maybe they only suspected it was me. Since we'd been running in the dark, they couldn't be sure. "I was visiting with a friend."

"Which friend?" Wagner asked.

"Doing what?" Lennox demanded, talking over him.

I scowled. "Messing around on computers, duh," I said, focusing on the second question and playing up the teen attitude. "It's literally what everyone does with their spare time." I frowned at Lennox. "Well, everyone but you probably. You look like you pull wings off bugs in your spare time."

Wagner couldn't hide his grin. Lennox took a threatening step toward me.

He froze when the door pushed open.

I stumbled back as a lady with a clipboard walked in. Her pink scrubs covered a plump body. She eyed the three of us. When nobody said anything, she waggled her clipboard. "The vehicle you wanted?"

Lennox spoke up, sounding almost hopeful. "Black? Older model? Long body?"

The nurse shook her head. "Security tapes show her driving a boxy purple vehicle."

My hands went clammy. They'd had hospital security check the car I was driving. They'd been hoping to find Randall's black Impala. I swallowed hard, feeling sick.

I eased behind the nurse and was out the door.

"That was great, kid," Frank said, he and Ollie following alongside me.

"Wait," came a call from behind us, the voice weak and thready.

I already knew it belonged to the ghost who had been staring out the window. He'd grown interested in our conversation when Frank had started talking to me. He'd been partly why I was so eager to escape.

"Can we help you?" Ollie asked, stopping to stall the man, which was the least he could do considering I'd been doing fine before he'd dragged me to Peyton's house. He had a lot to make up for.

"She can hear you, can't she?" the old ghost said.

I didn't so much as hesitate as I strode on.

Frank doubled back to Ollie. "Who, her? She's alive. The living can't hear us. You know that."

"But she heard you in there, didn't she?" The old ghost said, confused.

"Hey, listen to that, Ollie. We're getting better at this game." Frank chuckled. "We've been doing this for a while now, where we pretend we're still alive. Brings back a lot of nostalgia."

The old man said something wistful-sounding as I turned a corner, trying to make my way back through the maze of corridors. I kept my eyes focused in the distance lest I accidentally make eye-contact with forbidden persons.

Eventually, I hit the reception room, then headed straight for my car, where I found Wagner leaning against the driver's side door, waiting for me. At least it wasn't the redhead. The blond at least seemed contemplative and deliberate rather than feral and hostile.

My shoulders sagged in imitation of a moody teen. "What do you want?" I wasn't keen on being alone with him, but I wasn't about to show I was nervous.

He pulled himself to his full height, holding out a business card. He had an easy manner about him, relaxed and comfortable. "My partner is a bit high strung. We're in the middle of a case that concerns some major players in the crime world."

I took the card he handed me. It had his name printed on it, along with a phone number. A circular logo covered half the card proclaiming he was with GBI, the Georgia Bureau of Investigations.

"What is this, like the FBI for Georgia?" I asked with typical teenager attitude. They'd let me walk off after I'd mentioned questioning a minor. I only hoped he wouldn't ask for my driver's license.

"In some ways." He didn't seem bothered by my snotty attitude. "We investigate crimes. Some of them have been committed in Peach Grove, which is why we're here. I'm not sure how you fit into things yet. Unless I'm mistaken, you're on the outskirts of the operation we're after. I recommend you stay that way. Steer clear of anything suspicious."

By that, he meant steer clear of whatever was going down at the cemetery.

His eyes told me it wasn't a threat. He seemed to genuinely care for my well-being.

He gestured at the card in my hand. "You don't seem like the type to go looking for trouble. If it happens to find you, I want you to have my number. Call me, day or night, if you find yourself in the thick of things. I can help."

"I don't know what you think I'm involved in. I haven't done anything wrong." Except hit someone with my car. And kick a cop.

"Let's keep it that way." He circled around me and headed back toward the hospital waiting room. "Call if you see anything suspicious," he said over his shoulder.

Like the man who'd come after me with a knife in Peyton's yard? Frank had said his name was Gio. I still had his picture burning a hole in my back seat. I could hand it over. Something told me I could trust Wagner. I didn't trust his partner at all.

I decided to keep the photo to myself for now.

Ollie could stand guard over me. If my attacker's boss saw I wasn't saying anything to anyone, he would leave me be.

Was that wishful thinking? If my attacker was watching me right *now*, he'd know I was talking to a cop.

A nervous glance around showed the parking lot was empty but for Wagner's receding back.

I climbed in my car and locked the doors, my imagination in overdrive. If my attacker wanted me dead, there was a million ways I could think of for him to accomplish it, especially if he was tied to a criminal organization.

"We gonna sit here all day?" Frank asked.

I screamed when his voice came from the back seat.

"Woah. Calm down. It's me. Sheesh. You broads get all worked up sometimes."

Having caught my bearings, I glared at him in the rearview. "This *broad* is wondering if her car might blow up. I've got a target on my forehead and a killer, possibly from a cartel, after me. In case you haven't gotten hip with the times, grandpa, nobody says broad anymore."

"Well excuse me for breathing," he said.

"Technically, you don't breathe," Ollie said. "And if Gio-the-Cartel-Assassin is wanting to kill you to avoid questions, blowing up your car in the middle of a hospital parking lot would be the opposite of inconspicuous."

"I do too breathe," Frank insisted. "But otherwise, good point."

It was a good point. I still winced when I started the engine. My nerves were shot. I needed sleep. Luckily, Lexi only lived a mile from the hospital.

Ollie was quiet on the way home, which was weird. Words normally fell from his lips like he had a chronic case of verbal diarrhea. I hoped his silence would stick. If he engaged less with me, maybe he'd find it easier to focus on binding to somewhere else.

I really did feel terrible about his predicament with Peyton, but there was genuinely nothing I could do to help. Like I'd been saying all along, he was on his own.

Frank, on the other hand, talked non-stop. Instead of talking to me, he muttered to himself, which I found easy to ignore.

Before heading into Lexi's house, I paused, listening to the breeze rustle through the branches, trying to tell myself I was okay. It did nothing to dispel the tension in my muscles or the knot in my gut. I felt like I was on the edge of a cliff looking down a terrifying slope that led to a future filled with cops, crime, and conspiracy.

I reminded myself all I had to do was turn away from that cliff and stay where it was safe. If I didn't stick my nose where it didn't belong, maybe my neck wouldn't end up in a noose.

Work. Home. That was all. It was enough.

If I couldn't get rid of Ollie, I'd ignore him. I'd been ignoring ghosts all my life. This was no different.

Resolved, I entered the house, surprised to see the lights on in the kitchen. Lexi had said she was going to bed. Had she left the lights on for me?

I closed the door quietly, but froze when I heard voices. Lexi was talking with someone, and she was angry.

Bailey the Yorkipoo sat on the floor outside the kitchen, watching Lexi and her guest intently.

"I do not date my clients. Ever." Lexi's voice was firm. Judging by the generous undertones of annoyance, this wasn't the first time she'd said so. "The day I date a client is the day I give up my business, and I have worked too hard to be dependent on a man, especially one who likes to think the grass is greener on the other side. If you couldn't find love with who you had, you're not going to find it with me."

I reopened the door, then closed it again, hard enough to be heard. Bailey's eyes stayed locked on the kitchen. "Lexi?" I called. "You up?"

A beat of silence came before she responded. "Yes. My guest was just leaving."

I could picture Lexi's raised eyebrow as she gave the guy a challenging look. Lexi could do "no-nonsense" better than my mom, and that was saying something.

A guy stepped out of the kitchen, headed for the door.

Correction: *Guy* stepped out of the kitchen. He froze when he spotted me.

"How's the limp?" I asked.

Chapter 11

"You," Guy said, shocked to see me.

"You bailed on me." His limp couldn't be that bad if he'd walked a mile since leaving the hospital.

"Did you follow me here?"

Lexi stepped out of the kitchen, eyebrows furrowed in confusion. "She's my cousin. Enid." Her gaze looked from him to me and back. "How do you two know each other?"

"I ran into him with my car," I said, the same time Guy said, "She gave me a ride to the hospital."

Lexi blinked. Unsurprisingly, she didn't look any less confused.

"Why did you leave?" I asked Guy.

"By the time we got there, my leg was feeling much better," he lied. "It's almost good as new."

He'd still been in pain when we got to the hospital. I was glad he was okay, but it was stupid not to at least get checked out. "You left without saying anything."

"I tried. You disappeared, and I didn't know where you were."

"I went to park the car, remember? You're the one who suggested it. Are you hiding from the cops?"

"What?" The question had taken him off guard. "Why would I be hiding from the cops? It was a hospital, not a police station. There weren't any cops to hide from."

"Yeah, there were. I know because they pulled me into a back room and questioned me about my vehicular assault."

"Woah," Lexi said, holding up her hands. "Start from the beginning."

I caught her up on the accident, the hospital, and the special agents, leaving out the part about the cemetery and the interaction with Wagner in the parking lot.

"Honest," Guy said. "I went to the bathroom, and when I came out, you were nowhere to be seen. I figured maybe you decided to leave. I didn't blame you. I was fine. I realized how close I was to Lexi's house, so I decided to walk. I was on my way here anyway when I ran into Enid."

"You mean when Enid ran into you," Lexi said. "Why would you cross the street at night in dark clothes?"

"That's what I was thinking!" I said.

"Did you not see her headlights?" Lexi gave her head a sharp shake. "Actually, never mind. If you walked here, you're fine. I'm glad everyone is safe. Guy, do you need me to call you a ride home? I'd prefer you didn't walk considering your track record."

His shoulders slumped. "I don't live close enough to walk. I was in the area and decided to drop by."

Lexi's voice grew sharp. "Did I teach you nothing? Never, ever just drop by on a woman unless you're looking to piss her off. It's rude to assume she's got time to drop everything and deal with your inconsiderate self showing up out of the blue."

Guy gave a pained groan. "I know. I should have called first."

"You shouldn't have come at all. I was very clear with you. If we're done here, I'll call you a ride."

"I can call my own ride," he said glumly.

"Good. This is a safe neighborhood. Go wait outside for your ride." She gave him a shooing motion, then locked her eyes on me. "Enid and I need to talk."

Looking like a kicked puppy, Guy shuffled past me and out the door.

I waited to hear the click of the door closing before asking, "You don't date *clients*?" It was the closest she'd come to mentioning her revolving door of dating was a business.

Lexi sighed. "It's complicated."

That was fair. Lexi and I only knew each other so well. Our fathers were brothers, but she'd always lived in Georgia, and Denver is on the other side of the country. They only visited every couple years or so.

Lexi and I got along great, partly because we didn't pry into each other's lives. Since moving in, I'd felt like asking too many questions would ruin our newly upgraded relationship. Sharing a house with someone is already an invasion of privacy in a lot of ways. I didn't want to push it.

Still, this was too much to sweep under the rug. "Am I allowed to ask what your clients pay you for?" I held up a finger to give her pause. "It's none of my business, so don't feel like you have to answer that."

Honestly, I was a little afraid she would confirm what I was already thinking.

If it turned out she was prostituting herself for money, my biggest concern was that her clients knew where she lived. What she did in her own home on her own time wasn't for me to judge, but it wasn't a profession known for its safety record.

Plus, I was pretty sure it was illegal.

Lexi opened her mouth, then closed it and took a moment to figure out what she wanted to say. When she finally spoke, her words came out separately, like they were being carefully chosen. "I am a courtship education consultant for men."

That wasn't the phrasing I'd expected. I carefully kept my face clear of expression and my tone neutral. "You teach men how to be better..." I couldn't quite get out the "in bed" part. I assumed it was implied.

Lexi nodded. "Partners in their romantic relationships, yes." After a beat of awkward silence, she twitched as if startled. "Including the bedroom, but not including sex."

I frowned, thoroughly confused. "What do romantic partners do in the bedroom besides that?"

Her face went stony, and she raised a pointed finger. "Exactly. That's the mentality a lot of people have because it's the default. My job is to teach the male partners, who are typically the most focused on sex, that other things can and should be happening in there. That drive overrides the need for human connection. For talking or just being with one another without an agenda. There's nothing wrong with sex, but if that's the central aspect of the relationship, it's going to have a messy ending. The same goes for dating someone because they're hot. There's nothing wrong with looking good, but if you want a healthy *relationship*, there needs to be more."

My mind was still trying to leap the hurdle it had been tripping on for weeks now. "And you don't sleep with them," I reiterated.

She snorted and managed to make it sound delicate. "I sleep with them on occasion. I don't have sex with them. I don't make out with them. There is no contact with private parts. If they have trouble with that aspect, I know a great sex therapist. My services include everything else, up to and including kisses."

When I stopped focusing on prostitution, I had trouble imagining her scenario. It was my turn to say my words slowly. "Men pay you to teach them about the importance of cuddling?"

Lexi laughed, deep and throaty in a way that would catch the attention of any man around. She tipped her head to indicate we should move to the living room, then led the way. "That's a simplified view of what I do. First off, I only take clients that have referrals from someone I know and trust. I don't let random people in my home, which is a necessary part of my services. I interview the man before taking him on as a client to see what he's looking for. More often than not, though, a woman hires me on behalf of their man."

"Wait," I interrupted. "Women hire you to date their boyfriends?" What kind of reverse harem pimp show was this?

We took seats on separate arms of her blue, L-shaped couch, tilting our bodies to face one another. I wrapped my arms around a rust colored throw pillow with fringe along the edges and tucked my feet under me.

"Boyfriends or husbands."

I tried to imagine a man agreeing to sign up for boyfriend boot camp. It seemed far-fetched until I remembered Lexi was smoking hot with hair that framed her face in big silky waves and sultry topaz eyes. Suddenly, I could see how men would be eager to sign up, but it would take a damn confident girlfriend to get on board with that.

"And wives agree to this sort of thing?"

"Again, I only work by referral, so they know what I offer, and they trust that I won't overstep. Like I told Guy, I work hard for my reputation. I won't sacrifice by fooling around with one of them."

"And you're like a dog trainer, only with men?"

"I don't like the comparison between men and dogs. That being said, you can't expect a dog to know how to navigate the human world without instruction. A man isn't a dog, he's a human being. Still, for all that men and women speak the same language, there's a world of biological and societal issues that muddle communication."

That made sense. Relationship drama was everywhere. I'd seen it in others, even if I'd never had a boyfriend myself.

"Do you have some sort of training regimen?" I asked, more curious than when I'd thought she was a prostitute.

"Yes, though it's more a broad strokes outline. Every couple is different. I fine-tune my program to focus on what's needed."

That was assuming both sides agreed on what they needed to improve. "How do you determine if a person needs to change or if the partner needs to lower their expectations?"

Lexi raised an eyebrow, looking impressed. "That is a fantastic question. Relationships are a negotiation. If the gap between the expectation and the current behavior is too big, I ask them to evaluate whether or not their relationship is feasible. Sometimes, the deal breakers are too big. If you need a man with a stable schedule or you have panic attacks over the thought of someone you love coming to harm, law enforcement and first responders are not for you. Love comes with sacrifice. Know where your line is."

"Sounds prudent," I said.

The more she talked, the more impressed I was by her. She'd really thought this out.

"Sometimes, it's not that cut and dry," she admitted. "My first step is always to figure out what I'm being hired for. My services start with subtle things like advice on clothing and appearance, vocabulary, how to phrase things so they don't sound offensive, assuming that's not what they're going for."

"You tell guys how to dress?"

"If it's an issue," she said. "Take your man Gregor."

Remembering his sequined shirt gave me a chuckle. "Fair enough."

"Those are usually quick fixes. Most of my time is spent on behavior modification. Things like treating their partner with respect, active listening, the concept of mental load, and helping with housework."

A light bulb went off in my brain. "The cooking." That's why there were always fancy leftovers in the fridge.

"Yes." She smiled. "My clients are required to learn the basics of cooking if they don't know how to bake a meatloaf, but I also encourage them to learn how to cook one fancy dish for a special candle lit meal. It comes in handy on special occasions."

"They take you out to eat, too, though, don't they?"

"Yes. That's where'd I'd have told Gregor to leave his phone in the car," she said with a laugh. "Going out can't beat a candle-lit dinner in the privacy of your home, though. That's a skill that takes time, effort, forethought, planning, grocery shopping, and setup. It's so much more romantic than throwing money at wait staff. It can also go wrong at any point, so it's good to practice it."

It sounded like she turned out quality boyfriends. "Do they do the dishes after?"

She gave me a look that said of course they did.

A new thought crept into my head. I blew out a breath. "Am I ruining things for you? My being here? Sleeping on the couch?"

Lexi shook her head a little too quickly. "No. My clients hire me for a 3-day or 5-day package. They're here, then they're gone. They don't get a say in how I run my personal life." She flashed me a sly grin. "If I were doing sex therapy, that might be a different story."

I laughed, feeling my face flush. "I could see that being a problem." I fought to block the image that came to mind. I hadn't officially met any of her clients until tonight. Speaking of which...

"So Guy was trying to convince you to go out with him?"

Lexi pursed her lips, indicating the question was more complicated than it seemed. "More or less."

"I assume he wasn't recommended to you by his girlfriend."

She winced. "He was."

My mouth dropped open in surprise. "Wait, so he dumped his girlfriend to come after you? That's gotta be bad for business."

"That's putting it mildly." She let out a slow breath. "I'm not sure how much blowback I'll get for it, but honestly, I can't control what a man does. I can only control what I do. I make a point of letting all my clients know that dating me is not on the table and never will be, even after the work is done, regardless of anyone's dating status. That goes for sex, too. It's taken years to build my career, and I love it."

"Career," I said, sounding it out. "So this isn't just side work."

"I enjoy my freelance job. I feel like I make a bigger difference with this, though. My first client was my best friend's new husband. They've sent me a thank you card every year on their anniversary. They've got the kind of marriage people dream of. Granted, a lot of that is their own hard work and communication, but they're both convinced they'd have gotten divorced without a strong foundation."

"How long have they been married?"

She had a soft smile on her face. "Seven years."

I whistled. "Wow. You've been doing this a while."

"We were young. They married right out of high school." Her eyes grew distant, her expression wistful. "They didn't have the healthiest relationship, but teenagers are blind when it comes to love." She thought about it, then added, "Everyone's blind when it comes to love. Teenagers more than most."

"Not that I'd know." I hadn't meant to say it out loud.

Lexi studied me. "Your mother called to check on you a bit ago."

Of course she had. "I talked to her."

Lexi saw my grimace. Her expression softened. "Your mom was always hard on you. I know it was out of love. She wanted you to be happy, but I could see how pushing you to be 'normal' always came across as criticizing. I think she knew it, but she wasn't sure how to say it differently."

"Too bad it never occurred to her not to say anything at all." My tone was bitter.

Lexi's experience with my mom was limited. She hadn't seen the worst of it. I'd had a lifetime of badgering.

Why can't you walk in a straight line? Stop flinching. Why don't you at least *try* to make friends? Being alone isn't good for you. You spend too much time inside. What's wrong with you? You can't even go to the grocery store without whimpering like a kicked dog. How are you ever going to function as an adult? How many times do I have to tell you ghosts aren't real? You need to see a psychiatrist.

Criticism was like a song my mother played on repeat. Growing up with her was torture.

I did end up seeing a psychiatrist. I lied to him. When my mother insisted, he prescribed me pills. They didn't make the ghosts disappear, so eventually I stopped taking them.

I'd have thought I was crazy if my grandmother hadn't been able to see them as well.

Lexi let out a soft sigh. "I don't think it's in your mom's nature to let it slide when she thinks you're struggling."

She was right. Too bad since I would have struggled less without my mother's input.

Lexi watched me, reading my face. "Growing up is hard. It's harder when you're not accepted for who you are." She let the statement linger before giving me a smile. "I'm glad you came to stay with me. I hope you feel accepted here. Ghosts and all."

I froze in surprise. We hadn't talked about ghosts.

When I was younger, I used to talk about them with my family. Eventually, I learned not to say anything where my mother could hear. My father and sister were more tolerant. As I got older, I realized they were still uncomfortable when the subject came up. They just weren't as vocal.

Eventually, I stopped talking about it altogether. My family knew the signs, whether I said anything or not. We'd carefully tiptoed around the subject, especially when we had visitors.

"You remember that?" I felt a profound sense of disappointment. After all that work trying to keep it hidden, and it was still plain as day, even to my cousin living in another state.

"I'm older than you. You used to talk about them nonstop when you were a toddler. Eventually, you quit. By then, I'd had more than one conversation with Aunt Virginia."

Technically, my maternal grandma, Virginia, was her great-aunt-in-law. Or maybe her grand-aunt-in-law, since they were two generations apart.

My hand drifted up to my chest, where my grandmother's necklace hung, tucked beneath my shirt so it sat against my skin. She'd given it to me when I was ten, and I'd worn it every day since.

She'd been my best friend growing up. The only other person in the world who knew what I knew. She said my mom knew the truth but refused to face it. The ability had skipped right over my mom.

Curious, I asked, "What did grandma tell you?"

"She told me she saw ghosts, too. She was a sharp lady, so I didn't have any problem believing her. It probably helped that she seemed otherwise stable. I was just a kid when she told me, but she never came across as crazy. She warned me not to mention it to your mom, though. Did you know your mom threatened to ban her from seeing you at one point? I think you were maybe four at the time."

I hadn't known that. "Did she do it?"

Lexi adjusted herself on the couch cushion, a thoughtful look on her face. "No. She made your mom recount the first time you showed signs of seeing things. You weren't even a year old. Your eyes would track across the room, following something that wasn't there. You'd point at nothing. Before you turned two, you started talking to empty air, following random paths, and trying to snatch at things that weren't there."

All long before Grandma could have influenced me. "I never knew that."

Absently, I stroked the fringe of my throw pillow. "I didn't realize I'd shown so many signs. Early on, I talked about ghosts so much because it was clear nobody else was tracking them. It seemed so strange to me when they were right there in plain sight."

Lexi nodded. "When you were five, your mom said she was going to take you to a psychiatrist. Aunt Viv told her pills wouldn't help."

"Did Grandma ever take pills?"

"It sounded like she tried them at some point. She'd said there was a time she'd have done anything to make the visions go away, but you can't fix reality, and the ghosts were part of her."

You can't fix reality. I knew that better than most. "My mom took me in when I was fourteen. Grandma was right. It didn't help." That had been a year after Grandma died. My mom must have been waiting for that.

"I don't want to pry, but I've been dying to know more about these ghosts you see," Lexi said. "If it makes you uncomfortable, we can let it go."

"No. Talking is good." I felt a smile tug at my lips. "I wouldn't have thought you were a prostitute for so long if we'd talked earlier."

Lexi's eyes went wide, and she threw a second fringed pillow at me. "You thought I was *what?*" she asked, laughing.

I laughed, too. "I know. I should have assumed you were running a training program for husbands out of your house. In hindsight, that should have been my first guess."

"Fair enough. It is a singularly unique profession."

When our laughter died down, I said, "I'm open for questions. Ask away."

So she did. In rapid-fire.

"Does everyone become a ghost?"

"I think so. They don't all hang out. Most move on."

"To where?"

"No clue. For all I know, they're still here, I just can't see them."

She looked thoughtful at that. "How many can you see?"

"At the moment? None. Your house isn't haunted. Most of them congregate in busy places, like stores and restaurants, the bigger and busier, the ghostlier. Hospitals are the worst."

"That makes sense. Do you hate having to hide that you can see them?"

"I wish I couldn't see them at all."

She seemed surprised by that. "Really? You wouldn't mind one standing in the shower with you, invisible?"

"I would definitely mind, but only if I knew they were there."

"The ghosts that linger have unfinished business?"

"Yeah, mostly."

"So they're mostly murder victims?"

That was certainly Peyton's case. "Not usually. Some just haven't figured out how to let go of their old lives. Those putter around like they've always done, going through the motions. The ones with unfinished business usually leave behind loved ones. They watch over them."

"That's sweet. Do they bother you much?"

"Constantly. Especially if they find out I can see them. Suddenly, they're desperate to get a message to their loved ones."

"Do you ever pass those messages along?"

"I did when I was younger. It didn't go well. Ever. Sometimes it went spectacularly bad."

She winced. "Most people probably aren't ready to hear stuff like that."

"Certainly not from complete strangers. Especially not from kid strangers."

"What do you do now when ghosts ask you to deliver messages?"

"I do my best not to let them know I can see them. I have yet to meet a ghost who will take no for an answer. Eventually, they mention my ability to other ghosts, and I end up overrun with a crowd of invisible people trying to talk to me day and night. Those are the times I feel like I really am crazy."

"That sounds rough."

"It is." I traced the shape of my necklace beneath my shirt. "Grandma always understood."

Lexi's look turned tender. "Growing up with your mom was harder than I realized, wasn't it?"

I nodded. "My life would be so much easier if people could look past this one weird fact about me. Everything I am seems to boil down to the one thing once they find out about it."

"Your mom used to complain you didn't have friends. I figured your ghost friends were more entertaining."

I huffed out a bitter laugh. "I've got horror stories where ghosts are concerned. I'd have killed for a regular friend."

"I remember your mom mentioned a friend of yours."

"Back in second grade?"

"Around then."

"Mackenzie Murphy. She was my one and only friend. We hung out for most of a year before I told her about ghosts. She'd been scared of the dark. I told her we were safe because my friend Julia was watching over us. Mackenzie didn't believe I saw ghosts, so I proved it by having her hide in my closet and hold up fingers."

"And you told her how many fingers she had up," Lexi guessed.

"Yes. Simple and effective."

"I'm guessing it was too effective?"

"Correct. She started crying, and demanded we get her mom to pick her up. Within a week, she'd told the whole school I was crazy and thought ghosts were real."

"I know how mean kids can be," Lexi said sympathetically.

"Mackenzie hated me with a passion from then on. Mom got phone calls from the school."

"Did you get in trouble?"

"No. She said maybe now I'd listen to her and stop this nonsense about ghosts."

"Ouch."

I shrugged. "She got what she wanted. I quit talking about ghosts."

"At the cost of having any friends. The relationship mentor inside me is in a rage over this. Everyone needs a friend."

Everyone needed a lot of things. Some things just weren't in the cards.

Lexi stood, moving closer to me. "I hope you find someone willing to accept you, ghosts and all. Don't stop putting your heart out there." She bent down to give me a hug. "In the meantime, you can talk about them with me."

Her hug brought tears to my eyes. I hadn't hugged anyone since I'd said goodbye to my dad when I'd left home. It felt good.

Something buried deep inside me started scrabbling for purchase. It took me a moment to realize it was hope.

Chapter 12

I fell asleep way past my bedtime. When I woke, the living room was already bright with sunlight.

"About time." A grumpy Frank was half-seated on the couch armrest.

I stifled a yawn, glaring at him. "Why are you in my house?" It came out grumpy, as I'd intended.

My talk with Lexi last night had brought a lot of emotions to the surface. Having yet another ghost invade my personal space while I was already feeling vulnerable put me in a bad mood by default.

"Don't snap at me. I spent the night listening to Ollie pour his bleeding heart on the ground. Did you know he married that broad?"

I rubbed my eyes, fighting off another yawn. "Peyton?" It was like he'd started the conversation without me. I was having trouble keeping up.

"Yeah, her. The recently deceased."

I gave way to the next yawn, which came on full force. "I don't want to hear about it. I can't help her. I can't help Ollie. Things are going to have to play out how they play out. I've barely kept my sanity all these years as it is. I'm not about to jeopardize it by diving into ghost problems."

Frank studied me while I got out of bed, tucking the blankets and sheets neatly into the thin mattress. "What is wrong with you? Why are you so self-centered?"

I didn't expect him to understand. He'd come very, very late to this party. "What little I've done so far has had monumentally bad consequences. You guys handle your own issues. I'm ignoring anyone without a pulse."

I folded the bed back into the couch, replacing the cushions before pulling the mahogany coffee table, inlaid with glass, back from the far wall to where it belonged in front of the couch. My makeshift bedroom disappeared in under five minutes as if I had never been there. It felt apropos.

Frank watched me work in silence until I went to the bathroom.

I'd barely closed the door when he walked through the wall to stand with his torso sticking out of the sink. I gave him a hard stare.

He returned it.

"Can I help you?"

"Are you volunteering? I thought you were done with us ghosts."

"I am. I was indicating you should leave." My tone was patient, if strained.

Frank crossed his arms. "I'm good."

"You're going to sit here and watch me pee?"

"You'd rather I leave." He nodded to himself. "I get it. It's disappointing when someone ignores basic human decency because they're too wrapped up in being an asshole to do what's right."

I put my hands on my hips and glared at him. "What do you want me to do? Get arrested? Stabbed, maybe? How is that going to help anything?"

Frank gave me a disgusted look. "No, dummy. I want you to be a friend. I want you to talk to Ollie and actually hear him instead of whining about doing the bare minimum, then blaming him when something goes wrong. He didn't ask you to jump in front of a bullet for him. He asked you for a ride."

"A ride ended with me almost getting stabbed," I reminded him.

"He is not responsible for what some thug with a knife does. If Theo asked you to grab a pack of gum from a gas station, and it gets held up while you're in there, you gonna blame him for that?"

That was different. I couldn't pinpoint why, it just was.

"I didn't think so," Frank said, answering for me. "Maybe stop making Ollie feel like trash for trying to help the love of his life. Even if you're not friends, it's a pretty shitty thing to do to a person."

It was. I knew that. I could even admit he hadn't intended for me to be in danger.

That didn't make it any easier to reconcile his demands for help with me being tossed into a situation I wasn't equipped to handle. I liked his willingness to help Peyton, but it wasn't right for him to dump that on me.

My voice of self-doubt reared its head again. Was I a jerk for not even listening to him? If I stopped fighting so hard to block him out, we might be able to come to a mutual understanding. I'd tried that. It had mostly consisted of me talking.

On the other hand, if all he needed was someone to listen, he had Frank. They were friends. Why did he need me?

My face must have gone mulish. Frank made a sound of disgust. "If your goal is to steer clear of trouble, you better find a new job, quick."

Oh, great. He was threatening to blab if I stayed. It would take less than a day for a swarm of ghosts to find me. "With Ollie bound to me, leaving won't help," I said bitterly. "He'll just follow."

"I'm not talking about Ollie. I'm talking about your boss."

Confused, I said, "What does my boss have to do with anything?"

Frank shrugged. "What does it matter? You'll ignore me anyway." He turned and walked through the mirror, leaving me to stare at my own reflection.

My thick hair was easily tangled. At the moment, it looked like a rat's nest. I had pink blotches on my cheek from where I'd slept on my hand and a shimmer on one side of my mouth indicated I'd drooled in my sleep. I was a mess, inside and out.

I'd planned to go hiking. I doubted I could focus on reading with so much chaos in my life. Hiking would clear my head, only it wouldn't fix my problems. I needed to clear the air with Ollie.

I showered, my thoughts drifting back to what Frank had said about Theo when we'd first met. Something about Theo being in with bad people? It had been vague. I'd brushed it off.

Now I wondered.

My thoughts waffled between Theo and Ollie. I couldn't help Peyton. Maybe Randall could. He'd proved to be resourceful. And paranoid. Very, very paranoid.

He was also a big part of why the cops were after me.

By the time I'd dried off, dressed, and put Bailey on a leash, I'd mentally prepared myself to talk with Ollie. Frank had disappeared, which I was grateful for.

Lexi came out of her office. "Morning," she said, tapping out something on her phone. "I'm headed to the store. Do you need anything besides the basics?" Lexi's basics would make a professional chef jealous.

"I'm good." Normally, I did the grocery shopping, but she was co-ordinating something special for an upcoming boyfriend-of-the-week.

We headed out the door at the same time. Bailey sniffed at the tree in the front yard. I watched Lexi back out of the driveway in her silver sedan. As she passed the Phantom, I spotted two figures in my back seat.

While Ollie was bound to me, Frank could go anywhere he pleased. Despite that, he stayed with Ollie. It was sweet. He was a good friend.

The familiar fangs of jealousy tore into me. Even ghosts got to have friends.

It occurred to me my vicious knee-jerk reactions to Ollie stemmed from his love of Peyton. He'd loved and lost something I'd never get the opportunity to experience. It was easy to say I'd rather have loved and lost than never to have loved at all, but Ollie might argue with me on that. Was I actually the lucky one between us?

It was a depressing thought.

I headed around the house to the back woods, pausing to motion for the ghosts to follow. Bailey sniffed along, oblivious to the added company.

Frank looked expectant, but held his tongue. Ollie stared at the ground with a vacant gaze. His blue aura looked murky. Could a ghost's mood affect the color of their aura? For all that I'd been around them my whole life, I'd done surprisingly little to learn about them.

"Ollie?" I waited for him to look up at me with his big blue puppy eyes. They were cartoonishly adorable. They'd probably gotten him out of trouble a lot as a kid.

"I'm sorry. I've been a jerk. I don't have a very high opinion of most ghosts. You're one of the few to respect my privacy." I gave Frank a pointed look. "I still don't think I can help, but I'm willing to brainstorm with you. We'll see if we can come up with some way to help Peyton without putting me in danger."

When I said Peyton's name, Ollie's aura brightened subtly, as if the very thought of her brought him joy.

The claws of jealousy tore at me, bringing an almost tangible pain. I paused to push my feelings aside, reminding myself his love for her was sweet and that helping him was the right thing to do.

So why did I want to throat-punch him?

His lips parted, just barely, drawing my attention. They looked sensuous and kissable. For all I knew, Peyton had married him for those lips. Probably the eyes, too.

"You'd still be willing to do that after everything that happened?" he asked.

I bit the inside of my cheek, trying to focus on the conversation. "I'm not making any promises, but talking can't hurt. Tell me more about this business of being stuck here. You mentioned she needed to move on?"

Ghosts were stuck here all the time. I didn't see why he was so distressed over it. If Peyton moved on, he wouldn't get to see her any more. If he loved her so damn much, why did he want her gone?

Frank waved a hand dismissively. "Ghosts are kind of like a compilation of thoughts and memories. We are the essence of our former selves. Most ghosts die and move on immediately. Don't ask where. We don't know. Anyhow, the ones that stay put are snagged on something, mentally speaking. That mental snag has the ability to hold us here."

I gave an exaggerated nod to indicate I already knew that.

He stuck his hands in his pocket and gave Ollie a sideways look. "More often than not, it traps a ghost in a certain location."

"Like Peyton being stuck at home. Sure, sure," I said. "But you're not trying to unbind her from her house, right? You want her to move on to the hereafter."

"Right. The problem with being bound anywhere is that you lose your memories of the wider world. Everything narrows down, so to speak. You not only gotta help free Peyton, you gotta help free Ollie, too. Now that he's bound to you, he's losing his memories of everything else."

I blinked. "What? Why are his memories suddenly tied to me? And why is he losing them now? He's been dead for a while."

We were talking right past Ollie, though he seemed content to let Frank explain things, possibly because I bit his head off every time he opened his mouth.

Frank sighed. "Like I said, we're kinda made up of memories. Sort of. Not really, but you get the point."

I didn't. He continued before I could say so.

"Ollie and Peyton lived around here. When Ollie died, he was tied to Peyton. Not to her house. To *her*. That's an important distinction."

"Okay," I said, still confused.

"She goes shopping or to the movies or to work or wherever, and Ollie comes with. He's got freedom, see?"

"So Ollie's ghost boundary was basically the whole town?" I was sort of following.

"Originally, no, but since he was able to follow her everywhere, it helped him stretch his bond out until he could essentially go wherever, within reason."

"Wait, so are all ghosts bound when they die? The ones wandering around just figured out how to stretch out their bonds?"

"It gets complicated. For the sake of simplicity, we'll say yeah."

"Okay. Ollie's doing fine. Why not have Peyton stretch out her bond? They can travel the city together."

"That's where things get dicey." Frank reached up to adjust his hat. "Ollie died a while back, so Peyton's not tied to him. Being tied to a person is less common than you'd think."

"She's tied to her house," I said.

"She's tied to her murder. It's an event."

"How can you tell when she was murdered at home?"

Ollie said, "She didn't care about the house. Trust me on that."

"Keep up with me," Frank said. "This is the tricky part. Since Peyton's tied to an event, her focus is a lot more limited. If she was tied to the house, she'd have a bunch of memories to keep her grounded. Her murder was so quick she didn't even see who did it. That's not much to anchor someone."

I didn't need him to tell me what happened to ghosts who lost their memories. They became shambling zombie-ghosts, unaware of anything going on around them, shuffling around like they had advanced dementia.

One thing didn't fit. "If Peyton's tied to her murder, how come she remembers Ollie?"

"Because she's fresh," Frank said bluntly. "She's still got all her memories intact. The memories of her death will stay with her for a long time. Everything else is made of tissue paper. They'll break down in no time."

"Does it hurt to lose memories?" I asked, wondering what the big deal was. "If we solve her murder today or ten years from now, she'll still move on, right? Where's the urgency?"

Frank scratched the underside of his chin. "Moving on isn't automatic. If she's stuck here too long and loses all her memories, it'll be hard to get her to let go, or pass through her doorway, or follow the light at the end of the tunnel, or whatever metaphor you want to use. Once the path is open, she still has to take it."

I was starting to see the problem. "If she's too far gone to recognize it, she'll be stuck here permanently?"

He winced. "It's complicated, but yeah. Maybe not forever. Maybe one day she happens to notice that there's a path and takes it. All we know is the sooner their issues are resolved, the easier it is for them to cross over."

"Why isn't Ollie a zombie-ghost by now?" I asked. "Why aren't you?"

"That's complicated, too. That particular hole is deeper than you know. For now, let's focus on Peyton."

My brain was already starting to feel like scrambled eggs. I let it drop. "How long does Peyton have?"

"Depends. How long does it take someone to forget a fact they once knew? It varies. Sometimes days. Sometimes weeks. It's pretty rare for someone to last months, and that's with a firm tie. Peyton's murder won't keep her stable for long. You've got a week. Two at most."

She'd been dead most of a week already. I still had no clue how to help her.

I chewed my lip, thinking. I had the photo of my attacker, only turning that in could land me in hot water. I wondered if I could mail it in. Maybe Randall could hand it over. That would be less suspicious. He lived right next door to her.

Of course, they'd probably ask to see the camera footage. Anyone could doctor a photo these days. They would see me on there. That would tie me to Randall.

If Wagner and Lennox got wind of that, they'd probably search Randall's house. I doubted they'd find his secret stairway. They'd definitely find his Impala.

Prison bars danced before my eyes again.

"You heard me, right?" Frank asked. "About Ollie?"

I blinked. "What?"

"Ollie's bound to you."

"Right." My brain tried to recalculate route. "He used to be bound to Peyton. She's dead. Now he's bound to me. Is there a problem with that?"

Frank barked, "Ollie!"

He'd been staring off into space. Startled, he looked up. "Huh?"

"Tell Enid about the life you built with Peyton."

Ollie blinked once. Then again. "Peyton and I loved each other." He sounded dazed.

"Where did you meet?" Frank asked, though it was clear he'd heard the story before.

It took a minute for Ollie to answer. "In college. I was in the food court. I saw her coming and felt my soul just…connect with her." A soft smile touched his lips. "She didn't seem to notice, so I stuck my foot out and tripped her."

I covered my mouth with my hand, trying not to laugh. "You liked her, so you tripped her?"

"I caught her before she fell." His smile widened. His aura brightened as he talked, like it was bringing him back to life. "I didn't realize it, but she suspected it was on purpose. She brought me a coffee the next day as a thank you. She'd melted chocolate ex-lax into it."

I winced.

"Let's just say I missed my afternoon classes."

Peyton sounded like a girl who knew how to do payback right.

"It rained all the next day," he said, chuckling. "I waited until she was walking to her car after her last class of the day."

I groaned, already seeing where this was going.

"I pulled up alongside her and spun my wheels when she was passing a puddle. It sprayed her clear up to her armpits."

"Wow. I hope she punched you for that."

He shook his head, the grin on his face reflected in his eyes. His aura was notably brighter. Recalling the memories was helping him.

"She pulled me out of the car and gave me a full body hug. Jumped up and wrapped her legs around me and everything. We stood there like idiots, laughing in the middle of the lane."

When he closed his eyes, savoring the memory, he looked so peaceful it made me want to cry.

"She felt so right in my arms. I couldn't stand to let her go. I put her down in my passenger seat and kidnapped her. I drove her around for hours with the heater on blast, and we talked and talked."

They sounded like they were made for each other. "How long were you two together?"

"We got married a few months later. We planned epic practical jokes on each other the whole time we were dating. We had to call a cease fire for the wedding." His smile slipped, and his brow furrowed. "We were together two years before I died."

I swallowed hard, my throat suddenly tight.

"She was pregnant," he said softly. "We'd put together a party to tell both our families the big news over a Fourth of July barbecue."

His smile disappeared altogether.

My heart clenched in anticipation.

I hate scary movies. I hate sad movies. I hated emotionally bracing myself for impact.

Ollie gathered himself. "Peyton was acting weird that day. She snuck off after my parents showed up. After a couple minutes, I went looking for her. She wasn't in the house. She wasn't in the back yard. The garage door was open, but she wasn't in there, either. I cut through the garage to check the street. I heard voices at the side of the house, around the corner of the garage."

Knowing how the story ended did nothing to ease my tension as his story. I imagined reliving the good memories only made the bad ones hit harder.

He swallowed hard. "Peyton was whispering to someone. I don't even remember the words they said. Essentially, the baby was his, not mine. She didn't know if she should tell me or not. Everyone was already there for the party. It was too late to turn back."

I studied Ollie, expecting him to be angry, but the dominant emotion seemed to be horror.

"I was so stupid." He closed his eyes. This time, he looked tortured. His voice came out raw. "I still have no idea how I didn't see through her. I should have known. Oh, God. I should have *known*."

The heartbreak in his words made tears come to my eyes. This was the woman he'd clung to, even in death? He carried such a torch for her after all she'd done. She didn't deserve him.

His next words came in a whisper. "She would never do something like that to me."

My mind spun out thinking of all the ways it could have ended. Had Ollie killed himself over his cheating wife? What had happened to the baby? Had Peyton given it up? There had been no mention of a child when they were reunited. I couldn't bear the wait. "What did you do?"

Ollie shook his head in disgust. "I climbed in my car and tore out of there. I left everyone behind. Peyton came running from the side of the house with some guy in tow. I didn't recognize him. She called after me, but I just...couldn't look at her. I couldn't bear to hear one more word. So I drove...and drove...until I found a bar, and I drank it. I drank until I couldn't see straight."

That didn't leave much to the imagination. "Did you drive drunk?"

"No." He let out a humorless laugh. "I might have been better off if I had."

Frank had his arms crossed, listening with a grim expression. I was ready to pull my hair out to find out what happened.

"Peyton tried calling. So did my parents. I got calls from numbers I didn't recognize. At some point, I dropped my cell phone in a cup of water. I never did get it back." He sighed. "Eventually I climbed into my back seat and slept it off. By the time I woke up, the bar was closed. I'd sobered up enough to drive, but my head wasn't on right. I wasn't sure where to go or what to do. What *is* there to do when your whole life unravels?"

I had no answers for him, so I waited.

"I drove around aimlessly. I ended up misjudging a gap during a left-handed turn. I had a blinking yellow light and should have had time. I didn't realize the guy coming was doing almost double the speed limit. I got T-boned good. Next thing I know, I'm standing beside Peyton at my funeral."

Oh, no. That was terribly depressing. It made me feel better about my own love life that his had turned to dust before he'd died. I couldn't help but ask, "What happened to the baby? I didn't think Peyton had a kid. Did the dad take it?"

Ollie let out a hysterical laugh that sounded on the verge of tears. "*I* was the dad. The guy she'd been talking to had been part of a prank."

My mouth dropped open. Holy shit. There were practical jokes, then there was cruel and unusual punishment.

Chapter 13

"What'd she do, hire an actor?"

He gave a helpless shrug. "He was my brother." He shook his head like he couldn't believe his own words. "Peyton was so excited to tell my family about the baby. She wanted to tell the *whole* family, so she looked up my brother. He was a decade older than me. My birth was an accident," he said, laying out the facts in a straightforward manner.

"My parents never intended to have me. My brother had been a troubled teen. He'd moved out by the time I was five. He got strung out on drugs, and my parent lost touch with him. Apparently, he ended up cleaning himself up around the time Peyton and I first met. He met a girl, fell in love, and was engaged to be married, so he reached out to my parents in the hopes of mending bridges. He apologized for putting them through hell and wanted them to be part of the wedding. He wanted me there, too."

He took a steadying breath. "Peyton found out before me and told my parents she was going to plan a surprise reunion. She kept it a surprise from me by saying the party was for the big baby announcement. I didn't even know what my brother looked like. Nobody had heard from him in years. Peyton knew that, so she planned for the ultimate prank."

It sounded like a bad idea waiting to happen from my perspective, but their relationship had been built on pranks, so who was I to judge? "Your brother thought it was a good idea?" I asked dubiously.

"Peyton could be very persuasive when she put her mind to something. Honestly, it would have been epic if I hadn't overreacted. That was so out of character for me. It's like my brain shut down. If I'd stopped to think for even a minute, I would have known she'd never cheat on me, then pretend the baby was mine until the middle of a big party, where she'd reveal I *wasn't* the father in front of my parents and everything."

Honestly, I wasn't sure what Peyton's limits were. "The baby?" I asked. I assumed the baby was real.

He shook his head. "First trimester. She lost it. The stress of my death was too much. My overreaction killed myself *and* my baby."

His self-loathing was palpable, mixed with a sorrow I couldn't fathom. A tightness in my chest pressed below my ribs. Maybe it was better to never have loved, after all. Being alone would beat going through what he'd been through. Living with that burden had to be a special kind of hell.

Thinking over everything that had happened, his reaction to Peyton's prank had been reasonable. He hadn't done anything wrong. "You didn't kill anyone," I told him, my voice tight with emotion. "The guy speeding killed you."

My words were paltry in the face of his pain. Truth wasn't always as comforting as it should be.

Life sucked sometimes. They'd been perfect for each other. He didn't even blame her for her poor taste in jokes, even after everything that happened.

Like Frank said, he was trying to help the woman he loved the best he could. I'd made him feel like a jerk for that.

The pain in my chest shifted, a subtle twisting of the knife. Some memories had edges sharper than a blade.

"Peyton never forgave herself," Ollie said numbly. "She cut herself off from family. She spiraled into depression. Months went by where I didn't think she was going to make it."

His face was a mask of unfathomable pain laced with profound loneliness, of wanting so much to be a part of something acutely forbidden. How hard had it been to stay by Peyton's side, watching her process his death while losing their baby? My heart broke for them.

"She could barely get herself out of bed until the notice came in the mail that she was going to lose the house. That's when she rallied. The house was all she had left of me. All my things were still there. *Are* still there."

He relayed the events like he'd lived them. For all intents and purposes, he had.

"She started working again, paying the bills. She'd lost a ton of weight and finally started eating again."

Listening to him talk, I could feel his hope after watching her self-destruct, blaming himself the whole while. He must have wanted so badly for this to be the end of her torment, for her to have some semblance of a decent life.

I studied his face, noting where the muscles of his jaw twitched. Anger was buried deep there. Anger at Peyton? Or at the world?

"She didn't start dating until recently. I don't think she was ready for an actual relationship. She suddenly had the worst taste in men. It was like she purposely chose guys that treated her like crap."

After losing the love of her life, I could see why she'd be nervous about falling in love. Self-sabotage had to be easier than reliving that nightmare.

"I tried giving her space when she started dating. I'd check in on her every day, but it didn't feel right watching her date other guys. I wasn't jealous or anything. I just felt like I was intruding where I didn't belong. I really wanted her to find someone who would make her happy. She kept choosing losers."

Ollie looked up, his eyes finding mine. "When I found out you could see me, I hoped you could give her a message. I needed her to know that I figured out it was all a prank. That I didn't hate her, you know?"

In context, that request seemed so simple. Such a small thing to ask after such a colossal train wreck of heartbreak.

"I wasn't sure what the consequences of communicating with her would be, so I went to find Frank. I wanted to run it by him before I asked you to talk to her."

"We were at the Retro Cafe the night she died," Frank cut in. "He stopped talking mid-sentence and kinda froze. It was crazy weird."

"I felt her die," Ollie said in a near-whisper. "I couldn't move. I couldn't think. It was like my tether to the living world wobbled. Like a severed live wire flailing around, trying to find something to latch on to."

What must it have been like to have the one thing anchoring you to the world suddenly vanish? I had no context for comparison.

If I was very lucky, I'd never know.

"He stayed in a stupor all the next day. I left to take care of some other stuff. I came back every few hours to check on him."

"You left him there?" I asked.

Frank gave me a look. "I got a life, too. I can't just drop everything."

"He was catatonic," I said in exasperation.

"There wasn't anything I could do about that. Either he recovers or he don't. Holding his hand doesn't help him any." He saw my glare and rolled his eyes. "Look, you're coming at this from a living perspective, where someone in his condition might wander off and get hurt. He's a ghost. He can't fall down a hill or get hit by a car."

While that was true, it still felt heartless to abandon him. "You still could have sat with him."

"I could have," he agreed. "But like I said, I had stuff to do."

"It's okay," Ollie said. "He didn't do anything wrong. I didn't need him to sit with me. It turns out, all I really needed was you."

"Me?" I asked. It didn't take long to connect the dots. "When I showed up, you were suddenly bound to me."

He nodded. "I'm not sure if it's because you were the last person I'd been interested in or what, but I couldn't sense Peyton any more, and you'd been my focus when she died."

Lucky me.

"How's Peyton doing?" I asked.

"As of last night? Not great." His blue eyes were sad. That seemed to be his norm lately. "She's starting to fade. She doesn't remember how I proposed to her. She's losing herself."

"Already?" A marriage proposal should be harder to forget, especially when it was by the man of your dreams. "Does visiting her help? Talking to her, and reminding her of things?"

If so, we were screwed. I wasn't about to hang out in her yard every day for the rest of my life so the two of them could chat. Randall had welcomed my visits so far. He'd probably get suspicious if I showed up too often.

Plus, I had a life, even if it only involved sticking my nose in a book and wiping down counters.

"It slows down the deterioration. The only way to fix it is for her to move on."

Solving her murder wasn't in my wheelhouse. I hated that he kept putting that on my shoulders. I decided to shift the subject. "What about you? If she's what originally tied you here, will you go when she goes?"

Frank snorted. "Don't let the door hit you on the way out."

"That's not what I meant."

Ollie didn't make a point of misconstruing my meaning. He just shook his head and said, "I don't know." He stared off into space, deep in thought.

Frank wasn't my favorite person, but he hadn't been exaggerating about Ollie. He was in bad shape, hardly able to focus on the present. The idea of having a zombified ghost bound to me was not appealing. I pictured him floating through the air, toes scraping the ground once he forgot to move his legs in a pantomime of walking. Would he come in the house, or would he be right there, staring at me at all hours of the day and night like some macabre accessory.

I shuddered.

I'd talk to him where I could and hope the cops found out who had killed Peyton. Maybe we could lie to her. Would she move on if she thought she had closure? It wasn't like the truth would make any difference. She was already dead. Finding the true killer wouldn't change that.

We sat in silence for a long moment. My phone rang. It was Theo, asking if I could work the afternoon shift. He'd hired a new waitress who hadn't bothered to show up.

"Sure, Theo," I told him.

Frank and Ollie followed me back to the house. Frank grumbled all the way. "It's like passing gallstones to get you to talk to the person bound to you, but you're willing to help out the living if they breathe in the right direction."

"Taking an extra shift isn't the same thing as trying to solve a murder. I'm a waitress, Frank."

"Ya know talking to Ollie don't take no special skills, right? Ya just shut ya trap and open ya ears." His accent was growing with his temper.

He was starting to remind me of my mother. Some fights you couldn't win. I didn't have a problem with listening to Ollie's story. It was being pressured into risking my life to solve a murder I had a problem with. Frank couldn't separate the two.

"Yeah, Frank. I'll try to be a better listener."

I wasn't sure if he detected my sarcasm. I headed inside.

Thankfully, he stayed outside with Ollie until it was time for my shift. They were camped in the back of my car when it was time to head in to work.

Since Frank seemed to know so much, I had a burning desire to know what he had to say about my boss. "Frank? What is it you think Theo is tied up in?"

"I figured that caught your attention," he said smugly. "Took ya long enough to ask about it."

"Frank," I said in warning.

He sat up straighter. "Fine. I'll tell ya what I know. I'm a pushover like that."

I watched in the mirror as he adjusted his hat like he was about to give a performance on stage. My comparison wasn't far from the truth. His accent got thicker as he slipped into storyteller mode.

"I like the cafe. It always smells good in there on account of how Tunde—sorry, Theo—has that brown sugar bacon cooking at all hours. Anyhow, I typically sit in there and smell the coffee to wake myself up in the mornings."

He drew out the word "coffee" until it sounded like "cawfee."

"Is this going to be a memoir about you or Theo?" I asked. "You do realize the drive to work isn't that long, right?"

"Don't get in a tizzy," he said, glaring at me in the mirror. "I was just setting the stage."

Impatient, I focused on the road.

"As I was saying, I go there every morning. A few months back, Theo gets a new regular. Guy comes in almost every day during the slow times and sits at the high bar so he can chat with Theo while he's cooking. He's big on the friendly conversation so Theo takes to him like a duck in water."

That sounded like Theo. He could make friends with a brick wall.

"This new regular is all smiles, every day. Most congenial person ya ever met with a grin like a Cheshire cat."

My stomach dropped at the mention of smiles. There's only one person I'd seen like that. "Cheshire cat?" I muttered. It fit.

A thought hit me. "Weren't you dead before that movie came out?"

He blew out in a *pfft*. "Come on. I'm not that old." He sniffed, then said, "Actually, I am that old. I still know who the cat is. I do watch the boob tube on occasion. You living folk spend a third of your time sleeping, then a bunch more eating, changing clothes, doing dishes and laundry, sitting on the toilet, and let's not even talk about the number of hours ya spend working. Ghosts don't gotta worry about none of that, and you're surprised I got time to catch a flick every now and again? I can walk into any house and watch whatever's playing, free of charge."

"Good for you." I tried to refocus him on the man's description. "Does this guy have dark hair, slicked back, and a long face?"

"Eh. I'd call him rat-faced, but yeah. Looks like a snitch doing hard time."

That was an apt description. Watching Theo and Smiles interact, I'd known something was off between them. "I know who you're talking about. I call him Smiles. Go on."

"Got your attention now, eh? Okay, so one day I come in, and the guy is sitting in a booth. Theo's with him, and they're talking in low voices. The restaurant is empty except for an old guy reading a newspaper in the far corner. Not sure why it was so slow since that was about the time the morning rush usually started."

"Get on with it, Frank." I was a block from the cafe. I didn't have time for his rambling story about the smell of the coffee or why business was slow that day. "What happened?"

"Theo got angry. I'd only been in the cafe for a few seconds, so I didn't hear anything specific. Theo's voice rose, and he pointed at the door like he wanted the guy to leave, only the guy said something back, smiling all the while like a shark ready to pick his teeth after a good meal. That's when Theo got real quiet, real quick. I headed over, but the conversation was done. The guy got up and left, strolling out like he owned the place."

"I've seen that walk. And I've seen them talk. Theo won't let me near him."

"For good reason," Frank said. "When the guy left, I followed him back to his lair. Learned all sorts of things."

I grunted, not sure I wanted to know. Whatever Theo was into was his business, right? The whole situation felt off.

Frank didn't ask permission before he continued.

"Smiles's name is Craig."

That sounded familiar. "Didn't you say something about the guy who attacked me with the knife knowing Craig?"

Ollie spoke up from the back, his voice a monotone, like he was only half-listening to us. "He said the guy who attacked you had ties to Craig."

"Oh, yeah," Frank said. "Gio. He works for Craig. Craig the Crowbar."

That was a stupid name. "What does he do, work for the mafia?"

"Close. Your friend Randall's convinced there's a cartel in town. He's right."

"Craig works for the cartel?"

"Craig practically *is* the cartel. He's the second in command, so to speak, at least in the area. The local Saints are part of a bigger group that's spread out over more than a dozen states."

I was stunned. Once my brain processed the words, my body responded, my palms sweating and my thoughts screaming. "What the hell does the leader of a cartel covering half the Eastern seaboard want with the owner of a small cafe?"

I sounded hysterical, but we'd gone from a murdered girl to a killer after me to a law enforcement conspiracy to a cartel to the cartel leader wanting my head on a platter? That was more escalation than any sane person could cope with.

"Good. This is finally starting to sink into that stubborn noggin of yours."

I glared at him in the mirror. "What's that supposed to mean?"

"It means you're so worried about being in danger around Ollie's sweetheart—"

"Peyton," Ollie supplied.

Frank talked over him. "—ya don't even realize you're sitting in a viper's den. You're neck deep in danger every shift ya work. Before ya fill in for Theo again, ya might want to educate yourself on his unwanted associations."

Well, crap. I was positive I didn't want to hear the rest of this story, but if safety was any kind of priority, I'd be better off knowing.

"I'm listening," I said, my voice almost a growl.

Chapter 14

Barreling down Highway 70, I questioned my life choices while Frank told me why I should regret moving in with Lexi. "What's the connection between Theo and *Craig* the *Crowbar*?" I said, mocking the nickname.

Frank's tone shifted to something a history teacher might use in a lecture hall if that teacher also sounded like a gangster. "They call Craig the Crowbar because he's good at creating leverage. Since the Saints set up shop in Peach Grove, they've started recruiting businesses to launder money."

My response was automatic. "Theo would never launder money for a cartel."

The thought was ludicrous. He was *Theo*.

Still, some portion of my brain wondered if I knew Theo as well as I thought I did. I'd only been working for him a few weeks.

"I know. He's more wholesome than a loaf of nine-grain," Frank agreed. "That's where the crowbar comes in."

I didn't like the sound of that.

"Theo's got a daughter on scholarship at Georgia Tech. She's his pride and joy. The only child from his marriage before his wife died from some kind of illness or other."

I didn't like where this was going.

"Craig got the skinny on the daughter and threatened her if Theo didn't do what he wanted. From the sounds of it, Theo threatened to go to the police. Craig convinced him that he'd never be able to prove he was behind anything. Craig would have someone else take care of the daughter, and either way, no amount of justice would make up for the loss of his kid, right?"

"Theo caved," I said. What else could he do?

"Like a house of cards."

My shoulders slumped. I felt terrible for him. After losing his wife, the only family he has left gets threatened? His daughter, no less. He'd never forgive himself if anything ever happened to her.

For once, I genuinely wished I could help. Craig's pompous smile made me want to slap his sleazy face.

When I'd been new to the area, I'd turned in applications for over a dozen places. None of them called me back.

Lexi had pointed out I'd only held one prior job, and that was in Wyoming. My resume might as well have been blank. I didn't have a single person in the area that could vouch for me except Lexi, and she was family, so she didn't really count.

When I'd come in looking for a job application, Theo had invited me to sit, despite it being rush hour. He'd told me to have lunch on him, then we'd talk if I had the time. I'd spent the time observing the waitress, the cook, and the patrons. My hands had been sweaty, and I'd felt like I'd walked into a test unprepared. I hadn't planned on a live interview. I was sure he'd drill me on what I knew about his business, which was essentially nothing beyond it being a restaurant.

When the lunch rush had died down, he'd sat across from me in a booth. He'd asked me about my hobbies and interests and told me about his dream of owning a restaurant that felt like home, bringing people together over good food and conversation.

Peach Grove had seemed like the perfect place for the Retro Cafe. It was still new, in business only a year, but it had collected a few regulars. His little family of patrons was growing. He'd been so hopeful, despite being blackmailed by one of his customers, a predator threatening his child.

It made my blood boil.

I pulled into my usual parking spot. The shepherd was lying next to the dumpster, head on paws like one of those sad movies about a dog waiting for an owner who would never come. It was one more depressing blow. I exhaled slowly, trying to figure out how I'd gotten myself in such a mess.

I'd just wanted to work in a place without ghosts. When I'd taken the job, there hadn't been any.

That was before Ollie. Before the dog. Before Frank. I was attracting a crowd.

"Why do you bring me problems I can't fix, Frank?"

Because he was a ghost. It's what they did.

I shook my head, digging my wireless earbuds out of the center console. I stuck them in my pocket. I'd have to start wearing them regularly with Frank and Ollie following me around. It would keep me from having to hold my phone to my ear like I'd suddenly gotten a call as I talked to them.

When I got out of the Phantom, the dog immediately stood and did her routine, barking and circling behind the building before coming back.

Ollie had been so quiet in the car, it surprised her when he said, "That dog really wants your attention."

"I think it lost a toy or something." I watched the dog circle again. "Frank, maybe you can help it."

Frank moved off to one side, calling to the dog. It ignored him. "Nope. She wants you. And not for a ball if I had to guess."

I frowned at the dog. "What makes you say that?"

"You know what kind of dog that is?"

"German Shepherd?"

"Wrong. Belgian Malinois. It's one of four kinds of Belgian Shepherds. Specifically, the kind that's often mistaken for a GSD."

"GSD?"

"German Shepherd Dog."

I blinked at him. "Why do they add dog to the name? Everyone knows a German Shepherd is a dog. It's redundant."

"Your face is redundant." We stared at each other for a moment. "A Malinois is like a GSD on steroids. They're like the neurotic genius cousin of a GSD."

I watched the dog do its routine on repeat. "Neurotic for sure," I muttered. "Genius, maybe not so much."

"Cops and soldiers have been choosing Mals over GSDs more and more often in recent years. Not all Mals are trained canine officers but that," he said, pointing at the barking dog, "is almost certainly one of them."

"How can you tell?" I asked, squinting at the dog. "Extra neuroticism?"

Frank let out a grunt of exasperation. "If you can't tell that dog is well-trained and doing its absolute damnedest to communicate with you, then you'd probably benefit from dog training boot camp yourself. Sit. Stay. Come. It's not that hard to figure out which one it's trying to get you to do."

I couldn't argue with that. The dog was insistent and expressed itself about as clearly as it could without speaking English.

"You're questioning the dog's intelligence. In my book, you're the one with a thick skull," Frank said. "Follow the damned dog. It'll take you two minutes to figure out what it wants."

"What if it's trying to take me somewhere across the city?"

"Don't be stupid. It's a ghost. It's locked onto something here by the building. If it was interested in something across the city, it'd be looking for someone that could see it over there."

"You think something's back there?" I asked skeptically.

Frank gave me a patronizing grin. "You'll never know unless you try."

The parking lot was pretty empty. It was early in the afternoon and the slowest time of day, but it was a Saturday, so we'd be slammed come dinner time. For now, I could spare an extra minute or two.

"Okay, dog. What do you want?" When I approached, she started barking joyously, bounding back and forth like she wanted to play as she steadily led me past the dumpster and around the back of the building.

The trash truck had come the day before, so the smell wasn't as bad as it got near the end of the work week. Still, I breathed through my mouth, trying to keep the smell of rotten food out of my nostrils.

I peered down the length of the building, past the prancing dog. There was nothing but the flat brick back of the building with a recess and a stoop where the back door let out. That door was blocked with crates of supplies from the inside, so I knew it was locked.

A six-foot strip of grass separated the building from a ditch running parallel to it. The ditch was mostly empty except where bits of pine needles had gathered along the segmented lines of concrete. Beyond the ditch, past a couple dozen more feet of grass sat the drive-thru side of an Arby's building.

The dog turned in a circle, sniffed the wall, and sat next to the door. She stared at me.

Ollie walked alongside me. "Don't police dogs sit when they smell something they've been trained to identify?"

"They do," Frank said from over by the dumpsters. "Maybe you should check it out."

He'd been in my face all day, and now he was keeping his distance? "What is it trained to identify? Bombs?" I eyed Frank. "Why are you all the way over there?"

"Poor baby. You need someone to hold your hand?" he asked.

Jerk. A bomb wouldn't even hurt him.

"Maybe. If there's a bomb and I trigger it, I could get hurt, unlike you. For all your whining about ghost feelings, you're not keen on prioritizing my safety." I studied the ground, suddenly wondering if there was some kind of pressure plate buried in the dirt. The grass grew evenly around the back stoop.

"Why would anyone put a bomb back here?" Frank snorted. "Who would they blow up? Nobody even uses the back door. If they wanted to kill your boss, there's a lot easier ways to do it."

That was true enough. Still, the dog had triggered on something. I stepped closer, waiting for her to get up and dance away again.

She sat still, studying me with a gaze so intense it made my hair stand on end.

I reached out and slowly turned the handle. The door was locked, as it should be. "You're not just hoping to get inside, right?" I asked the dog. "You know you can't eat brown sugar bacon. You're dead."

The dog shifted her weight in an eager motion.

I scanned the wall, which ended at the roof. "Maybe she lost a ball on the roof."

"If Spiderman were a dog, he'd be a Mal. Trust me, if the dog needed to be on the roof, she'd be on the roof."

"She can't get on the roof," I scoffed.

"She can absolutely get on the roof," Frank said blandly.

I looked down at the dog. She licked her chops, then looked at the wall beside her, then back at me.

"It's a wall. I don't understand. What do you want?"

With a growling whine of frustration, she stood and pawed at the wall, digging at it furiously.

"All right, all right," I said, catching her urgency. Give me some space. I knelt beside her, and she backed off, barking once before going back to silently staring at me with the intensity of a thousand suns. "Psycho."

Frank laughed. "That's been used to describe them almost as often as neurotic genius."

I studied the bricks where the dog had been clawing. The mortar was recessed in places, creating grooves of uneven depths. Near the ground, there was a section of six bricks—three tall and two wide—where the mortar was noticeably missing, but only if you were looking straight into it. I stuck my fingertips into the grooves and tried to pry the bricks loose. The whole chunk wiggled, but I didn't have enough of a grip to pull it out.

The dog yipped, a high-pitched bark that made my ears hurt. She paced over to the where the grass sloped down to the ditch and started pawing at the ground, whining with frantic intensity.

"Seriously? I haven't even uncovered this mystery yet, and you want me digging up something else?" Despite my words, I was curious enough to check on the dog.

She pawed at a black stick. I picked it up, finding it wasn't a stick at all. It was a miniature crowbar about as big around as my middle finger and twice as long.

Ollie peered over my shoulder. "Why would something like that be lying out here?"

That was a very good question. It didn't escape me that the miniature crowbar's flat end was the perfect size to fit between the loose bricks. "I think I'm going to regret finding out."

The crowbar made quick work of the bricks. The two-by-three stack came out as a solid chunk, revealing a hidey hole with a plastic grocery bag shoved inside. I pulled it out to discover there were three grocery bags, triple layered to protect a black canvas pouch the shape of one of those pizza delivery pouches that kept the pizza boxes warm, only a quarter of the size.

"Do I want to know what's in here?" I was more than a little dubious.

"You could always put that thing back where it came from and pretend you didn't find it, but the dog's never gonna leave you alone," Frank remarked. "It wants you to do something with that."

The dog was staring at me like it wanted a treat. Maybe a steak. I was tempted to remind it food didn't work the same for ghosts, even when they were dogs.

Ollie spoke up. "You may as well see what's in it before you make that call."

He was right. I'd done the work of unearthing the pouch. Based on the dog's behavior, it held something of interest.

I pried apart the Velcro seal. "Holy crap."

Inside the pouch was a two-gallon Ziplock full of little clear baggies, each holding a handful of little white pills. "That's drugs." Prison bars floating in my mind's eye with "life sentence" printed across them.

Frank made his way over and squatted beside me, peering at the drugs. "Oxy," he said. "And a lot of it. It'll buy a damn lot of bread. Depending on the strength of the dosage, you could be looking at well over a million bucks there."

My mouth dropped open. "A million dollars?" Who left that kind of stash lying around?

"Best guess. Might be more."

I stared at him. "How do you know this stuff?"

He just shrugged. "Drugs are a booming business."

The evidence of that was in my hands. It was a drop in the bucket of a vast ocean of illegal activity, too. A cartel spanning a dozen states. "Blessed night," I muttered. "What do I do about this? I need to call the cops."

Ollie shifted behind me. "Won't you get in trouble for that? How do they know the drugs aren't yours?"

Darker thoughts went through my mind. The cops could be working with the cartel like Randall said. They could arrest me even if they knew the drugs weren't mine. I really hated not being able to rely on the authorities. I had no business messing with stuff like this.

I could take the drugs. Throw them in a dumpster somewhere.

Craig would think Theo had something to do with it. Over a million dollars was more money than my brain could comprehend. People killed for that kind of money. Craig the Crowbar probably killed people for fun. He didn't need a reason, though this would be one of hell of a doozy.

I could stick them back in the hole and seal it up. Pretend like I'd never found it. The problem was, I needed Craig gone. Out of Theo's life. This was the ticket to nabbing him.

My hands started to shake as I weighed my options, none of them good.

Calling the cops would get the drugs confiscated. It wouldn't tie them to Craig. It would just piss him off. A multi-state cartel probably had ways of getting information, like who turned in the drugs. That's if he didn't come gunning for Theo.

I shoved the bag of drugs back in its pouch, which was still inside the grocery bags. I slid it into the hole in the wall and replaced the bricks, their sides scraping as they slid bumpily into place.

How did I keep getting neck deep in problems I couldn't fix? Most women comforted friends after they got dumped or helped them find a new job. I didn't have friends, so even mundane problems felt daunting, but this was comical in a not-actually-funny kind of way.

"So what are you going to do?" Ollie asked.

"Honestly? No clue. For now, I'll help Theo by pulling my weight while I used the time to come up with something feasible. It's not like the drugs are going anywhere." I headed for the dumpsters, leaving the ghosts behind.

"You know your fingerprints are all over those bags now," Frank called after me.

I stopped and hung my head. He was right. I hadn't even thought of that. Good thing I'd determined calling the cops was a bad idea, especially with Wagner and his evil partner after me.

The tight ball of worry in my gut grew limbs and began clawing its way up my throat. I focused on breathing. I just had to keep moving. I'd figure something out.

Chapter 15

The dinner rush lasted well into the evening, which didn't give me much of a chance to chew over my problem. By the time we'd ushered out the last of the customers and finished with dishes, mopping, and wiping everything down, it was later than usual.

"You are troubled," Theo commented. He studied me while I removed the little plastic spouts from the soda machine so they could soak overnight in a clear bin of water.

I was about to repeat what I'd said the previous day, that it was nothing a good night of sleep wouldn't fix, but I made the mistake of looking at him, and the words died on my lips. He looked so genuinely concerned for my welfare that lying to him felt wrong. Sleep wouldn't fix anything. I needed answers.

"I'm in a bit of a situation," I said, trying to be as honest as I could. "I'm feeling stuck."

Theo nodded thoughtfully and returned to his task of wiping down the iced tea vats. "I have been stuck in many situations. Sometimes solutions are easy to find. Sometimes, not so much." We worked silently for a minute. "Would a raise help?"

I didn't know much about his financial situation, but starting a business cost money, and it was usually years before it became profitable. I doubted Theo was in a position to offer me more money. He'd done it anyway.

I smiled. "No. It's not a money problem." I caught the flash of relief on his face.

"If talking helps, know I am here." He gave me that special, fatherly smile of his.

Suddenly, all I could think about was his daughter, away at college, completely unaware that she was being used to blackmail her dad by terrible men. She'd grown up seeing that smile. If things went poorly for Theo, she might never see it again.

"I have a friend," I hedged. "He's in kind of a bind." I felt the story out as I told it. "He's got a situation where he's being bullied, in a way. He tried standing up for himself, but he can't make the bullies stop. They're big on intimidations, so if he goes to the authorities, they might hurt him."

Theo nodded again. "And you're worried about your friend's safety." He inhaled deeply through his nose, thinking.

"I'm willing to go to the authorities myself," I hedged, "but I don't know if that will blow back on him."

His lips pursed. "Maybe not, if they know you're the one who told, but that could put you in danger."

I'd been trying not to think about that.

Theo crossed his arms, staring up at the ceiling. "Do the bullies have a routine? Is it possible to lead the authorities to them so they catch the bullies doing the wrong thing?"

Special Agent Wagner's card had been burning a hole in my pocket all afternoon. He'd seemed level headed. I could call him, tell him what I found, only I couldn't prove the drugs were Craig's and not mine. Or Theo's.

"Possibly. I'll think on it." I let out a heavy sigh. "The problem will still be there tomorrow."

Theo put a hand on my shoulder. "You are a good person," he said. "You'll do the right thing."

If I could figure out what that was.

Twenty minutes later, the Retro Cafe was locked up, and we'd gotten in our respective cars. I pretended to get a phone call and waved Theo on. His insistence on walking me to my car every night seemed less paranoid now that I knew his situation.

I hadn't seen Ollie or Frank all evening. When my car started, they came out from behind the cafe with the dog in tow. The dog took up her usual stance by the dumpsters. Ollie and Frank walked into my car and took seats in back.

"Where have you guys been all night?" I asked.

"We were guarding the drugs," Frank said, like it should have been obvious.

"And playing with the dog," Ollie said with a goofy grin that lit his blue eyes.

He'd been so sad all day, his joy brought a sliver of relief from my anxiety. My life was a mess. I'd take the joy where I could get it.

Staring out my windshield, I tried to decide what to do. "I still don't have a plan," I admitted, reaching into my pocket to pull out Wagner's number.

I could call the police station anonymously. Something told me Wagner and his moody partner would find out it was me. They were covering major crimes. A million dollar bag of drugs would have them sniffing around for information. Maybe tipping Wagner off directly would earn me at least a few brownie points.

"You're not thinking of calling that guy, are you?" Frank was leaned over my shoulder from the back seat, frowning at the card.

"You got a better idea?"

"Sure. Leave the drugs where they are and forget about them."

"How does that help Theo?"

"It doesn't. How does you getting yourself arrested help Theo?"

My nose wrinkled. "I'm not going to get arrested."

"Need I remind you your prints are all over that bag?"

I'd considered that. It was an easy fix. I'd already taken an industrial strength disinfectant wipe from the cafe.

Before getting out of my car, I saved Wagner's number in my contacts. I'd call and feel him out. If it felt safe, I'd tell him what was going on. If he seemed inclined to be hostile, I could always make something up about why I'd called.

The prybar was next to the wall where I'd left it. Pulling out the bricks was easy enough the second time around. I pulled out the grocery bags, pried open the Velcro of the nylon pouch, and pulled out the giant Ziploc.

My heart raced knowing I was holding a damn long prison sentence in my hands. Or a death sentence.

The sanitizing wipe was starting to dry out. It was just wet enough to wipe down the bag and the outside of the nylon pouch.

I was about to seal everything back up when I remembered the pair of disposable gloves I'd also taken. I reached in my pocket to pull them out, but froze when the dog started growling. It was an ominous sound, deep in the back of her throat.

"We've got trouble," Frank said.

Staying crouched, I pivoted to see him staring at the Arby's, whose lights brightened the distant night until they were blotted out by a figure rising from the concrete ditch.

I swallowed hard. I couldn't make out details because the figure was backlit. He was slender and moved with a notable swagger. That was enough to identify him.

Ollie clenched his fists, a nervous gesture. "Oh, Enid. This is bad. He has a gun."

I fumbled an earbud from my pocket and slipped it into the ear closest to the cafe wall. I tapped it and said in a quiet voice, "Call Special Agent Wagner."

"How? Ghosts don't exactly get cell service," Ollie said.

He'd thought I'd been talking to him. Silly ghost.

My phone parroted my instructions back to me before it dialed. I heard the line ring. I'd barely saved his number, a fact that made me dizzy. Craig the Crowbar could make my body disappear so nobody ever found me. Even if he killed me, at least now someone would know what happened.

Assuming the good detective answered his phone.

On the fourth ring, he picked up. "Hello?" He was all business.

"It's Enid from the hospital," I whispered frantically. Craig was almost within hearing. "I'm behind the Retro Cafe with Craig the Crowbar."

Wagner's alarm was immediate. "Is he armed?"

I tried to make an uh-huh sound that came out strangled.

"Oh, good." Ollie's relief showed in his voice. "Smart move. Will he be able to make it here in time?"

That was a stupid question. How the hell would I know? The question irritated me.

I considered trying to hide the stash I'd been wiping down, but didn't see the point. Even if I managed to shove the bag back in the hole and return the bricks, there was no reason for me to be squatted by a locked door right where his stash was hidden.

Besides, he'd spotted me long before I knew he was watching. Playing dumb at this point was more likely to anger him than convince him I didn't know about his drugs.

Craig tipped his head as he approached. He was only a handful of steps away, and I thought he'd heard me answering Wagner. Hopefully it had just sounded like a whimper.

"I'm on my way. Are you okay?" Wagner asked, his words coming out in a staccato.

Of course I wasn't okay. I was in deep crap with no escape. How far away was he? Would I be dead before he got there?

I prayed Craig was as big a talker as he seemed. If he was a shoot-first, ask-questions-later kind of guy, I didn't have a chance.

I'd spent most of my teen years convinced my future would hold only loneliness. It wasn't much to live for. I'd never *wanted* to die, but it hadn't seemed like the worst thing that could happen. At least when I was dead, I wouldn't be an outcast.

With mortal peril only a few feet away, I was rethinking that stance.

Craig was too close for me to answer Wagner. I hunched in on myself, fear like a physical force assaulting my body.

Deep shadows distorted Craig's face until he was all angles, his classic, too-wide smile giving him a Doofenschmirtz look.

A hysterical laugh burbled up in my throat.

"I know you," he said. "You waitress here. I always wanted to chat with you. Theo's protective of his staff." He studied me, noting the bag in my hands.

I didn't say anything.

"You're a pretty little thing. Too nosy for my tastes. Hasn't anybody ever told you not to touch things that don't belong to you?"

The dog was crouched, her snarl an almost sub-audible frequency, radiating danger. Craig, oblivious, walked right by her.

Wagner had gone quiet, listening. Hopefully, he'd heard Craig mention the drugs weren't mine.

Frank came closer, his eyes locked on Craig, probably watching for tension in his trigger finger.

I could imagine him yelling "Look out!" just before a bullet entered my brain. Fat lot of good that would do me.

Some part of me had always known it would end like this, neck-deep in ghost problems.

Wagner said something in my ear. Blood pounded through my ears so loud I couldn't make it out. I stood and slowly backed away from the bag.

Craig looked down at where I'd left the disinfectant wipe. "Trying to clean your prints off the bag? That tells me you weren't planning to steal it, at least. I might kill you quick just for that."

He stepped around me, holding his gun close to his hip. His aim would be crap, but it wasn't that hard to hit someone from point-blank range.

Frank motioned for me to step away from the drugs. When I shuffled back, Craig focused on the pouch, nudging it with his toe. "Is it all there?"

My brain felt hot, like it was melting in my skull. "Of course. What would I want with drugs?"

Craig scoffed. "It's true that only certain kinds of people like drugs, but everybody likes money. And these drugs? They're worth a lot of money."

Keep him talking. If I could distract him long enough, Wagner would show up. I had the upper hand here, right? As far as Craig knew, the cafe was shut down, and we were standing in the dark, so there wasn't much chance of being interrupted. He had all night to hold me at gunpoint.

"Where would I sell them?" My voice came out hoarse, which felt weird. It had sounded fine a minute ago. "I assume you'd know if I tried to sell something like that anywhere within a hundred-mile radius of here."

He looked pleased I thought he was so competent. "Oh, I'd definitely know. I'm glad to hear you know that, too. One more reason to make your death a quick one. Theo, on the other hand, won't be so lucky."

The blood froze in my veins, and a chill swept through me. "Theo?"

Craig gestured down at the open hole in the wall. "How else would you know about this? I assume he spotted me out here at some point. His big mouth is gonna cost him in blood." He couldn't hide the excitement in his voice.

I wanted to object, to tell him Theo hadn't said anything about his drug stash, but he'd asked how else I would know about it. I eyed the dog. Trying to explain that the ghost of a K-9 drug-sniffer led me to it would not help my case.

If I couldn't explain, maybe I could use what I knew. "If you hurt Theo, you'll leave his daughter alone, right?" I said for Wagner's benefit. "She doesn't know anything about you leveraging her life to keep Theo from reporting you to the police."

Craig shrugged. "The deal was for Theo to keep his mouth shut. Obviously, he told you. Even if you're not police, you can cause trouble for me. That makes you a loose end. Theo as well. The last thing I need is for his daughter to start crying to the cops about how her daddy was blackmailed by the cartel. That shit'll be all over the news. We can't afford that kind of publicity."

"You're going to kill his daughter, too?" I stammered. "She doesn't know anything about this."

"I don't know that," he said, holding his hands out to the side. He was way too comfortable swinging his gun around. "And I'm not taking the chance."

I'd always known the guy was a creep, but that was pure evil.

"Theo didn't tell me about you," I said. "I could tell you weren't here for the grits. You kind of stand out."

His look turned thoughtful. "So you decided to snoop on me? Seems you've got a dangerously inquisitive streak." He tapped his gun on his thigh. "Maybe I can use that."

Dubious, I asked, "What do you mean?"

"I mean you could get paid to be a snoop. Of course, you'd have to convince Theo to keep his mouth shut. You'd have to keep yours shut, too."

It was baffling to think he'd misread me so badly. There was no part of me that would ever work with him.

Something in my expression must have given me away, because he paused to give me a pointed look. "You did want to keep Theo safe, right? And his daughter?"

He had me there.

"And you do like money, am I right? Working in food service can't possibly be your dream job."

He was right on both counts. I desperately needed a nest egg.

Granted, Wagner was on the way, but all I had to do was hang up the phone, warn Craig, and lie to Wagner once he got there.

Working for Craig would make me plenty of money in a hurry. I'd have a nest egg in no time. The cost? I'd be shackling myself to an organization that hurt innocent people. I'd never be able to leave without putting Theo and his daughter back in danger. I'd never be able to leave, period. Craig wouldn't let me go.

"Ask him about Peyton," Ollie said, his voice tight.

"What?" I asked.

Craig assumed I was talking to him. "You work for me or you die," he said bluntly. "I didn't get this far by taking chances. If someone even looks at me like they know something, I take them out. Usually, I have a little fun with them first." His eyes turned cold as he watched for my reaction.

I was distracted by Ollie, who said, "Peyton's boyfriend turned up dead. Randall says he died from right-handed injuries, but he was left-handed. Plus you were attacked outside her house."

"You're on to something," Frank said. "Peach Grove is a sleepy town. What are the chances two murders are a coincidence when there's a big drug cartel in town? They've gotta be connected."

I licked my lips. Craig was holding his gun in his right hand. That didn't mean much. Most people were right-handed. Still.

"What kind of loose end was Peyton?"

Craig sneered. "That stupid bitch would have been fine if she'd have been reasonable. She wouldn't let Victor back into her house to get his shit. She packed it all on the porch and changed the door locks, but he'd hid a bunch of our valuables up in her attic like a crack head."

He sighed and shook his head. "We gave him the chance to get it back. He failed, so we went in and got it ourselves."

That had been more of a confession than I'd bargained for.

I looked at Ollie, whose expression was halfway between horror and rage. He'd spent his entire afterlife tied to her, hoping to set things right. He didn't deserve to hear about her death in such a blunt, callous way.

It was astounding that Craig had admitted all this while trying to recruit me. Who wanted to work for a psychopath willing to brutally kill people's loved ones?

A deep and abiding love was hard to come by. Most people never got to experience that kind of steady devotion. It was rare and beautiful. Craig only saw it as a leverage point.

Craig circled me, a mangy, prowling hyena. Where the hell was Wagner?

I focused on keeping Craig talking. "What about Victor?" I blurted. "He was part of your gang, right? Why have him killed?"

"Sweet girl," he said, shaking his head. "Morons don't last long in our world. You're given a job, and you do it. If you don't, we make an example out of you." His words were bland, like he was stating the sky was blue.

"You're not taking my bait, which make you my current job. Next is Theo. Then his daughter. I'll have it all taken care of before the sun rises." His smile didn't reach his eyes. "Stupidity is not rewarded. Efficiency is. I'm not one to brag, but I am excellent at my job."

He raised the gun. The sound of the dog growling ratcheted up a notch. The only reason she hadn't attacked, I was sure, was because she knew she couldn't physically touch Craig. It was supremely frustrating to be in a situation that sucked this much without being able to make a difference.

"He's going to shoot, Enid. Run." Ollie's eyes were wide with panic, the emotion in his command bleeding into me, spiking my own desire to flee.

"No," Frank said sharply. "Don't run. He'll only shoot you in the back. You gotta keep him talking until Wagner shows up. It's too late to run. There's nowhere to hide."

He was right. My best chance would be to dive into the ditch, which wouldn't do much good. Regardless, I took slow, cautious steps, circling around him. "You don't want to shoot me," I said. "I've got something you want."

Craig seemed amused by that. "Then I'll take it off your corpse."

"It's not on me. It's in me. It's knowledge. You'll lose it forever if you kill me now."

"When I started out killing, I used to like listening to people beg. They came up with reasons not to die that sounded so creative to my young mind. By now, I've killed well over a hundred people and all the excuses sound the same. I have kids. I have information. I have money. I have power. You're not that evil. You'll end up in hell. Blah, blah, blah. You bore me."

His gun arm shifted higher. I knew I was out of time.

"I see ghosts," I blurted, backing slowly away from him. I edged closer to the ditch. It was a terrible option. It was the only one I had.

Hopefully, the darkness would throw off his aim. He'd chase me down, but it would give me a few precious seconds more.

Craig paused, dropping the gun a few inches. "That one's new. Congratulations. It's earned you an extra three seconds of life." He raised the gun again.

"Think about what that could mean. Ghosts could get information from anywhere, unseen." I didn't bother to point out that ghosts were self-centered and didn't do favors unless it got them something. A ghost spy network would be less than useless to the Saints, especially since ghosts couldn't be threatened.

"Remember what I said about efficiency?" Craig said. "Playing what-if is the opposite of that. You would die so quick in our organization. But then, you're dying pretty quick outside our organization, too."

He shrugged. Casual talk of my death didn't bother him in the slightest. He took one step toward me and squinted down the sights of his gun in one smooth motion. He shouldn't have needed the sights. He was barely beyond arm's reach. One bullet was all he'd need.

"No, stupid, they already have information," I said, hoping the insult might give him pause. "Information you want."

His grin widened. "Then that information will die with you."

It took me off guard when Special Agent Wagner suddenly yelled, "Freeze!"

I couldn't tell where he was because the sound through my headset was so loud. I screamed, jerking like I'd been tasered.

Either Wagner's sudden appearance or my scream startled Craig. He pulled the trigger.

White hot fire lanced through my shoulder, an inch below my left collarbone.

Ollie yelled "No!" and lunged for me.

The dog, already crouched and on edge, leapt at Craig's gun hand. She passed right through him and plowed into Ollie.

I stumbled back, tripped on my own feet, and fell with Ollie and the dog partially inside me, which was exactly as disturbing as it sounds. We disappeared into the ditch.

I should have cracked my head on the concrete. Maybe I did. If so, I didn't feel it. The world simply disappeared in a blink, leaving me in inky blackness so dark it was like negative color.

In the void, something snatched hold of me.

Chapter 16

Claws raked down my arm.

I tried to scream. No sound came out.

I tried to suck in air. There was none.

I was in some kind of vacuum where air didn't exist. My entire body strained against the nothingness, desperate for a return to normalcy, away from this state of utter wrongness.

Along with the atmosphere itself, sight and sound had disappeared. Had I died? Had I landed wrong in the ditch and caved in my skull?

That made less sense with each passing second as the burning in my lungs increased exponentially.

An odd pulsing throughout my body alarmed me. It took a moment to understand it was my heartbeat, the pounding blood unrecognizable without the accompanying throbbing in my ears as it rushed past.

My need to breathe was acute, triggering panic like I'd never known. I flailed, frantic, until I smacked blindly at whatever had gotten hold of me. I'd forgotten it was there. Briefly, I felt fur with one hand and clothes with the other.

Within seconds, my thrashing weakened, and my mind slowed. I gripped hold of something. It was holding me, too. An arm? Ollie? Had the fur been the dog?

As if in answer, a growl emanated from the darkness. It wasn't a sound so much as a deep, thrumming rumble just beyond the edges of hearing, more a vibration in my skull than anything. That was not the ghost dog.

The sound struck terror in me. Whatever it was, it was big. Huge. It brought skyscraper-sized dragons to mind.

Enough adrenaline can jump-start a heart, but it's no replacement for oxygen. I was far past the need for air. My awareness dwindled, my world narrowing to a single point of certainty: something in the darkness was going to murder me horribly.

With that thought, my consciousness winked out.

Time disappeared, then returned, hazy in the muddy recesses of my mind. It disappeared again, then returned. I couldn't tell how long had passed, a year or a few seconds. I detected the sensation of breath, only I wasn't sure if I was breathing or being breathed upon.

A burst of something went through me. Light? Power? It was like stepping from a cold cave into tropical sunshine, the warmth running through me like a shiver as my body tried to expel a cold rooted deep in my bones.

If there had been light, my eyes couldn't see it. I couldn't even comprehend the concept of sight, so far gone was my mind, my thoughts scattered like dandelion fluff in a stiff breeze.

Eventually, I came to my senses, amazed I was alive. The first sensation to return was fear, terror in my very soul. The idea of that thing in the darkness, infinitely powerful, dangerous, and *aware of me* was enough to induce a panic attack.

I lay on the ground, trembling so hard my bones ached for a long while.

A breeze shifted strands of hair hanging in my face. They stuck to my skin. Was I sweating?

"Enid? Are you okay?" Ollie asked from nearby. He sounded anxious.

The dog growled, a pitiful sound compared to the thing in the darkness.

"All right," Ollie said, placating. "I won't touch her, but I need to know she's okay."

I opened my eyes to more darkness, though this time it lacked the voidal quality of that terrible dream world I'd been in. Another breeze blew, rustling leaves overhead.

Ollie knelt on the ground a few paces off. I could see him if I peered past the dog's legs. She stood between us, guarding me.

When I lifted my head, pine needles stuck to my face. I wiped at them, surprised to find my cheeks wet with tears. They had run down to mat my hair in soggy clumps.

When I shifted, the dog turned so fast she was a blur. She came to me, licking my face, adding to the wetness.

"Ugh. Get off me," I mumbled, trying to ward her off. She ignored me. It wasn't until my fingers touched her fur that I realized I could feel her.

"You're alive." Ollie's relief was clear. "Are you okay?"

"Mmf," I said, trying again to dodge the dog's tongue. "Why is she licking me?" I managed in the brief second between me pushing her away and her rebounding like a magnet.

"She's been guarding you. Looks like she's pretty fond of you."

I shoved her away again. "Sit!" My forceful tone provoked an immediate response. The dog's butt dropped to the ground, ears up, and that intent look returned. She watched me like I was holding a giant steak.

I sat up and swiped at my face. "Why is her slobber on me? Why can I touch her?"

Ollie blinked stupidly at me. "You can feel her?"

"Did you not see me pushing at her just now?" It was fairly dark out, but the moon was most of the way to full, and there were plenty of stars. Where were we?

I scanned the area and spotted a familiar path. I was home. How had I gotten here?

"I thought she was pretending," Ollie said. "Like how dogs play keep-away when you try to get their ball from them. I didn't realize you were actually pushing her."

"Well, I was. Does that mean I'm dead?" My voice grew heated and more than a little panicky. "Am I dead, Ollie?"

He held up his hands as if warding me off. "Woah. I have no idea. Calm down."

The phrase immediately made me more mad. "First off," I said, holding up a finger, "nobody in the history of pissed-off people has *ever* calmed down because someone told them to. Second off," I held up another finger, "if I'm dead, that's a pretty damn good reason to get worked up. Answer the question, Ollie. Did you kill me?"

"What?" His voice went up an octave. "I didn't kill you."

"You plowed into me, then I fell into that ditch and ended up in that horrible nightmare place, and now I'm in the woods by my house with no explanation of how I got here."

I'd been shot before I fell. I'd felt the bullet go in. My hand felt at the wound, pawing clumsily at my shoulder. "And my bullet wound is *gone*." I almost yelled it at him, as if my magically healing wound were his fault. "*Why* is my bullet wound gone, Ollie?"

"I don't know." He sounded like a mouse squeaking objections at me.

"Where was that place? That nowhere place where light doesn't exist?"

His mouth opened and closed like a fish out of water. "I don't know." It came out as a stammer.

I took deep breaths in an effort not to lunge at him and shake him until answers fell out of his big, stupid brain. "I hate ghosts!" I screamed at the world.

Granted, I'd hated ghosts for a long time, but now my rage burned within me, a living thing.

"Uhh…Enid?" Ollie wrung his hands, his eyes widening in alarm. "You're starting to glow."

"What?" I looked down at my hands to see a pale, sage green aura around me. I was glowing. Just like a ghost.

I really was dead.

A voice called from off in the distance. "Call your therapist! People are trying to sleep!" It sounded like Lexi. In fact, given the proximity to her house, it might very well be her.

Ollie spoke slowly, his words weirdly drawn out. "That's weird."

When I looked at him, he motioned at me.

When I looked back down at my hands, the glow was gone. I breathed out. I'd never known a ghost's aura to flicker out of existence.

What the hell was going on? Was I dead or wasn't I?

The dog whined. She shifted in place like it was impossible to sit still for even a minute.

I ignored her. I had bigger things to worry about than entertaining a dog.

A car drove by along the street beyond the woods, and a thought came to me. I was on my feet in an instant, running through the woods for Lexi's house. I circled the driveway and barged in the front door.

Lexi had been heading for her bedroom. She spun when I entered, her hand going to her chest. "Enid! Girl, you scared the hell out of me."

"You can see me?" I asked. Before she answered, I came to the realization that I wasn't, in fact, dead. If I had been, I'd have gone through the door instead of opening it. Unless going through things was a learned skill.

"What?" She looked at me like I had three heads, which was valid considering my question.

"I mean, do you see the state I'm in?" I stumbled through the words, trying to sound less crazy. "I tripped in the woods, and now I've got pine needles in my hair and everything. Boy, what a mess."

She blinked. "Yes. A mess. Do you need medical attention?"

I blinked back. "No?" At least, I didn't think so.

"Then take yourself back outside, and brush yourself off before you dump more leaves on my living room floor." She put her hands on her hips and gave me her no-nonsense look.

"Right." I backed out the door, closing it on my way, reveling in the feel of the doorknob beneath my hand.

"And don't come barging in her like you've got the devil on your heels," she called after me.

"Sorry," I said. I closed the door behind me and stood on the front stoop.

Ollie was there, waiting for me. The dog passed through the door on her way *out* of the house. I hadn't even noticed her inside.

I walked out to the curb and sat with my head on my knees. A headache had been coming on since I'd awoken, and it quickly made its way to the top of my list of concerns. Maybe I'd hit my head after all.

"Ollie, what's going on?" I whispered it this time.

"I have no idea. I was there with you in that dark place." His voice was quiet. Oddly soothing. "I felt the presence there. It scared me, too. I have no clue what that was. Or *where* that was. I'm just glad you're not dead."

I was glad I wasn't dead, too. "I wouldn't be much use to you dead."

"That's not what I meant."

I wanted to glower at him, but he sounded so sincere.

"Maybe we can ask the Spirit Body if they know what happened."

"Tell me about them. What is the Spirit Body?"

"They're a committee of sorts full of really old ghosts. They keep the peace, maintain the rules, settle disputes, that sort of stuff. They're like the ghost government. If anybody would have answers, it's them."

My headache was growing worse by the second. My pulse pounded through me, setting off lightning bolts in my brain that ricocheted through my body all the way down to my toes. I groaned.

"Enid?"

"I hurt," I mumbled. "My head hates me."

He replied. I couldn't make out his words. I needed Tylenol. Or sleep.

By the time I reached the house, I stumbled inside and flopped down on the couch. I was out before my head hit the pillow, whether asleep or unconscious was up for debate.

My dreams were terrifying, full of unseen danger lurking over my shoulder as I lay curled in a ball, hoping that thing wouldn't notice me. A menacing rumble vibrated my bones, and I desperately prayed the darkness would disappear.

A voice broke through my sense of impending doom. "What is wrong with you?"

I jerked, inhaling like I'd come up from the bottom of a lake. Wild-eyed, I flailed, only to find I was curled up on Lexi's couch. She was standing over me, staring at me like she had no idea who I was. The dog lay across me, growling again.

"Stop that," I said. The dog's growl faded, and she licked her lips but kept her eyes on Lexi.

Lexi put her hands on her hips. "Stop what? You're the one covered in leaves curled up with your shoes on my couch, no blankets or pillow or anything. What is going on with you?"

Before I could answer, there was a knock at the door.

I stared at Lexi, who heaved an exasperated sigh and circled the couch to open it. "Can I help you?"

"Hello, ma'am. Sorry to bother you. Is this the residence of Enid Walsh?"

I knew that voice.

Lexi opened the door further, frowning at me.

Special Agent Wagner caught sight of me. His eyes narrowed. "Miss Walsh. Glad to see you made it home okay. Could I have a word with you?" He sounded robotic, like he was trying to keep his anger from showing. Not that it did much good when it was written all over his face.

My headache from the night before still hadn't subsided. I'd slept wrong. Every joint in my body whimpered in protest as I pushed myself up. I circled the dog and made my way to the door, mumbling an apology to Lexi as I slunk past her.

Wagner stepped aside to let me pass.

"Come find me when you're done out here," Lexi said, a warning that she wanted an explanation for my weird behavior. I nodded, and she closed the door.

Lexi didn't have much of a porch, so I walked down the sidewalk to stand in the driveway where there was more privacy and elbow room. Especially, I noted, since my car wasn't there. I assumed it was still at the Retro Cafe.

Wagner kept looking me up and down from different angles, circling me when I stopped. He stepped in and touched my left shoulder below the collarbone, flicking my hair out of the way. "You were shot." It was a simple statement.

I looked down at my shirt, brown with maroon paisley teardrops scattered across it. There was a neat, round hole with a half-inch ring of blood around it. I could make out smooth skin through the shirt.

I'd already determined the bullet wound had disappeared. I'd somehow failed to notice the hole in my shirt. With my hair down, it must have covered the hole enough for Lexi not to notice.

Ollie had been sitting by the garage. He spotted me and rose, nodding in greeting as he joined me, the detective, and the ever-present dog in the driveway.

It felt strangely good to have him near, like a knot of tension in my gut was eased. Whatever had happened, it had happened to both of us. We were in this together.

Wagner grew impatient at my silence. "Explain."

I tried to think up a believable lie. When none came to mind, I tried stalling. "Explain what, exactly?"

This question did nothing for Wagner's patience. His lips drew into a thin line. "How is it you were shot, only now you're uninjured? Why did you run off? *How* did you run off? You fell in that ditch and disappeared. I would have seen you if you ran."

"No you wouldn't. You were busy dealing with Craig the Crowbar," I reminded him.

"I shot him the same time he shot you. I got him in almost the same spot, even. His gun ended up not far from the ditch, so I secured that before cuffing him. You had fallen in the ditch seconds before I was over there looking for you, flashlight and all. The ditch was empty. You weren't anywhere to be found. I called for you, and you didn't answer. So I'll ask you again to explain yourself."

I opened my mouth, then paused. Eventually, I just shrugged. "I genuinely don't know. I fell in the ditch and blacked out. When I woke up, I was home. I've got a hole in my sweater and a killer headache. My body feels like I ran full-speed into a brick wall, and my memory is Swiss cheese. I wish I had answers for you," I said honestly. "You're the detective. If you figure out some explanation, please fill me in."

He gave me a hard stare for several beats before dropping his gaze. He lifted a hand to pinch the bridge of his nose. "I don't have any answers, Miss Walsh. That's what I came here to get from you."

Ollie reached my side and grimaced. "Poor planning on his part," he muttered.

We stood there awkwardly in the early morning sunlight. The air was brisk, and the trees were alive with bird sounds I normally would have found soothing. The various calls from different species were distorted by the throbbing in my head, making them chaotic and discordant. "So you got Craig? Is he still alive?"

Wagner nodded. "He's alive and in custody. We've got him under heavy guard while they treat him at the hospital."

"Good. He'll come after me if he ever gets out."

"We're hoping to put him away for the rest of his life after he tells us all he knows about the Saints."

"Why would he help you if he's going to get life in prison anyway?"

"He's getting life in prison either way, assuming he doesn't get the death penalty. If he doesn't want his stay in prison to end with a shiv in his throat, he'll cooperate. In return, we'll put him in a different prison than the one we put the Saints in."

I felt a wave of disgust for Craig, followed by a flash of fear. Only it wasn't fear for myself. It was fear for others. How many lives had Craig ruined? Theo had almost certainly been the last in a long line of good people he'd blackmailed. I was just glad his daughter was safe now.

Ollie stepped closer to me, hovering protectively at my side. It was odd not to resent his presence.

The dog stood at my other side, opposite Ollie. She edged in close, her side pressing against my leg. Was she jealous of Ollie's proximity to me? At least she'd stopped snarling at him.

If she was at my home, did that mean she was bound to me instead of the dumpster? I seemed to be collecting ghosts at an alarming rate.

Why could I *feel* a dog who could walk through walls? Was I somehow less corporeal than I had been last night? Was my spirit-self more solid?

Ollie had mentioned the Spirit Body might have answers. I wasn't sure I wanted them.

My whole life, I'd only ever wanted to be left alone. Did I really want to dive into the world of ghost governments? What would happen if an entire organization found out I could see them?

The answer was obvious. I'd never worry about nightmares again because I'd never get any sleep.

Chapter 17

Special Agent Wagner insisted I come down to the station to give a statement.

I had no clue how to avoid sounding crazy. Anyone reading the report would think I was lying.

I told him I'd be by later that morning. My hair was still a mess, and my clothes were rumpled.

He told me to come down as early as possible so the details would be fresh in my mind. I almost laughed. "Wouldn't want my detailed memory of events to fail me."

With a wry look, he headed for his car. The dog trotted along at his side, tail wagging. She liked Wagner. I was inclined to trust her judgment.

Thinking back, I second-guessed that instinct. She'd growled at Lexi. And at Ollie. But not at Frank, oddly enough. Why not?

Frank was some kind of detective, I was pretty sure. So was Wagner. Did the dog have a love of sleuths? Or maybe cops, specifically. Frank had known a lot about her breed in relation to law enforcement. He'd been positive she'd been a trained K-9 officer. Based on the drugs she'd located, I was inclined to agree.

Strange that she liked me.

Beside me, I felt Ollie's eyes on me. We hadn't really talked about everything yet. I wasn't sure I was ready to. It happened. It was terrifying. He'd already said he didn't have answers. Talking just brought it all back up again.

"Head feeling better?" he asked.

As if in response, I felt a throbbing begin behind my eyes. "Sort of."

"I'm sorry I got you into this."

"I know." And I did. He hadn't meant for any of this to happen. He'd lost a lot. I got that. It didn't matter enough for me to be okay with risking my life.

"Thank you for all you've done," he said. "I don't know your story. I can't pretend to know why you're so resistant to embracing your ability. When I see suffering, every fiber of my soul wants to help. I can't. I'm dead."

He moved to stand in front of me. His aura was brighter than I'd ever seen it, but his eyes were sad.

That heartfelt, somber look filled me with guilt. I looked away.

"Being dead means I have nothing to lose. You still have your life. I want to see you live it."

I could feel his eyes on me. Those blue, blue eyes that were way too beautiful.

The silence stretched until I glanced up.

His face was set in determination. He spoke like he'd deliberately chosen his words. "I swear to you, Enid, as long as I'm bound to you, I will do my best to keep you from harm."

It sounded like an oath. Was he pledging himself to my protection? It was odd to think of a ghost as more of a guardian angel than a greedy, manipulative bastard. From any other ghost, I'd think it was empty promises or a way of buttering me up.

Ollie didn't need to win my favor, though. We'd solved the case. Peyton could move on. When I took the time to think about it, I felt his sincerity was genuine. He'd tried to protect me from Craig. He'd gone through the place of darkness with me. He'd tried to comfort me afterward. To my surprise, I found I trusted him.

What did that mean for us? Were we...friends? Partners of a sort? Did it matter? When Peyton moved on, would Ollie leave, too?

Something in my chest clenched uncomfortably at the thought. Why did I feel like I was losing something I'd never had. It was silly. He'd move on, and I'd be ghost-free.

It was what I'd wanted. Now I was going to pout over it?

Ollie studied me, waiting for a reply to his solemn proclamation.

"Thanks," I said, feeling awkward. I bit my lip, not sure what else to say. "I'm going to shower. I'll be back out soon."

He stayed where he was, watching as I walked away. I felt an odd sense of regret, like I'd missed an opportunity. If he'd had a body, maybe I'd have taken his hand and given it a squeeze. Or given him a hug, my arms wrapped around his neck, his warm body pressed to mine, a steady presence that took away the aching feeling of utter loneliness I'd had for as long as I could remember.

I pulled my thoughts away. They would only lead to pain. I took a deep breath, resolved to focus on reality.

Inside, Lexi was making coffee in the kitchen. When I approached, she turned and raised an eyebrow. "Don't walk in like nothing's up. You're acting crazy. Spill."

Straight to the point, as usual.

I shoved my hands in my pockets and leaned against the counter. Lexi's kitchen had natural wood cabinets covering three sides of the room with a tiny island in the middle, all topped with creamy brown marble. The woodsy colors gave the room a sense of warmth.

Deciding to take a page from Lexi's book, I spoke bluntly. "There was an incident after work. A guy showed up with a gun. I called the police, they arrested him."

Lexi's mouth dropped open. "Were you hurt?"

I'd carefully arranged my hair to cover the bullet hole in my shirt. "No wounds. Just a little too much excitement for my taste." That much was true.

"The man at the door was with the police?"

I nodded. "He wants me to come down and give a statement."

From behind me, the dog whined. I turned my head and frowned at her. She sat near one corner of the dinner table, her eyes barely high enough to reach the table top. Her gaze was locked on the bowl in the center full of ornamental blue and beige balls.

Of course. The dog wanted a ball.

"Did you wrestle with the guy? Is that why you were covered in leaves when you came in?," Lexi asked. "You did look a bit keyed up last night. And you crashed hard. I tried to get you to change before I went to bed, but you were dead to the world."

Her phrasing brought to mind the dark place. A shiver ran down my spine.

People report seeing strange things when they die and are resuscitated, or even when they've just come really close to dying. I didn't think that was what had happened in my case. I hadn't been able to breathe, but by then, I'd already been in the lightless place.

Besides, a near-death experience wouldn't explain how I'd ended up in the woods behind my home.

"Enid?" Lexi asked, watching me.

I replayed what she'd said. She'd asked a question. "No, the gunman didn't touch me. I got a ride home since I was too shaken to drive, then I wandered out back to the woods to settle my nerves." It sounded like a legitimate excuse.

Lexi seemed to buy it. "Why did you come crashing through the door?"

I shrugged apologetically. "I was still wound up. I probably should have spent more time out there watching the stars or something."

Her expression softened. "I'm sorry you had such a hard night. I didn't help with that." She shook her head and turned to grab a mug out of the cabinet and pour herself a cup of coffee.

"You didn't do anything. You're right, I wasn't behaving like myself. I'm sorry I scared you when I came in."

She let out a musical laugh. "I was afraid something was chasing you."

The dog whined again. I turned to see her watching me. She looked to the balls and then back to me before shifting her weight impatiently. "No."

Lexi had turned back to me. She tipped her head. "Is there something you're seeing that I'm not?" She sounded amused.

I sighed. "You may have mixed feelings about this, but we seem to have adopted a dog. Or been adopted by one, at least."

"And this dog is..." she trailed off.

"A ghost."

"Uh huh." She sipped at her coffee. "I guess I don't mind, so long as Bailey's okay with it. What kind of dog is it?"

"Looks like a German Shepherd, but it's not. Something Belgian." She tried to remember what Frank had called it. "A Mal?"

"Its name is Mal?"

"No, that's what the breed is called, I think."

Bailey, having heard her name, wandered out of Lexi's room to come hang out with her humans. The Mal barely glanced at the little Yorkie-poo. On her way to Lexi, Bailey stopped to sniff at my ankles. I bent down and picked her up, running my fingers through her silky fur.

The Mal watched me for a moment before leaving the balls to come stand by my side, her nose tipped up so she could lay her chin on my hip and stare up at me with soulful eyes. "Jealous?" I asked.

I put Bailey down so she could go to Lexi.

"Do the dogs get along?" Lexi was fighting to hold in a smile.

"Bailey can't see my dog. The Mal's not happy to share me, not that she can do anything about it."

"Well, I guess she can stay."

"Good thing, since I can't make her leave."

It was odd to mention a ghost in the room without tension immediately filling the conversation. Lexi was so different from my mother. My father and sister weren't as critical, but they'd always been uncomfortable with the subject. Lexi was the first family member I'd found who didn't make me feel like I'd stepped out of line by mentioning the G-word.

The Mal shifted beside me, her neck craned to stare at the balls on the table.

I laughed. "We may need to swap out your table decorations. My dog seems really focused on the balls."

Lexi grinned. "I have a few table centers I swap out regularly. I'll pick something less round."

Her upbeat mood lifted mine. "Thanks. I'm going to hit the shower and change clothes. I'll wipe down the couch when I'm done."

"Yes, please." She sipped her coffee before calling after me. "Need a ride back to your car?"

"Yes, please," I parroted back.

I was glad Lexi knew about my dog. It made me sound less crazy when I demanded she stay out of the bathroom. Eventually, the Mal laid down outside the door, head up, staring at me with the intensity of a thousand blazing suns. Her focus was disconcerting.

I closed the door in her face, grumbling about personal boundaries as I stripped off my clothes.

My top would have to go in the trash. It was a scary reminder of how close to death I'd been.

Getting shot had hurt like blazes. In contrast, the shower felt fantastic. It felt normal. It felt cleansing. For those brief minutes, I could imagine there were no detectives, no cartels, no ghosts.

I'd given up my dreams of becoming anything useful to society before I'd been old enough to consider what I wanted to be. Even as a young child, I knew I had to stay out of the public eye. I needed a small and quiet life in a small and quiet place.

If I was lucky, I'd have a friend or two to go to lunch with. Not a husband or kids. I'd never even bothered to consider if I wanted that. What I mourned was the loss of the option.

It was okay. I was okay with solitude, really, but I still resented the ghosts who kept my life so limited.

I blocked out the negative thoughts swirling in my head and enjoyed the water, warm and soothing as it washed away the stress of the world. I zoned out for a moment, lost in sensation.

My eyes closed, the shower walls winking out. The darkness behind my eyelids grew darker at a rapid rate until I could feel that place, the voidal space, pressing in on me.

Gasping, I opened my eyes. My heart pounded, my breathing quick and shallow. Suddenly solitude wasn't so comforting. I nearly cried at the loss of that, too.

A wave of hopelessness washed over me, replacing the soothing warmth of the shower with a familiar, weighty dread.

I turned off the water and toweled off. The visions of darkness would fade over time. I just had to stay busy until then. If I kept my mind occupied, I wouldn't have time to focus on nightmares.

One step, then another. I got dressed, combed my hair, and got a ride to the cafe from Lexi, who dropped me off by my car.

Ollie and the dog hopped out of her back seat to stand beside me.

The stench from the dumpster had built up again. The container was emptied regularly only to slowly return to its previous state of disaster.

Rinse and repeat, just like my life. Every time I pressed reset, I seemed to find myself back in the same situation.

Ollie said, "You've got something on your car."

A yellow sticky note had been left on the windshield. I pulled it off to see a big question mark. "Theo. He must have seen my car this morning and wondered why it was here when the store was closed."

The dog wandered off to sniff at the grass. I hoped she wasn't looking for more drugs.

I headed for the cafe with Ollie at my side. The smell of sweet brown sugar bacon and buttery grits replaced the stench of garbage that lingered in my nose. Today, the smell of sage sausage was almost as strong.

My life was reverting to its normal state of ghost-filled chaos, but the quality of the stench, so to speak, was different with Ollie, Frank, and strangely, the dog at my side. I had a job with an awesome boss, an understanding cousin to live with, and friends of a sort.

Sure, I once more had ghosts invading my life, but they weren't all bad. They were kinda okay even, in small doses.

"Decent crowd for a Sunday," Ollie commented. The cafe was half-full of lingering patrons now that the breakfast rush had passed.

I caught Theo's eye. He made his way over. "Your car was here. You were not."

"I ended up finding another way home last night."

"Is your car not working?" he asked, a note of worry creeping in.

"No. My car works fine," I assured him.

Wagner must not have notified him of the events behind the cafe the night before. Presumably, he'd fill him in at some point in the day. I wasn't sure if he'd mind me spilling the beans first, but Wagner wasn't my priority.

I considered telling Theo what happened, but knew he wouldn't have time to hear the full story until things were slow. He'd have a lot of questions.

"It's a long story. I'll stop by around shift change this afternoon and fill you in."

He nodded.

Jade, one of the waitresses on shift, came up behind Theo and tapped him on the shoulder. "My customer says the eggs are cold." Her wry smile told us it was one of *those* customers. The ones who found reasons to complain.

Theo took the plate from her. "Okay. I'll cook him some new ones, just this once," he said, smiling as he headed for the grill.

I had no idea how he kept such a good attitude.

"If he hadn't spent twenty minutes talking while he picked at his waffle, he wouldn't have had this problem," Jade told me.

She worked the cafe most weekends and some weekdays, depending on the college courses she was taking any given semester. She was smart, capable, and generally the opposite of Jenna. We got along great whenever we worked together.

I chuckled. "Whoever said the customer is always right clearly didn't work in the service industry."

"A customer came up with that, guaranteed." Jade left to clear a table.

Theo had scraped the plate of cold food in the trash and cracked a couple eggs on the hot griddle. "You want breakfast?" he called to me. When I hesitated, he said, "Two eggs or four take the same amount of time to cook."

I hadn't eaten breakfast and wasn't sure when I'd get the chance, so I nodded and took a seat at the low bar.

"I'm going to look for Frank," Ollie said, wandering off to the back room.

Frank had to be curious about our sudden disappearance the night before. I was surprised he hadn't tracked me down at my house. He could be in the back room or behind the building.

Theo brought me a plate with eggs, toast, and a piece each of bacon and sausage. Before I'd taken three bites, he returned with a bowl of grits. I inhaled the aroma of cream and butter with a hint of salt. The smells brought a warm, cozy feeling to my gut.

The Retro Cafe felt more like home than my actual home ever had. Theo had a lot to do with that. He was so different from my parents, who rarely gave praise—to me, at least. My younger sister hadn't been showered with it, but the comparison between the weirdo and the normal kid had been pointed out often.

When you're a kid, you don't get a choice in where you live or what your home is like. As an adult, I hoped to create a home for myself.

I took a bite of my bacon and savored the sweet saltiness.

Just a few days ago, I'd been convinced I needed to move. After getting to know Ollie, talking with Lexi, and putting Craig behind bars, I had a new determination to stay. A few good people had made all the difference.

A flash of lime green color caught my eye. A ghost strode to the middle of the cafe and paused to scan the room, easy to spot by his knee-length jacket the color of spicy mustard with matching knee-pants, white stockings, and shoes that made me think of the Amish. The frilly lace at his neck had been popular somewhere around the Revolutionary War era.

His hair, beard, and mustache were trimmed close, the gray nearly blending with his pasty complexion. His lime green aura gave him a sickly look, and his frumpy expression seemed perfectly at home on his face.

I diverted my eyes before he noticed me. I already had three ghosts too many on my list of acquaintances.

Ollie wandered in through the soda machine and stopped in front of me. "I can't find Frank anywhere. He must have gone off on his own."

I tried to motion with my eyes that another ghost was in the room, but Ollie was scanning the parking lot through the big glass windows behind me.

"You there," the new ghost said.

I pulled my phone out of my pocket so I would have somewhere to focus my attention. I didn't trust myself to keep my facial reactions under control.

"Hi." Ollie said, surprised. "I didn't see you there. You haven't seen a guy named Frank around here, have you? Round head? Fedora?"

The lime green aura moved close enough for me to see it in my periphery. "I have not. My name is Brad. You would be?" He had a pompous way of speaking.

"Ollie."

"Ollie. Right," Brad said in a dismissive tone. "Well, Ollie, I'm the Shamus. What do you know about the power ripples emanating from the Styx?"

There was a brief pause. "The Styx? Like the river? Is that real?"

"No, Ollie. Not the river. It's a place."

My hand clenched around my phone, which wasn't even turned on. I didn't like Brad's condescending tone. Before I inadvertently glared at the new arrival, I jabbed the power button, hoping to find something to catch my eye on my phone screen.

Nothing happened. The screen stayed blank.

I swiped a finger across the screen. It lit up briefly, then flickered and went out. That was weird.

I hadn't charged it last night, so I'd plugged it in while I showered. The way the screen flickered indicated glitchiness, not a dying battery. My phone was only a couple years old. It had worked perfectly before now.

Brad said, "Something's stirred it up. That could mean big trouble in the spirit world, you know."

Obviously Ollie didn't know. He'd just said as much. Brad wasn't a very good listener.

"Uhh. Sorry. I don't know anything about a place called the Styx. Unless you mean, like, the run down part of town. Peach Grove doesn't have many neighborhoods that fit that description."

"It's not in this town," Brad said slowly, like Ollie was a child. "It's not anywhere on Earth, even."

Ollie sounded confused. "Then why would you be asking random ghosts if they know what's happening there?"

"Never mind. Clearly you aren't educated enough to answer my questions." Brad sounded disgusted at Ollie's ignorance. "We'll get to the bottom of it ourselves."

Ollie pivoted, looking around. "We?"

"Dear boy. I'm a member of the Spirit Body. Do you even know what that is?"

"I do. Hey, maybe you could help us with something."

I knew what he was going to ask. "Nope," I said, swiping at my blank screen as if I were talking to myself.

"With what?"

Judging by his attitude, Brad was often plagued by stupid questions.

Ollie ignored me like I often did to him. "We need to talk to the Spirit Body," he told Brad.

I made a mental note to strangle him the first opportunity I got.

Chapter 18

"We sort of fell into a land of darkness and it freaked us out," Ollie explained. "Then we were teleported to a new location. I know some ghosts can teleport, but I've never heard of that happening involuntarily. Could you tell us how to get an appointment or whatever?"

"We? Us? Who is us?" Brad asked, his tone suspicious.

Ollie gestured at me. "The two of us. Plus a dog." He caught the tight-lipped look on my face and blanched. "Sorry," he told me. "We're not going to get answers unless we talk to them."

Brad moved to stand beside Ollie. "You're still alive. You can see us?"

Resolved, I nodded.

I'd convinced myself the worst of the chaos was over. I could settle into this new life with my limited ghost friends.

Something told me that was going to blow up in my face.

"That is highly unusual." Brad crossed his arms, frowning at me like I was a naughty child. "The Spirit Body will want to speak with you, young lady."

Young lady? What was I, twelve? I hated this already.

I pushed my chair back, stood, and shoved my phone in my pocket.

"You can't leave," Brad said. "By the order of the Spirit Body, I demand you stop."

Ghosts didn't hold sway over the living. Brad couldn't do anything to stop me. At least, I didn't think so.

Besides, did he expect to have a conversation in the middle of a busy cafe? I'd talk to him in my car, though I had half a mind to make him chase me across town first.

I headed for the cash register and pulled my wallet from my back pocket. I'd never seen the point of a purse when pockets worked fine.

"Brenda!" Brad's voice went shrill behind me. "Brenda! I have a living here who sees into the spirit world. I told her to stop, but she's not listening."

I turned to see him shouting at the ceiling, head back, arms out, like he was in the middle of the Rapture or expecting a beam of light from a space ship to come down and beam him up. If only I were so lucky.

"Get someone down here *now*," he demanded.

The ceiling tiles did not respond.

Was this the equivalent of ghost 9-1-1? Were the Spirit Body police coming to arrest me? That should be interesting.

Ollie looked alarmed.

I gave him a flat "I told you so" look. Idiot.

He said something to Brad that I couldn't make out past Brad's yelling, but it sounded like a placating explanation. Brad either didn't hear him or ignored him.

Theo appeared behind the register. "I will see you this afternoon."

I tried to block out Brad, who continued to speak to the ceiling as if it was talking back. Was there a spirit-walkie-talkie type communication device? It was disconcerting to think the Spirit Body might have abilities I hadn't previously considered.

If Brenda was responding I couldn't hear it.

"Uh, yes," I told Theo, digging out a twenty.

"You don't pay for meals here," he said, already holding up a hand to stop me. "Family eats free."

My irritation at Brad leaked into my response. "Theo, *food* isn't free. If I'm not paying for it, you are. I ate it, I'm more than happy to pay for it."

"No, I insist." His accent grew thicker whenever he had strong feelings about a topic. "You have filled in for too many shifts this week. I feel bad asking so much of you. Please, take this token of apology and my heartfelt thanks. I don't know what I would do without you."

Theo had the market cornered on sincerity. All that, and he didn't even know his daughter was safe from the Saints.

At least, she should be.

I'd need to make sure Wagner had heard that part of my conversation with Craig. I'd have more news on Theo's daughter after visiting the police station.

"Thanks," I said, dropping my objections. "The eggs were fantastic."

Brad stormed over to me. "You will not depart from this place. I demand to know how you came by the ability to see spirits."

Ollie came up behind Brad. "Hey, man, leave her alone. I already told you she can't talk to you in public. Back off."

It was so strange to have a ghost back me up for once, even if he was about as threatening as a cartoon chipmunk.

Theo gave me his thousand-watt smile. "I am glad you enjoyed them. I'll see you later. I promise not to call you in to work," he joked.

Brad's domineering voice overshadowed Theo's. "According to our sources, the only way for the living to interact with the dead is through the proper rites and rituals of a seance as set forth in the Rules of Yore."

"She hasn't done anything wrong," Ollie snapped. "Leave her alone."

"You dare to interfere with Spirit Body business? Be very careful how you answer that lest you come to regret your decision."

As he blathered on, I tried to wrap up my conversation with Theo. "I should be by after the lunch rush." I didn't realize my volume was loud until Theo tipped his head, and I noticed patrons staring at me.

Rubbing my ear with a finger, I glared at Brad. "Sorry. I've got some kind of buzzing in my ear that's annoying me to death."

Brad inhaled like I'd slapped him. "How *dare* you. Insulting the Spirit Body Shamus comes with quite a penalty. You'll be hearing from my supervisors." He lowered his voice to something less overbearing and more menacing. "If I were you, I'd tread very carefully. You do not want to bring the full might of our enforcement team to bear."

Ollie disappeared through the back wall while Brad scolded me. When he'd finished delivering his threat, my dog bounded through the side wall, ears up as if looking for something. She spotted me. Brad had stepped close, trying to loom over me with what few inches he had over me.

My dog's lips pulled back silently to reveal her teeth. She stalked up behind Brad and ripped a snarl that sounded like a chainsaw.

Brad jumped and spun. Sadly, I couldn't see his look of horror, but his high-pitched scream of panic inspired a good mental image. He threw his hands in the air and took off running with the dog on his heels.

I smiled. "Would you look at that. The ringing in my ears just disappeared. I'll see you later, Theo. Have a great morning."

"You, too, Enid." He turned back to the grill. I headed out to my car.

Ollie was waiting for me outside. "The dog really loves her job."

I'd never wanted a dog, but I was growing quickly attached to this one. "She's a good girl." My smile fell as I remembered Brad. "I wish you'd consulted me before telling that loudmouth jerk I could see ghosts."

"Sorry. I thought we'd talked about it last night."

"Yeah, but I hadn't agreed. I figured I'd have time to think it over."

"I wasn't going to contact them behind your back or anything, but when he showed up, I figured it was as good a time as any."

I glanced around. There was no sign of Brad or my dog. "Can he actually do anything to me? I mean he's a ghost, and I have a body, right? That makes me untouchable?"

Ollie winced in a way I didn't like. "Maybe?" he hedged. "I've heard some things about what the Spirit Body can do to interact with the living world. I'm not sure how much of it's true. For the most part, they don't have any reason to mess with the living."

I didn't like that answer. "So what happens now that we've chased Brad off?"

"I have no idea. I wish Frank were here. He knows a lot more than I do."

It was a problem for another day. I had more immediate things to worry about. Wagner would be waiting for me at the station. If I was lucky, his red-head partner would be busy somewhere else. Lennox rubbed me the wrong way, and I'd just as soon not deal with his antagonism.

While I drove, I struggled to keep my mind off Brad. If the Spirit Body caused enough trouble, I might have to move after all. Blessed night. I couldn't seem to catch a break.

I'd gotten lucky with Theo. I felt like trash every time I thought of bailing on him. I really liked Peach Grove. The small town community had a soul all its own, and I was reminded of it every time I saw Theo or Lexi. Good people trying to help where they could.

I could leave. Start over. Something told me I'd just end up in the same situation again. I didn't have a lot of life experience yet, but it wasn't that hard to see I'd have to fight to carve out a life for myself if I ever wanted stability. What better chance would I have than now, with a solid home, a steady job, and my first ever friend to support me?

About a mile from work, I spotted a figure running down the sidewalk, arms pumping in an exaggerated motion, head thrown back like a cartoon character with my dog nipping at his heels. She was herding him.

I barked out a laugh.

Ollie shifted nervously in his seat. "Maybe we should call her off. I don't know that harassing someone from the Spirit Body will turn out well for us."

I fought back the urge to remind him Brad started it. The Spirit Body probably couldn't do anything to me, but Ollie was a ghost. They could do a lot more to him. "Fine," I grumbled. "Holler at her as we pass. I'll pull in to the parking lot up ahead."

He stood, his upper body sticking up through the top of the Phantom, and whistled. "Come!"

The dog broke away from the beleaguered man and made a mad dash for us. With my blinker on, I slowed to pull in at a little sandwich shop. The dog plowed into the back seat before I'd left the road, so I turned off my blinker and continued on.

"Good job," Ollie told the dog. Then to me, he said, "We should probably give her a name."

"She's already got one. We need to figure out what it is."

"Are you planning to get a book of dog names and try them out until she responds to one?"

"Something like that." If she was a K-9, Wagner might be able to provide a list of deceased dogs from the area.

In my rearview mirror, Brad had stopped running. He'd bent over, hands on knees, breathing hard. "Do ghosts get tired when they run?" I asked.

"Not like the living do. It's more a mental thing," he explained. "It's why we breathe and sigh and laugh like we're moving air with our lungs. Technically, we should be capable of talking clearly without even opening our mouths, but our brains find it easier to mimic the way we've always done things. Talking with your mind instead of your mouth is way harder than it sounds."

How had I never considered that before? "When ghosts talk, they're not actually talking. If they were, other people would hear them. So how do ghosts make sound?"

"I'm fuzzy on the details. I think it's a form of telepathy. We talk in each other's minds, but we're limited by our own concepts of reality. We end up limiting our projection to a radius that sound would travel in. If Frank were in a building next door, I can't talk to him because my brain tells me sound doesn't travel that far, even though we're not actually using sound."

"Your brain hobbles itself because it's applying the rules of the living," I said.

"Basically."

"But you know you're dead."

"Doesn't matter. It takes a ridiculous amount of work to break those mental barriers."

"So? You don't eat, sleep, or work. You're essentially immortal. You have all the time in the world to get the work done."

Ollie smiled. "You have the potential to become fluent in fifty languages. It would just take time and effort to accomplish. If you had all the time in the world, would you spend it on that?"

"No," I said with a snort. "But I don't need to know fifty languages."

"For the most part, ghosts don't need to know how to talk to people in another room. Besides, learning fifty languages would be easy in comparison."

I turned into the police station, scanning for a parking spot. "Easy how?"

"Nobody's come up with a study guide for changing ghost reality. Instead of learning fifty languages, say you only have to learn one, but it's an alien language you've never seen or heard, and there's not so much as an alphabet available for you to start with."

That would be harder. "Fair enough. Why is breathing and talking such an issue when walking through things isn't?"

"Walking through things is easy. New ghosts can't touch things even if they try. Usually, the floor is the only thing they don't pass through. Since the default is the opposite of what you expect to happen, the brain adjusts pretty fast. Once you figure out how to make things feel solid, it doesn't take long to get good at it, partly because we use that ability all day."

"If you learned how to speak in people's heads from a distance, you'd use that all the time, too," I said.

"True, but the normal way of doing things works fine, so it takes more work to convince yourself it's possible."

"Kind of like if you're in outer space, your brain tries to find a place to call the ground, even though you don't need to stand anywhere."

"Right. And when gravity exists, it's really hard to decide that any direction but down is down."

His explanation was making my head hurt, which went to prove his point. Interesting as the concept was, digging deeper would have to wait.

I pulled into a parking spot and focused on what I was going to put in my statement. It didn't take long to conclude memory loss would be my best defense. I had no logical explanation for my disappearance.

With Ollie on my right and the dog on my left, I headed inside. The lady at the front desk called for Wagner, who came to get me from the lobby.

"We'll take the elevator," he said, leading me off.

My dog padded after me, then sat patiently beside me, waiting for the doors to open. Ollie had already disappeared to check out the holding cells and see if Craig was in one. They may have moved him to a larger facility knowing his connections.

"Thank you for calling me last night, Miss Walsh. You helped us put away an important man. With luck, more will follow."

They'd try to use him to get to the rest of the cartel. So long as they didn't come for me, I was happy.

Speaking of which. "I have a picture of a man. He tried to attack me with a knife a few days ago outside Peyton's house. He's tied in with Craig's group. I think his name is Gio. If you can prioritize him, I'd feel much safer knowing he's off the streets."

The elevator arrived. The doors opened and two uniformed officers stepped out.

"Send it to me," he said. "We owe you for giving us such a strong foothold in this case."

We got on the elevator. He pressed the button for the second floor.

"If you mean that, I have another favor to ask. I'd love a list of deceased K-9 officers who've worked in this area?"

He looked bewildered. "Why?"

I'd thought of the answer to this before he'd asked. "I saw one outside. I'd like to say a prayer for them. To honor their sacrifice."

If my dog was a police dog, that list would narrow down possible names.

His expression was caught squarely between skepticism and consideration. "We'll be passing by my desk on the way. It should only take a minute to print it out."

"Thanks."

Retrieving the names took longer than a minute. After restarting his computer twice, Wagner gave up. "I'll have to get the tech guys to do something with this pile of junk," he said, shoving his keyboard away in disgust.

Ollie wandered through the large room full of strategically placed desks and spotted us. "Hey. There you are. Craig's in a cell here. I can't believe I've never wandered through the police station before now. To be honest, it's more boring than I would have thought. What are you guys up to?"

I pointedly eyed Wagner. "Wish I could help. Computers are not my forte."

Wagner sighed. "Didn't your generation grow up with computers?"

"Yes. Using one and fixing one are completely different skill sets."

Ollie made a thoughtful sound. "If his computer isn't working, that might be your fault."

I raised an eyebrow.

"Ghosts and computers don't mix."

I'd known that much. My parents had quit buying them early on after my second one went on the fritz. Both had died after only a few weeks of use when pesky ghosts had waltzed through them.

"We can make them freeze up or run slow, though it's not really obvious unless we're standing inside one. I know you're not a ghost, but whatever glowy thing you've started doing might affect them in the same way. For us, standing near one doesn't do much, but you might have a lot more electromagnetic force or whatever disrupting the computer."

I hadn't thought of that. My phone *had* been glitchy in the diner.

The glowy hand thing freaked me out whenever I thought about it. Ghosts had auras, not the living.

"Ah, well," Wagner said, standing to motion me across the room. "I'll send the list to your phone. You get texts okay?"

"Sure," I said. I hoped.

"What are we getting texts of?" Ollie asked.

I did my best to answer, following Wagner. "The K-9 officers will have names, right? I'd like to make the prayers as personal as I can."

"Yes," Wagner said. "That's not a problem. Newspapers usually announce when a K-9 officer is killed in the line of duty. The names aren't secret."

"Oh," Ollie said. "You're trying to figure out who your dog is."

"Thanks," I told Wagner. "I could do a search for them, but a list will save me a lot of time."

He smiled genially. "You saved me time. I'm happy to return the favor." He opened a door leading to a short hallway and ushered me in.

Chapter 19

My brain felt like pudding. Wagner had gone to get me a drink of water twenty minutes ago, leaving me alone with his partner.

The red beard and mustache gave Lennox a scruffy look. Combined with a classic smile that almost reached his eyes, he looked like a nice guy at first glance.

He paced, his steps deliberate and methodical, walking through Ollie, who had sprawled out on the floor while he patiently endured my interrogation.

"Do you have magic powers, Miss Walsh?" Lennox asked, dimples showing through his beard. "Powers of teleportation? Invisibility?"

He'd asked for an explanation of my disappearance about a million different ways. He was close to the truth, not that he'd believe me if I admitted to it.

I squirmed in my seat, my leg bumping against the dog. She'd tired of Lennox's posturing. She lay with head on paws, half under the table, her eyes tracking him.

"Look. I can't explain what happened while I was unconscious. I was behind the cafe. I fell. I woke up in the woods outside my home. That's all I know."

Lennox nodded. "You didn't see anything. You didn't hear anything. You don't know anything."

I knew he was being facetious. I nodded anyway.

He dropped his congenial approach and went for bluntness. "I don't believe you."

I shrugged. "Okay, fine. I have magic. I teleported." I let my frustration bleed through my words. "Only I don't know how I did it, so don't bother asking. Magic is new to me. Teleportation, especially. But as far as I know, magic isn't against the law. You can't arrest me for it since it doesn't officially exist, right?"

"Currently, magic isn't against the law. Impeding an investigation is."

I let my head drop back on my shoulders and let out a groan. "I didn't impede anything. I found stuff in the wall and got cornered by that Craig guy and immediately called Special Agent Wagner for help."

Lennox stopped to loom over me. "Right. Let's circle back to the millions of dollars in drugs you just happened to find hidden in the back wall of your workplace. I put those bricks back myself. The seam is pretty invisible unless you know what you're looking for. You just thought, 'Hey, maybe I'll take this convenient little pry bar and start ripping up the wall?'"

My irritation reached the breaking point, and I threw caution to the wind. "Blessed night. You are *such* an omelette."

He blinked, looking befuddled. If I hadn't been so ready to slap him, I'd have laughed, but my anger was too fired up. I was ready to melt steel.

"Is there a class for how to be the *most* annoying person on the planet? Do they train you to be so dense light bends around you? If you asked, I'd rate your personality zero stars. My only regret would be the lack of a negative rating. You suck on an epic scale."

Just as we renewed our glaring contest, Wagner returned, water bottle in hand.

It was possible to drown in a spoonful of water. I was tempted to try out that theory if it would get me away from Lennox.

"Sorry that took so long. None of the vending machines on this floor have water in stock." Wagner's long, clean-shaven face looked far more stern than his partner's. His blond hair was neatly combed over his prominent eye ridges, accentuating the straight lines of his nose.

Just going off looks, I'd have picked Lennox as the good cop, but his cheerful expression was like that fish with the dangly light that lured in prey.

I pressed my hands to the table and stood. "Are we done here? If so, I promise you won't hear from me again. The next time someone tries to shoot me, I'll take the bullet."

Wagner gave Lennox a dry look. "Have you been badgering Miss Walsh?"

Again with the charming smile. "I was on my best behavior, I swear. I didn't even ask her about the cemetery."

I matched his stupid grin. "I don't know what you're talking about. *Sometimes* I like to walk through cemeteries. I don't recall seeing anyone else around, though. Last I checked, it wasn't a crime to walk through a cemetery."

"So long as nothing's being vandalized, it's not," Wagner assured me.

Lennox tapped a finger on his chin. "Though why anyone would want to walk through a cemetery alone at night is beyond me. Now couples, I've seen. Cemeteries are a surprisingly common spot for teens who want a little privacy."

"Ew. You like to sneak up on teens making out in the cemetery at night?"

"Cemeteries can be spooky if you don't find something to occupy your time with."

I curled my lip in disgust. "I don't make out with people in cemeteries. And they're not spooky. They're a resting place for the dead. They were living once, just like us. The living aren't spooky. Why would the dead be any different?"

Wagner sat across the table from me. "We relate better to the living. They're easier to understand."

I shrugged, my belligerence dying down now that I was facing Wagner instead of Lennox. "The dead aren't so hard to understand."

He nodded sagely. "You say that with confidence. The dead seem pretty unknowable to me." Wagner had a quiet way of speaking that brought the tension in the room down.

"Sometimes the dead stay dead. Sometimes they want to be heard." It was a cryptic statement, but we'd been talking in circles since I'd arrived. Doublespeak was starting to sound normal.

Lennox leaned against the wall next to the only window in the room, letting Wagner take the lead.

"Have you seen anything strange in the cemetery?"

Wagner was giving me an opening to come clean without coming clean.

"No, but I heard there's a guy off the most wanted list buried somewhere around here. Maybe you could point me in the right direction. I was wondering what his grave marker looked like."

Wagner nodded. "I know the grave you're talking about. Notorious killer."

He was willing to talk about it. That was promising. "So I heard. Any idea why he's buried in a small town like Peach Grove?"

"He died in the area." When I looked interested, he continued. "I didn't work the case. Rumor has it his daughter was…mistreated…by some people around here. He came looking for revenge."

A hardened criminal cared what happened to his daughter? That seemed like a stretch. "Some kind of power move? Like his daughter was his property, so he came to reassert his claim on her or something?"

"From what I've heard, he was a pretty dedicated father."

Lennox snorted, looking out the window. "Scumbag with a conscience," he muttered.

"Not all bad people are bad in all ways," Wagner said. It sounded like an old argument between them.

A moment of silence passed before I broke it. "Are we done here?"

Wagner rapped his knuckles gently on the table where my signed statement lay. "I think so. That's all we need for now."

"But don't leave town," Lennox said, his voice candy cane sweet. "We may have more questions for you."

"Yay," I said, deadpan.

Ollie climbed to his feet. The dog took that as her signal to stir. She let out a heavy sigh and walked me to the door.

Wagner and Lennox exited on my heels.

"Random question," I said, thinking of how we'd almost opened up back in the interrogation room. Sorry, *interview* room. "Why might a criminal get a cop funeral, theoretically speaking?"

Wagner scanned the hall, which was empty. "Theoretically, there could be any number of reasons. If, for example, they changed their ways and worked with law enforcement to bring down high profile targets and if, say, they did something heroic, like take a bullet to protect an undercover officer, that could earn them such a funeral."

"It's pretty rare for a criminal to become a hero, though," Lennox said. The look he gave Wagner said he didn't believe tigers changed their stripes.

"Rare. Not impossible." Wagner said before leading the way to the elevators.

They were headed out to lunch, so we walked out to the parking lot together. I'd managed to park a handful of cars from them and had Wagner wait while I grabbed Gio's photo from my front seat.

I jogged over, unlocked my car, and snatched the folder. As I headed back to Wagner, a police cruiser pulled up beside me.

Ollie, who had not jogged alongside me, had a clear view through the front windshield. "Enid, that's Gio!"

I didn't get a chance to look at the driver. The passenger side, which was nearest me, swung open. Out stepped the last person I wanted to see: Craig the Crowbar.

"Wagner!" I screamed. He and Lennox had been talking. Both their heads swiveled in my direction. They took one look at Craig and bolted for us.

Craig didn't waste time. He grabbed hold of my arm and swung me into the side of the cruiser. My left side slammed into the unyielding metal. I could swear my bones creaked. Craig jerked me back and pulled open the rear door. Before he could shove me in, my dog lunged at him.

The strangest thing happened. She hit him.

Craig stumbled from the sudden impact of the dog's body and went sprawling, nearly taking me down with him. I managed to grab hold of the open doorway of the cruiser to stop my momentum.

The dog tried to latch onto Craig, but whatever ability she'd manifested disappeared like it had never existed. She snarled, snapping at Craig again and again only for her teeth to pass right through him.

I stared stupidly for a shocked moment. It turned out to be a dumb mistake.

Gio had come around the front of the car, moving with military efficiency. Since Craig had fallen near the rear of the cruiser, Gio took me off guard. He came up behind me and, using one strong hand, slammed my head against the car.

Seconds passed in a blur. The next thing I noticed was the awkward molding of the back seat as it dug into my stomach. Gio had tossed me in the car like I was an unruly puppy. He swung the door closed. My left foot hadn't cleared the opening.

The door slammed onto my foot. I screamed.

The door only slammed shut a second time as soon as I pulled my foot free. I bit my lip trying not to let out a string of curse words while I waited for the pain to subside enough to assess the damage. Luckily, I was wearing ankle boots, which offered some small level of protection.

Something hard shifted on the seat beneath me. I pulled it out from under my side. It was a pair of handcuffs, the ends open. Dimly, I realized they must have been on Craig not long ago. Ollie had said Craig was in jail. Gio must have staged a jail break.

A voice came from the back of the car. "Keep your mouth shut, you hear?" It sounded like Gio was warning Craig not to talk to the cops. Two seconds later, Gio was in the front seat. The doors locked with a *thunk*. The engine revved, and we took off, leaving Craig in our dust.

"Come!" Ollie hollered from the front seat.

The pain in my foot subsided enough for me to attempt to right myself. I pushed up with my arms only to have the dog leap into the car and land on my back, shoving me back down with an expelled breath.

She scrambled around, trying to find a place that wasn't atop me, but I was sprawled awkwardly, taking up almost all the available space.

Before we could separate, the car skidded around a corner, tossing the dog into the footwell. I barely avoided landing on her.

Gio cursed under his breath and took another sharp turn, tires squealing. As soon as the direction stabilized, he slammed on the gas, accelerating at an alarming rate.

I managed to right myself. We were barreling down Highway 70, headed back toward the cafe.

The dog jumped onto the passenger side back seat, claws scrabbling on the hard surface.

I'd never been in the back of a cop car. The back seating area was hard, molded plastic with an indentation in lieu of lower back support, probably to accommodate people with their hands cuffed behind their back. It was uncomfortable and slippery, which made it difficult to keep my seat when the car took another sharp turn.

"Are you okay?" Ollie asked from the front passenger seat. A wire grate separated the front and back of the car.

"Bruised," I said, scanning the door. I knew it wouldn't open. I couldn't resist checking anyway. There was an arm rest molded into the door with not even a handle to pull on, which made the feeling of being trapped grow until it was panic-inducing claustrophobia.

"Bruises are going to be the least of your worries," Gio said, taking another turn.

I gripped the grating ahead of me to keep from sliding into the dog, who leaned with her right side against the door.

I clenched my eyes shut and tried to steady my breathing. I'd been overwhelmed before. I knew how to deal with it, I just needed a moment to block everything out.

Gio said something else, but I'd unfocused my brain until everything around me was a distant buzzing. I zeroed in on my heart beating, my lungs breathing, the pull of my weight on my fingers as we took another turn, this time at a more normal speed. Within a handful of seconds, I'd grounded myself.

I opened my eyes. We were on a side street I drove often. It was on the way to the library from Lexi's house. A block later, we pulled back onto Highway 70. We passed the Retro Cafe another few blocks after that.

Two figures stood on the sidewalk out front, one with a lime green aura and a spicy mustard outfit, the other in a muddy orange-pink aura and a dingy yellow Victorian style ball gown.

"Brad," I said.

Ollie had spotted them, too. "Looks like he's got company."

As we drove past, traffic ahead slowed. Brad spotted me staring at him. He pointed and said something to the woman, who turned to look, her gaze sharp. She had a stern, matronly face framed by short bangs curled to within an inch of their lives. The rest of her hair was pulled back in a tight bun.

She'd look equally at home on the set of Pride and Prejudice or switching Little Orphan Annie's backside. I disliked her immediately.

Her head rose in a haughty manner, and she said something to Brad.

"I think we're in trouble," I muttered.

Ollie grunted in agreement. "Just what we need."

"Trouble doesn't get any bigger than what you're in," Gio said. "You're as good as dead."

Chapter 20

The four bodies in the police cruiser suddenly became six. Brad popped into the front seat between Gio and Ollie. The woman in the poofy dress ended up landing on the dog, who end up in my lap snarling and snapping at the lady.

"Goodness!" she exclaimed. "It's no wonder you've been detained by law enforcement. What a menace!"

"I told you that dog is violent," Brad said, turning clumsily in the front seat to glower at me. "She sent it to attack me."

"I did not send her after you," I objected.

Gio glanced at me in the rearview mirror. "Send who? The dead girl?"

He had to mean Peyton. It was the only female link between us. "No. Never mind."

The woman in the gown cast the dog a wary glance, but waved Brad off. "I'm less interested in her dog and more in the fact that she can see into the spirit world." She turned to address me. "What is your name, child?"

I couldn't put into words my distaste for the woman. Her entire demeanor was condescending and off-putting, just like Brad. Was the entire Spirit Body like this?

I kept my voice low so Gio wouldn't chime in. "I'm not a child. My name is Enid."

"Well, Miss Enid, we must determine—"

"No miss. Just Enid."

She glared daggers at me, indicating she hadn't been interrupted nearly often enough in her lifetime. "I am Miss Margarette, the Spirit Body Maven, but since you're too simple-minded for titles, I suppose you can call me Margie."

The car took a hard right turn, pressing me into my door. I was glad for the stability since I was balancing the dog on my lap while she faced Margie, head low and teeth bared.

The car straightened out, and I said, "I'm a little busy getting kidnapped right now. Could we have this conversation later?"

"I'm afraid this can't wait," Margie said, unsympathetic to my plight. "A living who can see the dead is an anomaly and a potentially dangerous one. It is my duty to determine the extent of that danger to the spirit world."

Ollie spoke up from the front seat. "Did you hear the part about being kidnapped? Her life is in danger right now. She needs to focus. Come back later. Having this conversation right now is insane."

"For me, it's typical," I told Ollie before turning to Margie. "I try to interact with your kind as infrequently as possible. I don't know what you do in your organization. I don't even know what your organization does. Probably nothing relevant to this century."

Margie the Maven went red in the face at my words. She spluttered a few times before saying, "Are you calling me dated?"

The car took another hard right.

I looked down at Margie's dress, outlined in her muddy, pinkish-brown aura, but didn't comment further.

Gio said, "Don't worry about my organization. You're giving me information, not the other way around. My job is getting answers, which is relevant in every century."

Another man appeared in the car, this one with a striking aubergine aura. He stood in the center of the car behind Brad. All I could make out was pinstriped suit pants since his upper body disappeared through the roof of the car like he'd created his own sunroof.

I hauled the dog further onto my lap before he sat on her head. She was too big to be a lap dog, but she let me manhandle her without trying to eat my face.

The new ghost was Asian, his classy suit paired with a white shirt and a dark, floral tie. He looked around, clearly taken aback at his surroundings. "My apologies for intruding," he told the car full of people.

"When I summoned you, we were on the street," Margie said. "We were forced to change locations lest this witch abscond with her attack dog."

The dog was too big to lay down, so her butt was planted firmly on my stomach, her paws precariously balanced on my knees.

The man's owlishly observant look made me wonder if he was a dog person. I didn't find him immediately intolerable, so that was promising.

The car slowed to a reasonable speed, probably to avoid being obvious. We were on a side road not far from the library I frequented.

The man in the suit dipped his head in deference to me. "I am Lisheng, the seventh embodiment."

Ollie let out a low whistle that told me this guy was important. I didn't get the impression Margie or Brad were, though they both acted like divas.

"Seventh embodiment. I don't know what that means," I admitted, remembering to keep my voice down.

He nodded as if he'd expected as much. "The Spirit Body contains the governing officials of the spirit world. There are 27 votaries and they are ranked by number, each with individual duties. I am number seven, thus the seventh embodiment."

"She's not impressed by titles," Margie said, sounding snotty.

Lisheng's demeanor didn't change. "The title is not meant to impress you, simply to notify you of the area I oversee." He gave Margie a hard look. "I am still new to my position, but my duty to investigate dangerous anomalies does not seem pertinent here. Yes, she is a living who can see the dead. I do not see an inherent danger in that alone. Please explain your insistence that I come here to confront this woman."

Margie raised an eyebrow at him. "Lisheng, if you cannot understand the danger here, you would do well to listen to my counsel. I have been deceased long enough to know that livings can only see the dead if they partake of the dark arts for a most nefarious purpose."

"Dark arts?" I blurted. "You think I stand over boiling cauldrons in my spare time, chanting phrases while I try to summon a demon or something?"

"What?" Gio said, baffled. "Are you seriously trying to scare me with magic?"

Margie's spine went stiff as a pole, and she turned a suspicious gaze on me. "Do you summon demons?"

When I didn't answer, she turned back to Lisheng. "It is vitally important that this woman be taken into custody. At the very least, she must be kept under strict supervision at all times from this point on. I know not what evil practices have earned her this ability, but I can assure you nothing good can come of her meddling in the spirit world."

My words came out in a hiss. "I don't want anything to do with you people. I'd like nothing more than for all the ghosts out there to leave me alone."

"Ha!" Margie pointed an accusing finger at me.

Gio didn't like my angry mutterings. "Quit it!" he said sharply, his words punctuated by the crash of his right elbow slamming into the divider.

Before I could blink, the dog lunged through the seat at him. Again, she should have gone through him. She went through the seat fine.

Gio yelped in pain and jerked the steering wheel. We jumped across the center line of the road, nearly colliding head-on with a minivan. He managed to jerk the car back at the last second. The minivan hadn't even had time to honk before it was past us.

"What the hell was that?" Gio screamed.

In the chaos, I'd grabbed the dog tight and hauled her back onto my lap. Her whole body vibrated with the strength of her growl. I wasn't sure what she'd done to him, but it easily could have killed us all. It's amazing how fast the gap closes when two cars are moving toward one another.

He turned on his blinker and turned at the next street, watching the minivan in his side mirror. If staying under the radar was the goal, he wasn't doing a great job of that.

Margie picked up where she'd left off, unperturbed by the erratic driving. "You admit to seeking the extinction of ghosts."

Ollie craned his neck around to stare at her. "Did you sniff glue as a child?"

I almost laughed, both at his comment and the absolute absurdity of the situation. I shook my head. "I just want to be left alone."

"Achievement unlocked," Gio said darkly.

He was definitely going to kill me, but terror is a strange thing. It comes on strong when you think about terrible things happening. One of the biggest deterrents to fear is distraction. If you can think about something else, fear has a hard time crippling you. Brad and his buddies were doing a fantastic job at that.

"Do you object to being observed?" Brad asked.

"Obviously." I pointed at Ollie. "I've already got someone watching me all the time, and I can barely stand him. I don't need more of you people in my business, talking to me, interrupting my life with dead-people stuff at the worst possible time. Case in point." I gestured to the car full of ghosts.

Gio said, "You won't mind the dead-people stuff when you're one of them. Trust me. Dead people are my specialty."

"Shut *up*," I fumed. There didn't seem to be much point in pacifying him. He was going to kill me either way. "My conversation doesn't involve you. Mind your business."

"Wow." He chuckled. "I'm going to kill you so slow. You're going to scream until your voice gives out. You're young. Pretty. All that clean, unbroken skin." The mood in the car shifted to something darker, malicious. "You've never felt a knife part your muscles, have you? If I can get you to tighten a muscle right before I slice through the tendon, it's like watching a rubber band snap. That'll get your attention real quick."

His goals hadn't been a secret. I'd known he was planning to kill me. Somehow, it hadn't sunken in that he was a straight up psycho.

Trees lined the road ahead. We'd left behind buildings and businesses. I couldn't tell which direction we were headed. Wagner and his friends would have a hell of a time finding us on some back country highway.

Was Gio going to pull off, take me down some dirt side road, and bury me in a shallow grave where nobody would ever find me?

The ghosts had gone quiet at the worst possible time, leaving room for fear to finally dig its claws into me like jagged blades into overripe cantaloupe. My heart pounded. My breath came fast. I suddenly felt like I was walking a tight rope strung out between the tops of skyscrapers, terrified of the fall. My hands trembled.

Everything narrowed to me, Gio, and the dog between us. Nothing else mattered. I needed a way out of this car. A way to put distance between us.

As I saw it, my possibilities were limited to exactly one option. The dog's muscles were coiled tight, ready for action.

"Get him," I hissed, giving the dog's sides a sharp tap. She was so lean I could feel her ribs.

That was all the encouragement she needed. Almost before my fingers touched her sides, she lunged at Gio again, her face going through the seat.

He screamed.

Briefly, I wondered if he could feel ghosts. Was he allergic to their presence?

When a splatter of blood hit the grating, I knew that wasn't the case. A single drop hung from one of the wire strips, dangling for a moment before dripping to the bar below it.

That was no allergy. The dog was biting him.

Ghosts could interact with solid objects, but that was a one-way trick. Ghosts had no impact on objects. A ghost could choose to go through a pillow or sit on top of it, but the pillow wouldn't sink beneath them.

Somehow, the dog had figured out a way to make part of herself solid, then sink her teeth into Gio while keeping the rest of her incorporeal. I'd never heard of anything like it.

The car drifted to the right side of the road, crossing over into grass. I pulled my dog back to me, afraid we'd crash. Gio had leaned forward, pressing himself against the steering wheel in an effort to get away from my dog. Blood smeared the back of his neck and stained the ribbed collar of his gray t-shirt.

Frantic, he turned to look at me, blind to the fact that we'd left the road and were fast approaching the broad, shallow ditch lining the highway.

I could warn him, but I paused. A crash was my best chance of taking him out. Of course, that could kill me, as well since neither of us were wearing seatbelts.

The car tipped, leaning precariously to one side as we skirted the border of the ditch.

I scrambled for my seatbelt, fumbling to get it buckled before we rolled over.

I almost made it. Almost.

Chapter 21

I screamed. At least, I think I screamed. The chaos of experiencing what clothes must feel like in a dryer was too disorienting to be sure.

Just as Gio registered the angle of the car, we hit a raised patch of ground and went flying, intermittently spinning and crunching upon impact. I'd gotten my arm through the seatbelt, which tried to rip me in two because I'd failed to latch it.

By the time the jostling ended, the car was upside down. I'd gotten lucky. At least one of the flips had happened with me in mid-air. The hard plastic seat didn't give me anything to grip onto, but it also didn't grip me back.

The buzzing in my ears resolved into a tinny echo. I was sprawled out on the roof of the car. A bleary glance around showed the car was free of ghosts. Small blessings. I'd count it a win.

Up front, the airbag had deployed.

Gio groaned, shifted, then jerked with a pained yowl before collapsing in an awkward heap.

The doors were still closed. I was still stuck. My best bet was to close my eyes and hope he thought I was dead. That quickly became difficult when my dog plowed into the car, whining and licking my face. Carefully shifting my arm, I blocked my eyes, nose, and mouth from access.

She licked my cheek and ear between worried snuffling along my body. I suspected she was checking for blood. I didn't feel the sharp sting of sliced skin anywhere. The lack of sharp objects in the back seat was probably by design.

In the blessed quiet apart from the dog's whimpers and snuffles, I listened to Gio.

He shifted, scrambling around until he got the passenger side door partway opened. It must have stuck because he shoved at it, grunting, then climbed out.

With the door open, I could hear sirens wailing in the distance, too far to be within sight. It was still comforting to hear. If they drove down this road, they'd see our overturned vehicle. We'd been lucky to land in a ditch full of knee-high grass instead of big, leafy bushes.

The latch on the door inches from my head made a clicking noise. Gio tried the handle a half dozen times, but the door wouldn't budge. We must have landed on that side of the vehicle at some point during our car-gymnastics, effectively jamming the door.

Ollie showed up. "Enid! Are you okay? Please tell me you're still alive."

I meant to let out a quiet "Mm hmm" but it came out as a weak groan. I sounded half dead. Come to think of it, I *felt* half dead. My body slowly cataloged aches in places I didn't know existed. I hadn't even tried moving yet. That was going to be loads of fun.

I kept my eyes closed, trying to breathe as shallowly as possible. The sirens drew closer. Gio cursed and kicked my door. He could probably break the glass in the window if he tried.

All my training ignoring ghost jump-scares made it easy to stay still at the sharp sound his foot made. Judging by the volume, he'd left dents in the metal.

"The living are such drama," Margie said with a sigh.

With her arrival came the other ghosts.

"This is most worrisome," Lisheng said, concern showing through. "Are you conscious, Miss Walsh?"

"She's awake," Ollie reported. "She's trying not to let him know, though. He can't get to her easily. If he thinks she's dead, he might just leave."

Margie had the nerve to be annoyed by the interruptions. "There's no point in wasting even more time. If she's awake, let us recommence."

I could have strangled her. It would be awesome if they'd shut up long enough for me to determine if Gio was going to smash the window in. Hopefully Ollie was keeping an eye on him.

"I propose we keep her contained," Margie said. "The disruption to the Styx is problematic enough. We don't need a rogue living meddling in our affairs."

"What is the Styx again?" Ollie asked.

Brad said, "It's above your pay grade."

Lisheng answered. "It is where the recently deceased cross over. There is much we do not know about it, but it is a dangerous place of great power."

"We should be focusing on that, not her," Margie said. "I say we put her somewhere she can't cause trouble until we have the time to do a proper evaluation."

"He's running off," Ollie reported. "He's taking off into the woods." A moment later, he said, "He's gone. You're safe, Enid."

I opened my eyes to see him crouched in front of me, eyes worried. I gave him a grateful look.

Shifting slowly, I tested my limbs. The good news was nothing was broken. The mixed news was I had so many bruises my foot didn't stand out as any more painful than the rest of me. The bad news was the same as always: ghosts were interfering with my life.

My dog got all excited when I moved, trying to lick at my face while simultaneously prancing around. I wrapped an arm around her neck to keep her from bowling me over.

"I'm solid, you're not," I said, grunting as I tried to position myself. I had to sit with my head in the footwell because the plastic seating overhead was too low. The roof had been caved in several inches. "How are you planning to stash me somewhere?"

Margie gave a dry chuckle. "We have our ways, child."

Despite her cryptic bravado, she cast a wary glance at my dog, who sat between my sprawled legs, leaning her shoulder against my chest.

"Containment isn't warranted at this point," Lisheng said.

"Then we'll watch her," Brad countered.

"You people need to leave me alone. Mind your own business and stay out of mine."

"You have nothing to hide. Why would you object?" Margie said, baiting me.

"Do you have any idea what happens to living people who start talking to the air?"

She sniffed. "They're burned at the stake for witchcraft, which is right and fitting."

My mouth dropped open. "Right and fitting?"

"Absolutely. They burned witches in my day. If you can see ghosts, you're a witch." She said, matter-of-fact.

I blinked stupidly at her.

"Just because it happened doesn't make it right," Ollie said. He looked a little green.

Margie gave me a sly smile. "You look shocked. Did you think we didn't know about your magic?" She laughed, like the idea was absurd. "You even have a familiar. It's not possible to hide what you are, *Miss* Walsh." She emphasized the "Miss" to annoy me. "Do you take us for morons?"

Ollie muttered something under his breath I didn't catch.

I was stuck on the word "familiar." Like a black cat? It took me a moment to realize she was talking about my dog. Did she think my dog was some kind of witch's familiar? "In the stories, familiars are living animals, not invisible ghost pets. And those are stories. Fantasy. Make believe."

Besides, witches had more than just familiars. They had real magic. Sure, I could see ghosts, but it's not like I could hex people or throw fireballs.

Or were fireballs more a wizard thing?

Margie turned expectantly to Lisheng. "Her powers are uncommon, but I can tell you with certainty that the only livings I've ever heard of who could see spirits were those who had succeeded in extinguishing a soul."

Woah. This conversation was getting out of hand so fast it made my head spin. We'd gone from attack dog to witchcraft to...murder?

For once, Ollie spoke up. "Miss Margaret, I can assure you Enid hasn't murdered anyone. In fact, she was nearly murdered herself last night."

"Yeah," I spluttered. "The police were there and arrested the guy. I didn't even kill him, much less anyone else."

I very purposely didn't mention the man I ran over with my car the night before that.

The distant police sirens had drawn closer. With Gio gone, there was a good chance I'd make it out of this alive. I just needed to get the ghosts off my back.

"You misunderstand," Lisheng explained. "To extinguish a soul is to kill a spirit."

Ollie and I exchanged a look of bafflement. I'd definitely never killed a ghost. How was that even possible?

Ollie's look of confusion shifted to something sickening.

My thoughts scrabbled to make whatever connection he had. I came up blank.

He wasn't saying anything, so I followed suit and didn't ask.

Lisheng said, "Miss Margaret, this is a very serious accusation. Do you have any proof that a soul has been exterminated?"

"Besides her familiar and magical abilities? No. Not yet. That's why I propose she be watched closely. It's clear she's entrenched in the dark arts. She'll slip up eventually. When she does, I want to know about it immediately."

"This is absurd," I said, louder than I intended. "I haven't done anything wrong. I refuse to stand by while you monitor me like some kind of criminal. If anyone's been out of line here, it's you."

"Enid," Ollie said, sounding wary.

I didn't want to hear what he had to say. Anger coursed through me. My skin felt flushed from all the adrenaline of getting dragged into yet another crazy scenario. "Ghosts have been ruining my life since I was an infant. All I've ever wanted was to be left alone."

"Enid!" Ollie's tone was sharp this time.

I turned to face him, my hands raised like I wanted to strangle him.

That's when I noticed the sage green glow had returned.

Unlike ghost auras, my skin didn't produce a steady glow so much as it emitted flickering wafts of green smoke, like early-morning fog on a breezy day. I'd never seen anything like it.

Everyone got a good look at me before the streaks faded and disappeared. Any argument I had against magic was out the window after that display.

The police sirens suddenly increased in volume, as if they'd come over a rise, allowing the sound to travel farther.

Lisheng cleared his throat. "I believe monitoring is necessary."

"I'll do it," Ollie said quickly, staring at my hands. "I'll keep an eye on her."

"You're a nobody," Brad said. "You wouldn't even know what to look for or how to report something once you'd seen it. I'll watch her."

His words finally pulled me out of my shock. "Forget it. You don't know how to interact with someone in the living world. I wouldn't trust you to watch paint dry."

"What are you saying?" he asked, somehow affronted.

With the police closing in on my location, I didn't have time to talk him through it. I resolved to be as blunt as possible. "You're a complete idiot. Wind blows straight through your ears. I think your gene pool needed a lifeguard. What's the rate of inbreeding in your family?"

His eyes were almost as wide as his open mouth by the time I'd finished.

"Oh, man," Ollie groaned, burying his face in his hands.

Margie gave me a cold smile. "You cannot watch her, Bradley. You're the Shamus. I'll watch her."

"But you're the Maven," he objected.

"I'll. Watch. Her," Margie insisted, enunciating each word.

"Not a chance," I said firmly. "You're intolerable and even more clueless than he is." Remember how offended she'd been at being called dated, I threw in, "And your dress looks like it came from the 1500s equivalent of a JC Penney clearance rack."

Her mouth dropped open almost as wide as Brad's had. Maybe if I insulted them enough, they'd finally leave me alone.

I could only see the grass on all sides of the car, but flashing police lights created a strobe effect on the ground, a sign that my salvation was near. Or was it a portent of things to come?

Lisheng raised his hands to ward off further arguments. "The young man will watch the girl. The Shamus will check in periodically and report to the Maven. If anything requires attention, it can be brought to the appropriate embodiment. As it stands, I agree there is reason to be wary, though it is premature to label the witch dangerous, so for now, observation will suffice."

"Surely, you jest," Margie said.

"As Maven, your duty is to filter information," Lisheng said, his voice growing sharp. "Surely *you* know the difference between the potential for danger and the reality of it. For example, continuing with your objections once I have made my decree, without further evidence of wrongdoing on the witch's part, would be dangerous for you, but the potential for danger does not equal certainty. The difference between the two lies in your actions, as it does for the girl." The warning was clear.

Margie reluctantly bowed her head, acceding the argument.

"I have other duties to attend to, many a far greater danger than this. Do not interrupt my day without confirming the need for it first," he told her. To me, he said simply, "Behave and we will have no further need of meeting."

With that, he disappeared like a popped bubble.

Margie turned her glare on me. "Don't try to leave the area. It won't do you any good. Bradley can find you anywhere. He'll check on you regularly."

I wasn't sure how often "regularly" meant, but I was sure it would be too often.

"Fine. If there are people around, Ollie will talk on my behalf so I won't sound crazy." I turned to Brad. "Can you grasp that or is your skull too thick for simple concepts?"

"I'm not an idiot," Brad huffed.

"If you were any dumber, I'd have to water you twice a week. I don't know what your job normally entails. I'm guessing subtlety isn't part of your standard skill set."

Margie waved her arms around as if to physically swipe the words out of the air before focusing on Ollie. "You are bound by the laws laid forth by the Spirit Body to report any behavior that could pose a threat to any spirit. Is that clear?"

"Yep," Ollie said, deadpan.

"You will report to Bradley whenever he shall appear. If he suspects you aren't being forthcoming, he'll replace you with someone more capable of truthfulness. You'll be confined for your dishonesty. Is that clear?"

Ollie nodded, looking bored.

"Wait a minute," I said. "Brad better have proof if he wants to claim we're being dishonest. And I don't want other ghosts to know I can see them. Brad's not the only oblivious ghost. You people chatter at me while I'm driving, working, or even mid-conversation. Some of you have tried far worse than that."

I'd had some close calls as a kid. A shiver ran through me at long-buried memories.

Margie sniffed. "The affairs of the living don't concern me, except where it affects the spirit world. Your inconveniences are of no import to me."

"Her problem *is* the spirit world," Ollie pointed out.

"So long as the spirits aren't being harmed, I don't care," Margie said.

"Enid has a spirit," Ollie said slowly, as if talking to a child. "It just happens to be housed in a body at the moment."

Margie cast a gaze skyward. "When she's dead, she'll be under my protection. Until then, she'll have to deal with her own problems."

She motioned to Brad. Together, they disappeared.

Chapter 22

I'd hoped the Spirit Body would give me answers. Instead, they'd given me more questions. Was the dog really my familiar? Why was she suddenly following me around when she'd been stuck at the cafe all week?

She'd come with me through the darkness. That was the first I'd seen her away from the cafe. It was also the first time my hands started glowing. Had the darkness done something to me? What was the monster lurking in there? The most pressing question of all was: Could it come out?

Instead of jumping out of the frying pan and into the fire, I'd gone straight to drowning in lava.

I couldn't even handle ghosts, now I was supposed to handle magic, murders, kidnappings, and cartels? "What am I supposed to do now?"

Ollie shifted uneasily. "I'd ask Frank for advice, only I'm not sure where he is."

Suddenly I understood his earlier look of dawning horror when Lisheng mentioned killing ghosts. "We haven't seen Frank since we went into the dark place." Had he come in with us? Had the thing in there gotten him?

I shuddered.

Boots arrived beside the car. A moment later, knees touched down, and a uniformed police officer peered through the window.

I gave him a little finger wave. Don't mind me, I'll just hang out until someone shows up with the jaws of life.

"You okay?" he called, his voice muffled.

"Yeah."

He pulled on the door. To my surprise, it opened. The rear passenger side had been jammed. The driver's side functioned fine. It must have escaped being crushed.

I crawled out, then sucked in a breath when I tried to stand. My left ankle hadn't stuck out in my sea of pain until I stepped on it.

Officer Pane, according to his name tag, stood aside while I crawled out of the car on my hands and knees. He had me sit on the ground while we waited for the ambulance.

With Ollie's help, I indicated which way Gio had run. He had a decent head start, so the officer called it in and moved on to cataloging my injuries. They were many, but minor.

Wagner and Lennox showed up before the ambulance did. Wagner helped me up the hill to the road. Lennox walked alongside me, watching me with suspicion.

I had to get checked out by the EMTs before Wagner would agree to take me back to the station. My foot was bruised and swelling, though I could walk on it gingerly. The EMTs wrapped it in an ACE bandage and let me go.

At the station, I ended up giving another statement, which went faster than the first one. I skipped any explanation for how I knew Gio, explaining he'd been helping with the jail break when Craig made him stop to grab me. Simple words. Short sentences.

Wagner waited patiently for me to sign it.

Lennox watched quietly, his vapid smile edged with something dark. "For a couple of thugs, they snatched you up pretty quick. We were right there and still lost you. There one minute, gone the next. Poof. You two were like the wind."

The words were innocuous. His tone was leading. I sensed a trap. "It's a good thing you guys have trackers on your cars," I said after a long moment of him staring at me like I was food.

"It *is* a good thing. Unfortunately, the car you were in had a malfunctioning unit."

Which meant they hadn't track me through the car. I cocked my head. "Did you track my phone?"

Wagner said, "That takes too long."

Lennox pointed at his partner like he'd hit the nail on the head.

I already didn't like this game. "Spit it out. I'm done guessing."

His shark-like grin bunched his cheeks. "We got a call about a police car driving erratically. The caller told us which road you were on."

There was more to the story.

Lennox held his anticipatory silence, which gnawed at me.

I rolled my hand in a "get on with it" gesture. My foot was throbbing, my back, head, and spine ached, and the scrape on my hand stung.

His eyes narrowed in annoyance. "The call came in over our car radio."

He stood, circling behind me so he could lean over my left shoulder. Always with the theatrics. "Only it didn't come from a cop."

He straightened, pacing like an irritated panther. "It didn't come from dispatch, either. No 9-1-1 call. Nothing official. Just a random guy getting through our encoded system to give us live updates on where your car was. He sounded pretty urgent. Almost like he was worried about you."

Oh, boy. I knew exactly one person who might be capable of pulling something like that off. I'd have to pay him a visit.

Lennox pivoted on his heel to face me. "Friend of yours?"

My innocent look didn't fool him.

Too bad. I knew when to keep my mouth shut.

He continued to make leading comments until Wagner made him stop. He looked disappointed but thanked me for my time and offered a police escort home.

I declined.

We parted ways at the elevator, where I pressed the button for the ground floor. When the doors closed, I was alone except for Ollie and the dog.

"How are you so calm?" Ollie asked. "I'd be screaming mad. At Lennox. At Brad. At Margie. It's like they can't keep from poking at you."

Stretching gingerly, I let out a tired breath. "I'm used to it. My life is nothing but hassle."

The dog whined beside me.

I looked down into those intelligent eyes. "You're a hassle, too. But you're also pretty helpful." I stroked the top of her head. She leaned into my hand. "You saved my life today."

"I'm sorry I dragged you into all this," Ollie said. "I can see why you hate ghosts."

"No. You were right to bug me. Peyton deserves closure. Ghosts are a pain. That doesn't mean their problems aren't real. I hope she ends up in a better place."

Her house was my next stop. In the car, my screen kept flickering on and off randomly while I tried in vain to navigate.

"The directions aren't hard," Ollie said. "I can tell you where to turn."

Frustrated, I turned my phone off. "You make a good navigation system. How well can you impersonate a search engine, a weather forecaster, a messenger app, and a news generator?"

"Not super well," he confided.

"This is going to get old so quick." Starting the engine, I pulled out of the lot and turned left, heading for Highway 70. "I'm hoping it's some weird after-effect of the dark place that'll fade soon. I don't care what Brad says, ghosts are real. Magic isn't."

Ollie stared out the window, and I knew he was thinking what I was thinking. Margie seemed convinced I'd killed a ghost. Where was Frank? I felt a longing to see the old grouch again, just to know he was okay.

When I pulled up at Peyton's, I sent Ollie ahead to check out the house. I didn't need another run-in with Gio.

He came back to give the all-clear a minute later.

We circled to the back of the house, my dog at my side. I'd be less conspicuous back there.

Peyton looked small standing alone in the middle of her barren concrete patio. Her eyes were glassy and empty, her aura visually diminished. She'd been perky and emotional only a few days ago. Now, she was listless and faded. The contrast was stark.

I'd seen ghosts worse than her, wandering blindly, oblivious to what was happening in the real world. I'd assumed the condition had come on after decades, possibly centuries, stuck in the same place. Peyton's rapid decline was alarming.

"Oh, Ollie," I breathed. "Is she going to be okay?"

"I don't know," he said. "I hope so."

He went to her, his arms circling her protectively. "Peyton, honey, we found your killer." His voice cracked like he was on the verge of tears. He cleared his throat and leaned back enough to look her in the eye. "He's in prison."

"The boyfriend you kicked out was running drugs," I added, feeling awkward. I started rambling, which was usually Ollie's thing. "He'd hidden something pricey in your attic, which is why he kept trying to get inside after you put his stuff on the porch. The gang leaders killed your boyfriend. I wasn't sure if you'd heard." I scanned her back yard. "Or if you'd seen him around."

The last thing she needed was to be pestered by her boyfriend in the afterlife.

According to Wagner, Craig was already singing like a caged bird. They were putting together warrants and raids left and right.

The botched jail break had Craig convinced the cartel would cut their losses and have him killed rather than risk a second jail break now that the cops were on high alert. His best shot at survival was to talk. It would be a busy week for the Saints and the task force both.

"It's over," Ollie said, kissing Peyton's forehead. "The whole group of drug runners is going down. I'm so sorry I wasn't with you when you were…you know. We could have found your killer earlier. But it's done."

The pain shone in his eyes as he studied her, waiting for something to happen.

His pronouncement was only met with sad doe eyes.

"I'm glad you weren't there," she said before admitting, "I'm glad it happened. Since you died, my life has been a wreck. All I ever wanted was you." She let out a depressed laugh. "They say you only get one true love in this life and I had it. I knew I had it, and I blew it. There's nothing left after you lose something like that."

"No, honey," Ollie said, his voice rough. "You didn't blow it. I should have had more faith in you. I ran off. If anyone blew it, I did." He wrapped her up in a hug and squeezed her tight. "We could have recovered, though. It was one bad night. We could have recovered if it hadn't been for the accident. Don't blame yourself."

She squeezed him back, her arms frail and skinny. "Then don't you blame *your*self," she said, her words muffled by his shirt.

They were like a Hallmark movie gone wrong. I stood there feeling like a third wheel, trying not to cry on behalf of the future they'd lost. Peyton's long auburn hair and Ollie's dreamy blue eyes would have made for one heck of an adorable child. I hated that they'd lost everything just when their lives were getting started.

With guys like Gregor out there in the world, it was tragic that people who loved with their whole hearts were torn apart.

"So long as you know the truth," Ollie said into Peyton's hair. They stood there for a long moment, slowly rocking. "It killed me watching you spiral, knowing you blamed yourself. And the baby...." he trailed off.

Peyton pulled back to look at him with tears streaming down her face.

I hadn't known ghosts could cry.

"Oh, Ollie. The baby." She buried her face in his chest. Her shoulders shook with sobs.

Their pain was unfathomable to me. Peyton's heartbreak over such a tragic loss made my chest want to cave in on itself.

I'd never be married. Never get pregnant. Maybe that was a good thing.

"I was with you when you found out," Ollie said, gently rocking her. "I was with you through it all. I watched you die a little more each day, and I'm so, so sorry you had to go through that."

She must have felt so alone. All the while, he'd been right there, watching the life they'd built crumble to dust.

It was a bleak reminder that some wrongs could never be made right. Sometimes all you could do was pick up the pieces and limp along. They'd both been limping for a long time.

"Thank you." Peyton sniffled back tears and gave him a wobbly smile. "I think I knew that deep down. I felt you with me. I convinced myself it was all in my head. You were my guardian angel."

He let out a weak laugh. "It didn't do you much good in the end."

"Don't say that," she said, running her fingers through his hair. "You did the best you could. We were given a crap hand. You're here now. I can see you. I can feel you." She gazed into his eyes for a long, long time.

I almost slipped back around the house and left them in peace. Almost.

Ollie's smile slowly fell. His eyes grew sad. "I wish we could stay here together." He closed his eyes and rested his forehead against hers.

"But I have to go," she whispered. "I can feel it pulling me. I don't belong here."

He nodded. "I wish I could go, too. I still have more to do. My work isn't done."

She clutched at him, pulling him close. "I'll wait. We'll go together."

"No," he said, swallowing hard. "The baby is there, on the other side, waiting for you." Slowly, he pushed her back and held her at arms' length. "It's been without you far too long. I'll be there when it's my time."

"All this time, I'd been so afraid of loving someone else because it hurt so much to lose you." She gave him a smile full of warmth and love, forgiveness and farewell. "Only I'd never really lost you at all."

"You could never lose me," he said.

"Until we meet again." She looked around her, eyes focused on something far beyond the neighboring house. "Promise me you'll find happiness where you can, Ollie. Of all the things I wish for you, that is the one I wish for most. You've got a heart the size of a mountain. Put it to good use." As she spoke, she began to fade into a transparent, low-glowing mist, the defined lines of her body growing hazy.

"Say hello to our child for me."

With one final nod, she was gone, her misty shape evaporating in the noonday sun.

A breeze ruffled my hair.

Ollie stood frozen, staring at the empty space his wife had left behind.

Chapter 23

"Are you okay?" I wasn't sure if Ollie was supposed to disappear like Peyton had. I hoped he wouldn't, not that I finally needed something from a ghost.

Ollie was supposed to keep tabs on me for Brad and Margie. If he left, one of those two meat heads would end up ruining my life.

"I'm okay," he said. "I just need a minute."

He looked so sad. I felt bad for thinking about myself. I hated to admit it, but I liked having Ollie around for more than his role as a buffer. He was genuinely good company most of the time and, unlike most ghosts, he understood how to work around the living world. It had been nice to have a companion over the past few days of chaos, and his connection to Frank had been invaluable.

With Peyton gone, I was reluctant to leave him, though if anyone could respect the need for space, it was me. If he was going to cross over, there was nothing I could do about it by lingering.

"Okay," I said, resolved to give him privacy to grieve. "I need to talk to Randall, anyway. I'll wait for you there. Take your time."

I looked around for my dog, who had been sniffing around the yard while Ollie and Peyton talked. She was nowhere in sight now. I debated on whistling for her, but figured she'd track me down or end up hanging out with Ollie until he was ready to rejoin me.

Besides, I didn't want to disturb Ollie.

When I cast him one last look, I saw something that made my heart leap in my throat.

A strangled sound alerted Ollie to my distress. He turned to look behind him, following my gaze to where Gio bore down on us. He'd rounded the corner of the house, spotted us, and looked ready for murder.

I'd have run for Randall's house, but I knew Gio couldn't hurt me. He was outlined in an aura, marking him as dead. He closed the distance between us in seconds, his face set in a mask of rage.

"Ollie, look out!" I hissed, worried for his safety.

"Enid, run!" he shouted back, lunging for Gio's legs in a tackle.

It turned out to be a good move since Gio was bulkier than Ollie. A head-on collision would have ended in Gio's favor, but with his legs taken out from under him, he ended up doing a face plant.

The two men grappled, each one trying to get ahold of the other. Gio wrapped Ollie in a bear hug around the hips, lifted him onto his shoulder, then slammed him down in a brutal wrestling move.

I winced. Could ghosts get hurt? They didn't have bones or brains to damage. Clearly they had something tangible, at least in whatever plane they existed on. I wanted to help, but I'd go right through a ghost.

Gio hauled Ollie up by his shirt front, spun him around, and put him in a headlock. He did something fancy with his arms, interlocking them in a way that kept Ollie on his toes, hanging from Gio's forearm.

His arms flexed. Ollie went rigid with pain. It appeared ghosts *could* get hurt.

"Wait!" I yelled. "You don't want to do that."

Gio's eyes blazed with anger. "What I want is to kill you slowly," he told me.

Did he know he was dead? If not, I might be able to trick him into thinking he could touch me.

"Then trade him for me," I said. "You've got no problem with him."

It was true only because he didn't know Ollie had been the one to recognize him when he'd come in to pester me at work.

"True. I was lucky to find you. I didn't even know you were still alive. Now that I've got you, why should I choose? I'm happy to kill you both."

My mind raced to come up with a way to stall him. I wasn't good at inventing lies. "He's under the protection of an organization more powerful than yours."

Technically, the Spirit Body was only more powerful than the cartel for the dead, but Gio was definitely dead.

Ollie frantically waved me off. It was clear he wanted me to leave him, even though I wasn't the one who would get hurt. I realized he was trying to mouth something when his hand fluttered to his face. He had to mouth it twice before I could make it out.

Trust me.

Trusting ghosts wasn't my strong suit. In Ollie's case, I would have trusted him to have my back. I didn't trust him at all not to die in some noble gesture of self-sacrifice. After seeing his devotion to Peyton, I wouldn't put that past him.

His eyes pleaded with me. He mouthed one more word. *Go.* Then he held up three fingers, too low for Gio to see, and counted down.

Confronted with a timer, I had to face the facts. I had no way to keep Ollie safe. The most I could do was watch him get his neck snapped. If he had a plan that required me to run, I'd run.

When his last finger came down to make a fist, he disappeared.

Gio stumbled into the suddenly empty space between his arms. "Hey. Where'd you go?"

I stood there dumbly for a heartbeat before I saw Ollie behind him, waving manically for me to run. I felt like an idiot. Ollie could pop in and out of places like Frank, Brad, and Margie could. If I stayed near Gio, Ollie was stuck near him, too.

Finally understanding, I turned and bolted. Three strides later, I realized I'd waited too long. Gio's fist grabbed hold of my hair, yanking my head back.

I gasped in pain, stumbling back until my shoulder blades slammed into his chest. He chuckled in my ear, a sinister sound.

My attention was focused on a warmth growing along my sternum. Reflexively, my hand went up, pressing on the necklace that sat against my skin.

My grandmother's necklace.

The warmth rippled through me in a fast-moving wave. I jerked from the strength of the power bursting out of me in a flash of green light.

With a grunt, Gio was flung back from me. He plowed into Ollie, who had tried coming to my rescue. They both fell in a tangled heap.

Ollie tried to get an arm around Gio's neck for a choke hold of his own. Gio twisted, half-rolling until he was up in a crouch over Ollie. He cocked back a fist, ready to knock teeth lose, when a fur-missile flew past me, latching onto the upraised arm with a snarl like a pissed-off Ducati.

Gio screamed as my dog twisted and writhed, using her entire body to yank on the tender flesh of his arm. Gio wrapped his free arm around my dog, then bit down on her ear.

She let out a pained cry, releasing her hold on his arm, then renewed her snarl. He'd lifted her off the ground. One hind paw found purchase on his bent knee, allowing her to lunge upward. Her teeth latched onto his throat.

Gio shoved her away, teeth tearing a large gouge out of his neck.

There was no blood. Gio didn't have a body. Instead, he leaked black aura like a belching diesel truck. He stumbled off a dozen paces before collapsing. He didn't move.

My dog sneezed, then came to stand by my side, licking her snout as she stared at the downed ghost with her hackles up.

"What was that?" I asked. "How did he grab me?"

Ollie pushed himself up to his feet. "I was afraid he might be able to. That's why I tried to get you to run. I don't think he realized he was a ghost, but a black aura means he's a ghost of vengeance."

He was definitely a ghost and definitely after vengeance. "Why does that matter?"

"Remember how I mentioned ghosts are limited by what they can imagine as real?"

I nodded.

"A ghost of vengeance doesn't even register limitations. When they die, they're new as ghosts, so they don't even realize there *are* limitations. They're so focused on the one thing that they do what's impossible to most of us without even realizing it."

That was a scary prospect. "So he blamed me for his death, then found me without even knowing he was looking for me?"

"Weirder things have happened. There's a range of really rare things that are possible with ghosts."

"How rare are we talking?"

"I honestly don't know. Near mythical in rarity."

My hand went up to my sternum. Feeling the necklace helped calm my nerves.

It consisted of a gold chain, delicate but sturdy, and a silver-dollar-sized pendant made of three slender crescent moons intertwined around a cantaloupe-colored gem. While the moons were outlined in gold, their surfaces were obsidian engraved with strange runic symbols.

"How'd you get him off you?" he asked.

I wasn't sure I wanted to mention my necklace. Caution told me to figure out more about it before I shared its secrets with others.

"He just flew back. Maybe his ability only lets him touch the living briefly?"

He made an ambiguous sound. "Good thing your dog showed up."

"She makes a good guard dog," I agreed. "She bit him when he was alive, too. Does that mean she's got some kind of rare ghost power?"

Ollie's gaze had drifted back to where Peyton had last stood. "I'm not sure," he said, absently. "I don't know much about ghost animals. They don't usually stick around."

It was clear his mind was back on Peyton. "Do you still need a minute?"

He didn't answer.

"I'll be over at Randall's. I'll come check on you when I'm done. Take your time," I said quietly.

Randall's house would keep me safe from anyone living. The dog could keep me safe from ghosts. I had no idea what my necklace would protect me from, but I was glad to have it on hand.

I'd been attacked three times in less than a day. I could use all the protection I could get.

Gio's ghost looked oddly misshapen. I passed it on my way to Randall's, giving it a wide berth. His aura had stopped leaking, though he looked like he was slowly deflating, the color draining from him.

Margie had accused me of extinguishing a soul. I wasn't sure what had happened to Frank, but there was no doubt in my mind that Gio was now a soul corpse.

He'd tried to kill me multiple times. His perma-death shouldn't bother me. He'd earned his fate.

I tried to tell myself that, averting my eyes from his decaying form. I didn't come close to believing it.

Death was scary for most people to witness, whether it comes in the form of a long decline or an abrupt end. It reminds us of our own mortality.

Death wasn't as big a deal to me. I had a unique perspective. This soul death was a new, scary concept. I wasn't sure anybody deserved to cease existing completely, in any form.

My conflicted thoughts followed me to Randall's house.

He opened the door almost before I knocked, glancing across the street at Peyton's house. It was clear he'd seen me arrive and circle her house, but he didn't ask. "Glad to see you safe. Cops catch up in time?"

"I'm starting to think you're a stalker," I said, only half joking.

"Everyone needs a stalker when they've got luck like yours." He invited me inside with a tip of his head. "I wasn't sure if you were better off with the cartel or the cops."

"The cops are fine," I said, launching into a lengthy explanation of why they'd been reburying a criminal in the cemetery.

We headed to the kitchen as we talked. Randall automatically started making tea.

When I finished, he looked thoughtful. "I heard about Quill's daughter. The authorities did a good job keeping attention focused on his death. Even *I* didn't know he was still alive until I caught wind of the second funeral."

A voice from the living room surprised me. "There you are!"

Frank stood there, looking exasperated.

"Hey!" I said, before catching myself. To Randall, I said, "Can I use your restroom?"

He nodded. I headed through the living room, giving Frank a pointed look.

When we were both cozied up inside with the dog squished between us, I closed and locked the door. "Frank! Where have you been?" I asked, excited.

He squinted at me. "Where have I been? One minute you're standing in the grass and the next you, Ollie, and the dog have gone poof." He waved his fingers like an on-stage magician, growing more animated as he talked.

"You're not at the cafe or at home, so I'm looking for you at the hospital, thinking you're half-dead from a coma with your spirit hanging out of your body or something. I've checked back at this cuckoo's house three times already." He gestured at all of Randall's house. "Where have *you* been?"

That was a long story. He didn't pause long enough for me to answer.

"I gotta go all the way to the Spirit Body to hear rumors of you from big-mouth Bradley about a living witch who can see ghosts with a dog familiar? What's this crap about you having magic?"

That was an even longer story. My mouth opened, but no words came out.

My magic, if that's what it was, had come and gone in brief flickers, much like my interference with computers. As far as I could tell, all it did was give me a headache and make me question my sanity.

"What are you, a fish?" Frank asked. "Where's Ollie? You two okay?"

I found my voice. "Ollie is at Peyton's. In the back yard. She crossed over a few minutes ago. Go easy on the questions. Let me talk to Randall for a minute. I'll fill you in on the way home."

"Yeah, yeah," he said, clearly annoyed. He disappeared.

I flushed the toilet, ran the tap, then headed back to the kitchen. "If I haven't already said it, thanks for sending the cops after Gio."

Randall shrugged. "That was risky. I had to burn through some equipment that could identify me, but I'm glad it worked out. Once he took you on the back highways, I couldn't track you through the traffic cameras. Sounds like he crashed the car?"

"He did." I didn't mention the ghost dog biting him. She sat beside me, her head turning to look at whichever of us was talking. "He turned around to yell at me, lost control of the vehicle, and ended up flipping it."

"You're lucky you survived," he said.

"We both did. Gio tried to get at me, only the door was jammed. He'd have broken the window if the sirens hadn't been closing in. I owe you my life."

Randall shifted uncomfortably at the praise. "It was probably good the door was jammed. They found Gio's body a half hour ago. He bled out less than a mile from the crash, his throat ripped out by some kind of animal."

My blood ran cold. I'd known he was dead. I could have guessed my dog's wounds had killed him. She'd killed him twice.

Randall went still. When I looked up, he was studying me. "Sorry. I could have said that more tactfully," he said. "At least you know he won't be coming after you again."

That was true only after his second death. His first death hadn't stopped him at all.

Chapter 24

On the way home, I filled Frank in on everything that had happened. Ollie was quiet, lost in the past, probably running through his list of regrets.

Maybe I was projecting. I definitely had regrets. Surprisingly, helping Ollie and Peyton wasn't one of them. That part felt good, as did helping Theo.

I still needed to stop in at the café. First I needed to shower, change, and take some Tylenol.

"Margie's full of hot air," Frank said. "She likes drama, and everybody knows it. Don't take her threats too seriously."

I hoped he was right. He'd dragged Gio's body into the ground where nobody would find it. The last thing I needed was Margie finding proof we'd soul-killed someone. Drama queen or not, she could stir up plenty of trouble.

Between Randall's observations, my dog's protective streak, and Frank's willingness to hide bodies, I was questioning my new friendships.

"You going to be okay, Ollie?" I asked.

"No. But I'll get there." He met my eyes in the rearview mirror. The dog had insisted on riding shotgun. "Thank you for helping us. I wouldn't have been able to live with myself if she'd been stuck here. It feels like she's been stuck here since I died. I couldn't watch her waste away."

Of course not. Ollie loved with his whole heart. It was something I'd come to admire in him.

My phone gave a warbling ping. I had a message, though the sound was distorted. At the next light, I saw it was Wagner, informing me they'd found Gio's body in the woods. He died from an unknown animal attack.

The message had an attachment titled *K-9s*.

The light turned green. I passed a sea of buildings, lost in thought. It had been a crazy week. I'd been through a lot. Ollie had been through more. Seeing his devotion to Peyton made my heart ache for his loss. He'd loved deeply and without reservation. Now, he was bound to me.

I wasn't sure what that meant, but anyone capable of that depth of emotion was someone I was lucky to count as a friend. He was a sweet, caring, heart-on-his-sleeve, defending-honor, white-knight type of man.

He wouldn't judge me for talking to the air, only because he was a ghost. I trusted him not to interrupt my work life now that his big mission had been accomplished. I wasn't sure how long he'd be stuck to me, but I was determined to enjoy his presence while he was here. My life was less lonely with friends in it. Even if they were ghosts.

When I got home, I pulled up the list Wagner sent over. It was longer than I expected, chronologically covering every dog in the Atlanta metro area going back decades.

Twenty minutes later, I was down to the last few entries with no luck.

"Robyn," I said, eying the dog in the passenger seat.

She stared at me, mouth open, tongue lolling.

"Lela?" No reaction. I skipped over the next dozen names, which were all male, before landing on a girl name. "Sarah?" Still no reaction from the dog. "Andrea? Yeah, that doesn't fit you at all."

"What about that one?" Frank asked. "Second to last name."

"Waffles," I read aloud.

The dog barked.

I eyed her suspiciously. "Waffles? Really? That's your name?"

She barked again and started licking my face, leaving something akin to slobber on me that dissipated after a second or two.

"Ew." I pushed her back, but scratched her on top of her head, her tail slamming against the door.

"Okay, okay. Sit." I waited until she was settled. "Waffles, huh? A ridiculous, goofy name for a ridiculous, goofy dog."

She barked again, a high-pitched yip that hurt my ears. I winced.

"You know we serve you for breakfast, right?" I wondered if that had been a joke among the police officers. Send in the crazy dog and say, "Breakfast is served." I chuckled at the thought.

My eyes wandered back to the entry:

Waffles - Belgian Malinois - Female

With just over five years on the police force, K-9 Waffles died in the line of duty after a high-speed chase that ended in a shootout on a bridge in which her handler was injured. K-9 Waffles pursued the suspect, who—in an attempt at evasion—leapt from the bridge with Waffles attached to his arm.

She was highly decorated, with awards from both narcotics detection and rescue divisions. Named after her favorite food, she was credited with extreme bravery in the face of danger multiple times throughout her career. She was a credit to her breed in providing extraordinary service to her organization. She will greatly missed by those who knew her and those she saved.

"Wow," I said. "Look at you. You're a hero."

Frank snorted. "You're surprised at that?"

"Not really," I admitted.

"She's a great dog," Ollie said, reaching over the headrest to pet Waffles, who looked pleased with herself.

"She'd be better if she stopped slobbering on me," I joked.

Frank said, "The living are never happy. You're gonna be late for your meeting with Theo. Get your sorry tuckus inside."

I turned to look at him. "My sorry tuckus?"

"Would you rather I curse? I thought ladies didn't like that sort of thing. I guess times change. Excuse me for thinking of your precious feelings, Princess."

Grumbling, I got out of the car and held the door open. "You coming, Waffles?"

She jumped out of the car and padded along at my side. I got the feeling she was happy to have a partner. Sitting by the dumpster all day had to have been miserable for her.

"I'm sorry you had to wait by the garbage," I told her. "The dumpster stinks. You can come to work with me. Bacon smells way better."

She looked up at me with a look that made me think she might actually understand what I was saying.

"But everyone knows Waffles are the best."

Her joyful bark told me she agreed.

Check out the rest of the series on Amazon!

About the Author

Jen Bair is an Air Force brat, Army veteran, and military wife. She loves traveling with her family to foreign places, real or imaginary, whenever she can.

Her family is her life. Her writing is her passion.

www.facebook.com/JenBairAuthor

www.JenBair.com

Made in the USA
Columbia, SC
28 April 2025